MISS LONELYHEARTS

&

THE DAY

OF THE

LOCUST

Two Novels by

NATHANAEL WEST

THE MODERN LIBRARY

NEW YORK

LIBRARY OF CONGRESS CATALOGING-IN-PUBLICATION DATA
West, Nathanael, 1903–1940
[Miss Lonelyhearts]
Miss Lonelyhearts; and, The day of the locust/Nathanael West.
p.   cm.
ISBN 0-679-60278-X
1. Advice columnists—New York (State)—New York—Fiction.
2. Motion picture industry—California—Los Angeles—Fiction.
I. West, Nathanael, 1903–1940. Day of the locust.
II. Title. III. Title: Day of the locust.
PS3545.E8334M5   1998
813'.52—dc21   97-39828

Modern Library website address:
www.randomhouse.com/modernlibrary/

NATHANAEL WEST

Nathanael West, an idiosyncratic, bitterly comic novelist who focused on the breakdown of the American dream in the 1930s using an innovative style that introduced surrealism and black humor into American literature, was born in New York City on October 17, 1903. His given name was Nathan Weinstein; he was the eldest child of Anna and Max Weinstein, his father a Lithuanian Jewish immigrant who prospered as a building contractor. West was an indifferent student who failed to graduate from high school and was later dismissed from Tufts College. Nevertheless, West was an avid and precocious reader, well versed in the English classics and Russian masters along with the latest French avant-garde writers. West graduated in 1924 from Brown University, where he formed a lasting friendship with classmate S. J. Perelman and was a frequent contributor to the school magazine *Casements*. Afterward, he worked intermittently in his father's construction business and made a brief literary pilgrimage to Paris before dwindling finances forced him to return to New York. From 1927 to

1933 West managed two family-owned residence hotels, Kenmore Hall and the Sutton Club, often providing free lodging for struggling writers such as Erskine Caldwell, Lillian Hellman, and Dashiell Hammett.

While employed at the Sutton Club Hotel, West completed his first novel. *The Dream Life of Balso Snell,* published as a limited edition in 1931, is a surrealist fantasy that parodies the ideals of Western civilization, and it received little initial critical or popular attention. During this period he also edited the quarterly journal *Contact* with William Carlos Williams and launched the short-lived satirical magazine *Americana.* In 1932 he and S. J. Perelman, who had married West's sister Laura, purchased a sizable farm in Bucks County, Pennsylvania, where West spent time writing and enjoyed hunting with local farmers.

West achieved a modicum of critical acclaim, though little remuneration, for his next book, *Miss Lonelyhearts,* which came out in 1933. Conceived as "a novel in the form of a comic strip," it tells of an advice-to-the-lovelorn columnist who becomes tragically embroiled in the desperate lives of his readers. "*Miss Lonelyhearts* is the perfect short novel . . . a prose poem of human suffering and self-delusion in extremis," judged novelist and screenwriter Budd Schulberg. And Malcolm Cowley noted: "*Miss Lonelyhearts* has brilliance, but it also has honest tenderness, a sense of the author's personality, and a reckless freedom of imagination—qualities that are even rarer today than when it was first published." V. S. Pritchett agreed: "*Miss Lonelyhearts* is very nearly faultless . . . a selection of hard, diamond-fine miniatures, a true American fable."

A Cool Million, West's third novel, appeared to disappointing sales and reviews in 1934. Subtitled "The Dismantling of Lemuel Pitkin," it is a satirical Horatio Alger story set in the midst of the Depression. The following year West headed for Hollywood and began working as a screenwriter of grade-B movies at Republic Productions and later at RKO Pictures. During this time West frequented the Stanley Rose Bookstore, a literary hangout on Hollywood Boulevard where he fraternized with William Faulkner, F. Scott Fitzgerald, John O'Hara, William Saroyan, Budd Schulberg, and other writers.

The Day of the Locust, West's Hollywood novel based on his experiences at the seedy fringes of the movie industry, came out in 1939. "*The Day of the Locust* has scenes of extraordinary power," wrote F. Scott Fitzgerald. "Especially I was impressed by the pathological crowd at the premiere, the character and handling of the aspirant actress, and the uncanny almost medieval feeling of some of West's Hollywood background set off by those vividly drawn grotesques." "This is the Hollywood that needs telling about," said Dashiell Hammett, and Dorothy Parker deemed it "brilliant, savage, and arresting—a truly good novel."

Budd Schulberg observed: "*The Day of the Locust* is a terrifying little masterpiece . . . a time bomb of a Hollywood novel . . . so irresistible in its wild daring and originality that not only do you not put it down, you are tempted to turn right back to page one and read it through again. . . . What makes this book so special is West's absolutely original way of illuminating his dark canvas with lightning flashes of wild humor—true gallows humor. . . . The orgiastic crowd, loving you this moment, destroying you the next, is the very essence of Hollywood—as Hollywood may be the essence of our success-driven culture. How truly West has caught it and recorded it in acid."

Following a brief courtship West married Eileen McKenney, who had achieved some celebrity as the subject of her sister Ruth McKenney's popular memoir, *My Sister Eileen* (1938), on April 19, 1940. Returning from a weekend hunting trip in Mexico, Nathanael West and his wife were killed in an automobile accident near El Centro, California, on December 22, 1940.

West's novels remained largely ignored until 1957 when the posthumous publication of *The Complete Works of Nathanael West* brought them critical recognition. "The work of Nathanael West, savagely, comically, tragically original, has come into its own," judged Budd Schulberg. "A new public [has] discovered in the writings of West a brilliant reflection of its own sense of chaos and helplessness in a world running more to madness than to reason." And Stanley Edgar Hyman reflected: "Nathanael West was a true pioneer and culture hero, making it possible for the younger symbolists and fantasists who came after him, and who include our best writers, to do with relative ease what he did in defiance of the temper of his time, for so little reward, in isolation and in pain."

CONTENTS

MISS
LONELYHEARTS

Miss Lonelyhearts, Help me, Help Me

The Miss Lonelyhearts of the New York *Post-Dispatch* (Are you in trouble?—Do-you-need-advice?—Write-to-Miss-Lonelyhearts-and-she-will-help-you) sat at his desk and stared at a piece of white cardboard. On it a prayer had been printed by Shrike, the feature editor.

> *"Soul of Miss L, glorify me.*
> *Body of Miss L, nourish me.*
> *Blood of Miss L, intoxicate me.*
> *Tears of Miss L, wash me.*
> *Oh good Miss L, excuse my plea,*
> *And hide me in your heart,*
> *And defend me from mine enemies.*
> *Help me, Miss L, help me, help me.*
> *In sæcula sæculorum. Amen."*

Although the deadline was less than a quarter of an hour away, he was still working on his leader. He had gone as far as: "Life *is* worth while, for it is full of dreams and peace, gentleness and ecstasy, and faith that burns like a clear white flame on a grim dark altar." But he found it impossible to continue. The letters were no longer funny. He could not go on finding the same joke funny thirty times a day for months on end. And on most days he received more than thirty letters, all of them alike, stamped from the dough of suffering with a heart-shaped cookie knife.

On his desk were piled those he had received this morning. He started through them again, searching for some clue to a sincere answer.

Dear Miss Lonelyhearts—

I am in such pain I don't know what to do sometimes I think I will kill myself my kidneys hurt so much. My husband thinks no woman can be a good catholic and not have children irregardless of the pain. I was married honorable from our church but I never knew what married life meant as I never was told about man and wife. My grandmother never told me and she was the only mother I had but made a big mistake by not telling me as it dont pay to be inocent and is only a big disapointment. I have 7 children in 12 years and ever since the last 2 I have been so sick. I was operatored on twice and my husband promised no more children on the doctors advice as he said I might die but when I got back from the hospital he broke his promise and now I am going to have a baby and I don't think I can stand it my kidneys hurts so much. I am so sick and scared because I cant have an abortion on account of being a catholic and my husband so religious. I cry all the time it hurts so much and I dont know what to do.

Yours respectfully
Sick-of-it-all

Miss Lonelyhearts threw the letter into an open drawer and lit a cigarette.

Dear Miss Lonelyhearts—

I am sixteen years old now and I dont know what to do and would appreciate it if you could tell me what to do. When I was a little girl it was not so bad because I got used to the kids on the block makeing fun of me, but now I would like to have boy friends like the other girls and go out on Saturday nites, but no boy will take me because I was born without a nose— although I am a good dancer and have a nice shape and my father buys me pretty clothes.

I sit and look at myself all day and cry. I have a big hole in the middle of my face that scares people even myself so I cant blame the boys for not wanting to take me out. My mother loves me, but she crys terrible when she looks at me.

What did I do to deserve such a terrible bad fate? Even if I did do some bad things I didn't do any before I was a year old and I was born this way. I asked Papa and he says he doesnt know, but that maybe I did something in the other world before I was born or that maybe I was being punished for his sins. I dont believe that because he is a very nice man. Ought I commit suicide?

Sincerely yours,
Desperate

The cigarette was imperfect and refused to draw. Miss Lonelyhearts took it out of his mouth and stared at it furiously. He fought himself quiet, then lit another one.

Dear Miss Lonelyhearts—

    I am writing to you for my little sister Gracie because something awfull hapened to her and I am afraid to tell mother about it. I am 15 years old and Gracie is 13 and we live in Brooklyn. Gracie is deaf and dumb and biger than me but not very smart on account of being deaf and dumb. She plays on the roof of our house and dont go to school except to deaf and dumb school twice a week on tuesdays and thursdays. Mother makes her play on the roof because we dont want her to get run over as she aint very smart. Last week a man came on the roof and did something dirty to her. She told me about it and I dont know what to do as I am afraid to tell mother on account of her being lible to beat Gracie up. I am afraid that Gracie is going to have a baby and I listened to her stomach last night for a long time to see if I could hear the baby but I couldn't. If I tell mother she will beat Gracie up awfull because I am the only one who loves her and last time when she tore her dress they loked her in the closet for 2 days and if the boys on the blok hear about it they will say dirty things like they did on Peewee Conors sister the time she got caught in the lots. So please what would you do if the same hapened in your family.

Yours truly,
Harold S.

    He stopped reading. Christ was the answer, but, if he did not want to get sick, he had to stay away from the Christ business. Besides, Christ was Shrike's particular joke. "Soul of Miss L, glorify me. Body of Miss L, save me. Blood of . . ." He turned to his typewriter.

    Although his cheap clothes had too much style, he still looked like the son of a Baptist minister. A beard would become him, would accent his Old-Testament look. But even without a beard no one could fail to recognize the New England puritan. His forehead was high and narrow. His nose was long and fleshless. His bony chin was shaped and cleft like a hoof. On seeing him for the first time, Shrike had smiled and said, "The Susan Chesters, the Beatrice Fairfaxes and the Miss Lonelyhearts are the priests of twentieth-century America."

A copy boy came up to tell him that Shrike wanted to know if the stuff was ready. He bent over the typewriter and began pounding its keys.

But before he had written a dozen words, Shrike leaned over his shoulder. "The same old stuff," Shrike said. "Why don't you give them something new and hopeful? Tell them about art. Here, I'll dictate:

"Art Is a Way Out.

"Do not let life overwhelm you. When the old paths are choked with the débris of failure, look for newer and fresher paths. Art is just such a path. Art is distilled from suffering. As Mr. Polnikoff exclaimed through his fine Russian beard, when, at the age of eighty-six, he gave up his business to learn Chinese, 'We are, as yet, only at the beginning. . . .'

"Art Is One of Life's Richest Offerings.

"For those who have not the talent to create, there is appreciation. For those . . .

"Go on from there."

Miss Lonelyhearts

and the

Dead Pan

When Miss Lonelyhearts quit work, he found that the weather had turned warm and that the air smelt as though it had been artificially heated. He decided to walk to Delehanty's speakeasy for a drink. In order to get there, it was necessary to cross a little park.

He entered the park at the North Gate and swallowed mouthfuls of the heavy shade that curtained its arch. He walked into the shadow of a lamp-post that lay on the path like a spear. It pierced him like a spear.

As far as he could discover, there were no signs of spring. The decay that covered the surface of the mottled ground was not the kind in which life generates. Last year, he remembered, May had failed to quicken these soiled fields. It had taken all the brutality of July to torture a few green spikes through the exhausted dirt.

What the little park needed, even more than he did, was a drink. Neither alcohol nor rain would do. Tomorrow, in his column, he would ask Broken-hearted, Sick-of-it-all, Desperate, Disillusioned-with-tubercular-husband and the rest of his correspondents to come here and water the soil with their tears. Flowers would then spring up, flowers that smelled of feet.

"Ah, humanity . . ." But he was heavy with shadow and the joke went into a dying fall. He tried to break its fall by laughing at himself.

Why laugh at himself, however, when Shrike was waiting at the speakeasy to do a much better job? "Miss Lonelyhearts, my friend, I advise you to give your readers stones. When they ask for bread don't give them crackers as does the Church, and don't, like the State, tell them to eat cake. Explain that man cannot live by bread alone and give them stones. Teach them to pray each morning: 'Give us this day our daily stone.' "

He had given his readers many stones; so many, in fact, that he had only one left—the stone that had formed in his gut.

Suddenly tired, he sat down on a bench. If he could only throw the stone. He searched the sky for a target. But the gray sky looked as if it had been rubbed with a soiled eraser. It held no angels, flaming crosses, olive-bearing doves, wheels within wheels. Only a newspaper struggled in the air like a kite with a broken spine. He got up and started again for the speakeasy.

Delehanty's was in the cellar of a brownstone house that differed from its more respectable neighbors by having an armored door. He pressed a concealed button and a little round window opened in its center. A blood-shot eye appeared, glowing like a ruby in an antique iron ring.

The bar was only half full. Miss Lonelyhearts looked around apprehensively for Shrike and was relieved at not finding him. However, after a third drink, just as he was settling into the warm mud of alcoholic gloom, Shrike caught his arm.

"Ah, my young friend!" he shouted. "How do I find you? Brooding again, I take it."

"For Christ's sake, shut up."

Shrike ignored the interruption. "You're morbid, my friend, morbid. Forget the crucifixion, remember the Renaissance. There were no brooders then." He raised his glass, and the whole Borgia family was in his gesture. "I give you the Renaissance. What a period! What pageantry! Drunken popes . . . Beautiful courtesans . . . Illegitimate children. . . ."

Although his gestures were elaborate, his face was blank. He practiced a trick used much by moving-picture comedians—the dead pan. No matter how fantastic or excited his speech, he never changed his expression. Under the shining white globe of his brow, his features huddled together in a dead, gray triangle.

"To the Renaissance!" he kept shouting. "To the Renaissance! To the brown Greek manuscripts and mistresses with the great smooth marbly limbs. . . . But that reminds me, I'm expecting one of my admirers—a cow-eyed girl of great intelligence." He illustrated the word *intelligence* by carving two enormous breasts in the air with his hands. "She works in a book store, but wait until you see her behind."

Miss Lonelyhearts made the mistake of showing his annoyance.

"Oh, so you don't care for women, eh? J. C. is your only sweetheart, eh? Jesus Christ, the King of Kings, the Miss Lonelyhearts of Miss Lonelyhearts. . . ."

At this moment, fortunately for Miss Lonelyhearts, the

young woman expected by Shrike came up to the bar. She had long legs, thick ankles, big hands, a powerful body, a slender neck and a childish face made tiny by a man's haircut.

"Miss Farkis," Shrike said, making her bow as a ventriloquist does his doll, "Miss Farkis, I want you to meet Miss Lonelyhearts. Show him the same respect you show me. He, too, is a comforter of the poor in spirit and a lover of God."

She acknowledged the introduction with a masculine handshake.

"Miss Farkis," Shrike said, "Miss Farkis works in a book store and writes on the side." He patted her rump.

"What were you talking about so excitedly?" she asked.

"Religion."

"Get me a drink and please continue. I'm very much interested in the new thomistic synthesis."

This was just the kind of remark for which Shrike was waiting. "St. Thomas!" he shouted. "What do you take us for—stinking intellectuals? We're not fake Europeans. We were discussing Christ, the Miss Lonelyhearts of Miss Lonelyhearts. America has her own religions. If you need a synthesis, here is the kind of material to use." He took a clipping from his wallet and slapped it on the bar.

"ADDING MACHINE USED IN RITUAL OF WESTERN SECT . . . *Figures Will Be Used for Prayers for Condemned Slayer of Aged Recluse*. . . . DENVER, COLO., Feb. 2 (A. P.) Frank H. Rice, Supreme Pontiff of the Liberal Church of America has announced he will carry out his plan for a 'goat and adding machine' ritual for William Moya, condemned slayer, despite objection to his program by a Cardinal of the sect. Rice declared the goat would be used as part of a 'sack cloth and ashes' service shortly before and after Moya's execution, set for the week of June 20. Prayers for the condemned man's soul will be offered on an adding machine. Numbers, he explained, constitute the only universal language. Moya killed Joseph Zemp, an aged recluse, in an argument over a small amount of money."

———

Miss Farkis laughed and Shrike raised his fist as though to strike her. His actions shocked the bartender, who hurriedly asked them to go into the back room. Miss Lonelyhearts did not want to go along, but Shrike insisted and he was too tired to argue.

They seated themselves at a table inside one of the booths. Shrike again raised his fist, but when Miss Farkis drew back, he changed the gesture to a caress. The trick worked. She gave in to his hand until he became too daring, then pushed him away.

Shrike again began to shout and this time Miss Lonelyhearts understood that he was making a seduction speech.

"I am a great saint," Shrike cried, "I can walk on my own water. Haven't you ever heard of Shrike's Passion in the Luncheonette, or the Agony in the Soda Fountain? Then I compared the wounds in Christ's body to the mouths of a miraculous purse in which we deposit the small change of our sins. It is indeed an excellent conceit. But now let us consider the holes in our own bodies and into what these congenital wounds open. Under the skin of man is a wondrous jungle where veins like lush tropical growths hang along over-ripe organs and weed-like entrails writhe in squirming tangles of red and yellow. In this jungle, flitting from rock-gray lungs to golden intestines, from liver to lights and back to liver again, lives a bird called the soul.

The Catholic hunts this bird with bread and wine, the Hebrew with a golden ruler, the Protestant on leaden feet with leaden words, the Buddhist with gestures, the Negro with blood. I spit on them all. Phooh! And I call upon you to spit. Phooh! Do you stuff birds? No, my dears, taxidermy is not religion. No! A thousand times no. Better, I say unto you, better a live bird in the jungle of the body than two stuffed birds on the library table."

His caresses kept pace with the sermon. When he had reached the end, he buried his triangular face like the blade of a hatchet in her neck.

Miss Lonelyhearts

and the

Lamb

Miss Lonelyhearts went home in a taxi. He lived by himself in a room that was as full of shadows as an old steel engraving. It held a bed, a table and two chairs. The walls were bare except for an ivory Christ that hung opposite the foot of the bed. He had removed the figure from the cross to which it had been fastened and had nailed it to the wall with large spikes. But the desired effect had not been obtained. Instead of writhing, the Christ remained calmly decorative.

He got undressed immediately and took a cigarette and a copy of *The Brothers Karamazov* to bed. The marker was in a chapter devoted to Father Zossima.

"Love a man even in his sin, for that is the semblance of Divine Love and is the highest love on earth. Love all God's creation, the whole and every grain of sand in it. Love the animals, love the plants, love everything. If you love everything, you will perceive the divine mystery in things. Once you perceive it, you will begin to comprehend it better every day. And you will come at last to love the whole world with an all-embracing love."

It was excellent advice. If he followed it, he would be a big success. His column would be syndicated and the whole world would learn to love. The Kingdom of Heaven would arrive. He would sit on the right hand of the Lamb.

But seriously, he realized, even if Shrike had not made a sane view of this Christ business impossible, there would be little use in his fooling himself. His vocation was of a different sort. As a boy in his father's church, he had discovered that something stirred in him when he shouted the name of Christ, something secret and enormously powerful. He had played with this thing, but had never allowed it to come alive.

He knew now what this thing was—hysteria, a snake whose scales are tiny mirrors in which the dead world takes on a semblance of life. And how dead the world is . . . a world of doorknobs. He wondered if hysteria were really too steep a price to pay for bringing it to life.

For him, Christ was the most natural of excitements. Fixing his eyes on the image that hung on the wall, he began to chant: "Christ, Christ, Jesus Christ. Christ, Christ, Jesus Christ." But the moment the snake started to uncoil in his brain, he became frightened and closed his eyes.

With sleep, a dream came in which he found himself on the stage of a crowded theater. He was a magician who did tricks with doorknobs. At his command, they bled, flowered, spoke. After his act was finished, he tried to lead his audience in prayer. But no matter how hard he struggled, his prayer was one Shrike had taught him and his voice was that of a conductor calling stations.

"Oh, Lord, we are not of those who wash in wine, water, urine, vinegar, fire, oil, bay rum, milk, brandy, or boric acid. Oh, Lord, we are of those who wash solely in the Blood of the Lamb."

The scene of the dream changed. He found himself in his college dormitory. With him were Steve Garvey and Jud Hume. They had been arguing the existence of God from midnight until dawn, and now, having run out of whisky, they decided to go to the market for some apple-jack.

Their way led through the streets of the sleeping town into the open fields beyond. It was spring. The sun and the smell of vegetable birth renewed their drunkenness and they reeled between the loaded carts. The farmers took their horseplay good-naturedly. Boys from the college on a spree.

They found the bootlegger and bought a gallon jug of applejack, then wandered to the section where livestock was sold. They stopped to fool with some lambs. Jud suggested buying one to roast over a fire in the woods. Miss Lonelyhearts agreed, but on the condition that they sacrifice it to God before barbecuing it.

Steve was sent to the cutlery stand for a butcher knife, while the other two remained to bargain for a lamb. After a long, Armenian-like argument, during which Jud exhibited his farm training, the youngest was selected, a little, stiff-legged thing, all head.

They paraded the lamb through the market. Miss Lonelyhearts went first, carrying the knife, the others followed, Steve with the jug and Jud with the animal. As they marched, they sang an obscene version of "Mary Had a Little Lamb."

Between the market and the hill on which they intended to perform the sacrifice was a meadow. While going through it, they picked daisies and buttercups. Half way up the hill, they found a rock and covered it with the flowers. They laid the lamb among the flowers. Miss Lonelyhearts was elected priest, with Steve and Jud as his attendants. While they held the lamb, Miss Lonelyhearts crouched over it and began to chant.

"Christ, Christ, Jesus Christ. Christ, Christ, Jesus Christ."

When they had worked themselves into a frenzy, he brought the knife down hard. The blow was inaccurate and made a flesh wound. He raised the knife again and this time the lamb's violent struggles made him miss altogether. The knife broke on the altar. Steve and Jud pulled the animal's head back for him to saw at its throat, but only a small piece of blade remained in the handle and he was unable to cut through the matted wool.

Their hands were covered with slimy blood and the lamb slipped free. It crawled off into the underbrush.

As the bright sun outlined the altar rock with narrow shadows, the scene appeared to gather itself for some new violence. They bolted. Down the hill they fled until they reached the meadow, where they fell exhausted in the tall grass.

After some time had passed, Miss Lonelyhearts begged them to go back and put the lamb out of its misery. They refused to go. He went back alone and found it under a bush. He crushed its head with a stone and left the carcass to the flies that swarmed around the bloody altar flowers.

MISS LONELYHEARTS

AND THE

FAT THUMB

Miss Lonelyhearts found himself developing an almost insane sensitiveness to order. Everything had to form a pattern: the shoes under the bed, the ties in the holder, the pencils on the table. When he looked out of a window, he composed the skyline by balancing one building against another. If a bird flew across this arrangement, he closed his eyes angrily until it was gone.

For a little while, he seemed to hold his own but one day he found himself with his back to the wall. On that day all the inanimate things over which he had tried to obtain control took the field against him. When he touched something, it spilled or rolled to the floor. The collar buttons disappeared under the bed, the point of the pencil broke, the handle of the razor fell off, the window shade refused to stay down. He fought back, but with too much violence, and was decisively defeated by the spring of the alarm clock.

He fled to the street, but there chaos was multiple. Broken groups of people hurried past, forming neither stars nor squares. The lamp-posts were badly spaced and the flagging was of different sizes. Nor could he do anything with the harsh clanging sound of street cars and the raw shouts of hucksters. No repeated group of words would fit their rhythm and no scale could give them meaning.

He stood quietly against a wall, trying not to see or hear. Then he remembered Betty. She had often made him feel that when she straightened his tie, she straightened much more. And he had once thought that if her world were larger, were *the* world, she might order it as finally as the objects on her dressing table.

He gave Betty's address to a cab driver and told him to hurry. But she lived on the other side of the city and by the time he got there, his panic had turned to irritation.

She came to the door of her apartment in a crisp, white linen dressing-robe that yellowed into brown at the edges. She held out both her hands to him and her arms showed round and smooth like wood that has been turned by the sea.

With the return of self-consciousness, he knew that only violence could make him supple. It was Betty, however, that he criticized. Her world was not the world and could never include the readers of his column. Her sureness was based on the power to limit experience arbitrarily. Moreover, his confusion was significant, while her order was not.

He tried to reply to her greeting and discovered that his tongue had become a fat thumb. To avoid talking, he awkwardly forced a kiss, then found it necessary to apologize.

"Too much lover's return business, I know, and I . . ." He stumbled purposely, so that she would take his confusion for honest feeling. But the trick failed and she waited for him to continue:

"Please eat dinner with me."

"I'm afraid I can't."

Her smile opened into a laugh.

She was laughing at him. On the defense, he examined her laugh for "bitterness," "sour-grapes," "a-broken-heart," "the-devil-may-care." But to his confusion, he found nothing at which to laugh back. Her smile had opened naturally, not like an umbrella, and while he watched her laugh folded and became a smile again, a smile that was neither "wry," "ironical" nor "mysterious."

As they moved into the living-room, his irritation increased. She sat down on a studio couch with her bare legs under and her back straight. Behind her a silver tree flowered in the lemon wallpaper. He remained standing.

"Betty the Buddha," he said. "Betty the Buddha. You have the smug smile; all you need is the pot belly."

His voice was so full of hatred that he himself was surprised. He fidgeted for a while in silence and finally sat down beside her on the couch to take her hand.

More than two months had passed since he had sat with her on this same couch and had asked her to marry him. Then she had accepted him and they had planned their life after marriage, his job and her gingham apron, his slippers beside the fireplace and her ability to cook. He had avoided her since. He did not feel guilty; he was merely annoyed at having been fooled into thinking that such a solution was possible.

He soon grew tired of holding hands and began to fidget again. He remembered that towards the end of his last visit he had put his hand inside her clothes. Unable to think of anything else to do, he now repeated the gesture. She was naked under her robe and he found her breast.

She made no sign to show that she was aware of his hand. He would have welcomed a slap, but even when he caught at her nipple, she remained silent.

"Let me pluck this rose," he said, giving a sharp tug. "I want to wear it in my buttonhole."

Betty reached for his brow. "What's the matter?" she asked. "Are you sick?"

He began to shout at her, accompanying his shouts with gestures that were too appropriate, like those of an old-fashioned actor.

"What a kind bitch you are. As soon as any one acts viciously, you say he's sick. Wife-torturers, rapers of small children, according to you they're all sick. No morality, only medicine. Well, I'm not sick. I don't need any of your damned aspirin. I've got a Christ complex. Humanity . . . I'm a humanity lover. All the broken bastards . . ." He finished with a short laugh that was like a bark.

She had left the couch for a red chair that was swollen with padding and tense with live springs. In the lap of this leather monster, all trace of the serene Buddha disappeared.

But his anger was not appeased. "What's the matter, sweetheart?" he asked, patting her shoulder threateningly. "Didn't you like the performance?"

Instead of answering, she raised her arm as though to ward off a blow. She was like a kitten whose soft helplessness makes one ache to hurt it.

"What's the matter?" he demanded over and over again. "What's the matter? What's the matter?"

Her face took on the expression of an inexperienced gambler about to venture all on a last throw. He was turning for his hat, when she spoke.

"I love you."

"You what?"

The need for repeating flustered her, yet she managed to keep her manner undramatic.

"I love you."

"And I love you," he said. "You and your damned smiling through tears."

"Why don't you let me alone?" She had begun to cry. "I felt swell before you came, and now I feel lousy. Go away. Please go away."

Miss Lonelyhearts

and the

Clean Old Man

In the street again, Miss Lonelyhearts wondered what to do next. He was too excited to eat and afraid to go home. He felt as though his heart were a bomb, a complicated bomb that would result in a simple explosion, wrecking the world without rocking it.

He decided to go to Delehanty's for a drink. In the speakeasy, he discovered a group of his friends at the bar. They greeted him and went on talking. One of them was complaining about the number of female writers.

"And they've all got three names," he said. "Mary Roberts Wilcox, Ella Wheeler Catheter, Ford Mary Rinehart. . . ."

Then some one started a train of stories by suggesting that what they all needed was a good rape.

"I knew a gal who was regular until she fell in with a group and went literary. She began writing for the little magazines about how much Beauty hurt her and ditched the boy friend who set up pins in a bowling alley. The guys on the block got sore and took her into the lots one night. About eight of them. They ganged her proper. . . ."

"That's like the one they tell about another female writer. When this hard-boiled stuff first came in, she dropped the trick English accent and went in for scram and lam. She got to hanging around with a lot of mugs in a speak, gathering material for a novel. Well, the mugs didn't know they were picturesque and thought she was regular until the barkeep put them wise. They got her into the back room to teach her a new word and put the boots to her. They didn't let her out for three days. On the last day they sold tickets to niggers. . . ."

Miss Lonelyhearts stopped listening. His friends would go on telling these stories until they were too drunk to talk. They were aware of their childishness, but did not know how else to revenge themselves. At college, and perhaps for a year afterwards, they had believed in literature, had believed in Beauty and in personal expression as an absolute end. When they lost this belief, they lost everything. Money and fame meant nothing to them. They were not worldly men.

Miss Lonelyhearts drank steadily. He was smiling an innocent, amused smile, the smile of an anarchist sitting in the movies with a bomb in his pocket. If the people around him only knew what was in his pocket. In a little while he would leave to kill the President.

Not until he heard his own name mentioned did he stop smiling and again begin to listen.

"He's a leper licker. Shrike says he wants to lick lepers. Barkeep, a leper for the gent."

"If you haven't got a leper, give him a Hungarian."

"Well, that's the trouble with his approach to God. It's

too damn literary—plain song, Latin poetry, medieval painting, Huysmans, stained-glass windows and crap like that."

"Even if he were to have a genuine religious experience, it would be personal and so meaningless, except to a psychologist."

"The trouble with him, the trouble with all of us, is that we have no outer life, only an inner one, and that by necessity."

"He's an escapist. He wants to cultivate his interior garden. But you can't escape, and where is he going to find a market for the fruits of his personality? The Farm Board is a failure.

"What I say is, after all one has to earn a living. We can't all believe in Christ, and what does the farmer care about art? He takes his shoes off to get the warm feel of the rich earth between his toes. You can't take your shoes off in church."

Miss Lonelyhearts had again begun to smile. Like Shrike, the man they imitated, they were machines for making jokes. A button machine makes buttons, no matter what the power used, foot, steam or electricity. They, no matter what the motivating force, death, love or God, made jokes.

"Was their nonsense the only barrier?" he asked himself. "Had he been thwarted by such a low hurdle?"

The whisky was good and he felt warm and sure. Through the light-blue tobacco smoke, the mahogany bar shone like wet gold. The glasses and bottles, their high lights exploding, rang like a battery of little bells when the bartender touched them together. He forgot that his heart was a bomb to remember an incident of his childhood.

One winter evening, he had been waiting with his little sister for their father to come home from church. She was eight years old then, and he was twelve. Made sad by the pause between playing and eating, he had gone to the piano and had begun a piece by Mozart. It was the first time he had ever voluntarily gone to the piano. His sister left her picture book to dance to his music. She had never danced before. She danced gravely and carefully, a simple dance yet formal.... As Miss Lonelyhearts stood at the bar, swaying slightly to the remembered music, he thought of children dancing. Square replacing oblong and being replaced by circle. Every child, everywhere; in the whole world there was not one child who was not gravely, sweetly dancing.

He stepped away from the bar and accidentally collided with a man holding a glass of beer. When he turned to beg the man's pardon, he received a punch in the mouth. Later he found himself at a table in the back room, playing with a loose tooth. He wondered why his hat did not fit and discovered a lump on the back of his head. He must have fallen. The hurdle was higher than he had thought.

His anger swung in large drunken circles. What in Christ's name was this Christ business? And children gravely dancing? He would ask Shrike to be transferred to the sports department.

Ned Gates came in to see how he was getting along and suggested the fresh air. Gates was also very drunk. When they left the speakeasy together, they found that it was snowing.

Miss Lonelyhearts' anger grew cold and sodden like the snow. He and his companion staggered along with their heads down, turning corners at random, until they found themselves in front of the little park. A light was burning in the comfort station and they went in to warm up.

An old man was sitting on one of the toilets. The door of his booth was propped open and he was sitting on the turned-down toilet cover.

Gates hailed him. "Well, well, smug as a bug in a rug, eh?"

The old man jumped with fright, but finally managed to speak. "What do you want? Please let me alone." His voice was like a flute; it did not vibrate.

"If you can't get a woman, get a clean old man," Gates sang.

The old man looked as if he were going to cry, but suddenly laughed instead. A terrible cough started under his laugh, and catching at the bottom of his lungs, it ripped into his throat. He turned away to wipe his mouth.

Miss Lonelyhearts tried to get Gates to leave, but he refused to go without the old man. They both grabbed him and pulled him out of the stall and through the door of the comfort station. He went soft in their arms and started to giggle. Miss Lonelyhearts fought off a desire to hit him.

The snow had stopped falling and it had grown very cold. The old man did not have an overcoat, but said that he found the cold exhilarating. He carried a cane and wore gloves because, as he said, he detested red hands.

Instead of going back to Delehanty's, they went to an Italian cellar close by the park. The old man tried to get them to drink coffee, but they told him to mind his own business and drank rye. The whisky burned Miss Lonelyhearts' cut lip.

Gates was annoyed by the old man's elaborate manners. "Listen, you," he said, "cut out the gentlemanly stuff and tell us the story of your life."

The old man drew himself up like a little girl making a muscle.

"Aw, come off," Gates said. "We're scientists. He's Havelock Ellis and I'm Krafft-Ebing. When did you first discover homosexualistic tendencies in yourself?"

"What do you mean, sir? I . . ."

"Yeh, I know, but how about your difference from other men?"

"How dare you . . ." He gave a little scream of indignation.

"Now, now," Miss Lonelyhearts said, "he didn't mean to insult you. Scientists have terribly bad manners. . . . But you are a pervert, aren't you?"

The old man raised his cane to strike him. Gates grabbed it from behind and wrenched it out of his hand. He began to cough violently and held his black satin tie to his mouth. Still coughing he dragged himself to a chair in the back of a room.

Miss Lonelyhearts felt as he had felt years before, when he had accidentally stepped on a small frog. Its spilled guts had filled him with pity, but when its suffering had become real to his senses, his pity had turned to rage and he had beaten it frantically until it was dead.

"I'll get the bastard's life story," he shouted, and started after him. Gates followed laughing.

At their approach, the old man jumped to his feet. Miss Lonelyhearts caught him and forced him back into his chair.

"We're psychologists," he said. "We want to help you. What's your name?"

"George B. Simpson."

"What does the B stand for?"

"Bramhall."

"Your age, please, and the nature of your quest?"

"By what right do you ask?"

"Science gives me the right."

"Let's drop it," Gates said. "The old fag is going to cry."

"No, Krafft-Ebing, sentiment must never be permitted to interfere with the probings of science."

Miss Lonelyhearts put his arm around the old man. "Tell us the story of your life," he said, loading his voice with sympathy.

"I have no story."

"You must have. Every one has a life story."

The old man began to sob.

"Yes, I know, your tale is a sad one. Tell it, damn you, tell it."

When the old man still remained silent, he took his arm and twisted it. Gates tried to tear him away, but he refused to let go. He was twisting the arm of all the sick and miserable, broken and betrayed, inarticulate and impotent. He was twisting the arm of Desperate, Broken-hearted, Sick-of-it-all, Disillusioned-with-tubercular-husband.

The old man began to scream. Somebody hit Miss Lonelyhearts from behind with a chair.

Miss Lonelyhearts

and

Mrs. Shrike

Miss Lonelyhearts lay on his bed fully dressed, just as he had been dumped the night before. His head ached and his thoughts revolved inside the pain like a wheel within a wheel. When he opened his eyes, the room, like a third wheel, revolved around the pain in his head.

From where he lay he could see the alarm clock. It was half past three. When the telephone rang, he crawled out of the sour pile of bed clothes. Shrike wanted to know if he intended to show up at the office. He answered that he was drunk but would try to get there.

He undressed slowly and took a bath. The hot water made his body feel good, but his heart remained a congealed lump of icy fat. After drying himself, he found a little whisky in the medicine chest and drank it. The alcohol warmed only the lining of his stomach.

He shaved, put on a clean shirt and a freshly pressed suit and went out to get something to eat. When he had finished his second cup of scalding coffee, it was too late for him to go to work. But he had nothing to worry about, for Shrike would never fire him. He made too perfect a butt for Shrike's jokes. Once he had tried to get fired by recommending suicide in his column. All that Shrike had said was: "Remember, please, that your job is to increase the circulation of our paper. Suicide, it is only reasonable to think, must defeat this purpose."

He paid for his breakfast and left the cafeteria. Some exercise might warm him. He decided to take a brisk walk, but he soon grew tired and when he reached the little park, he slumped down on a bench opposite the Mexican War obelisk.

The stone shaft cast a long, rigid shadow on the walk in front of him. He sat staring at it without knowing why until he noticed that it was lengthening in rapid jerks, not as shadows usually lengthen. He grew frightened and looked up quickly at the monument. It seemed red and swollen in the dying sun, as though it were about to spout a load of granite seed.

He hurried away. When he had regained the street, he started to laugh. Although he had tried hot water, whisky, coffee, exercise, he had completely forgotten sex. What he really needed was a woman. He laughed again, remembering that at college all his friends had believed intercourse capable of steadying the nerves, relaxing the muscles and clearing the blood.

But he knew only two women who would tolerate him. He had spoiled his chances with Betty, so it would have to be Mary Shrike.

When he kissed Shrike's wife, he felt less like a joke. She returned his kisses because she hated Shrike. But even there Shrike had beaten him. No matter how hard he begged her to give Shrike horns, she refused to sleep with him.

Although Mary always grunted and upset her eyes, she would not associate what she felt with the sexual act. When he forced this association, she became very angry. He had been convinced that her grunts were genuine by the change that took place in her when he kissed her heavily. Then her body gave off an odor that enriched the synthetic flower scent she used behind her ears and in the hollows of her neck. No similar change ever took place in his own body, however. Like a dead man, only friction could make him warm or violence make him mobile.

He decided to get a few drinks and then call Mary from Delehanty's. It was quite early and the speakeasy was empty. The bartender served him and went back to his newspaper.

On the mirror behind the bar hung a poster advertising a mineral water. It showed a naked girl made modest by the mist that rose from the spring at her feet. The artist had taken a great deal of care in drawing her breasts and their nipples stuck out like tiny red hats.

He tried to excite himself into eagerness by thinking of the play Mary made with her breasts. She used them as the coquettes of long ago had used their fans. One of her tricks was to wear a medal low down on her chest. Whenever he asked to see it, instead of drawing it out she leaned over for him to look. Although he had often asked to see the medal, he had not yet found out what it represented.

But the excitement refused to come. If anything, he felt colder than before he had started to think of women. It was not his line. Nevertheless, he persisted in it, out of desperation, and went to the telephone to call Mary.

"Is that you?" she asked, then added before he could

reply, "I must see you at once. I've quarreled with him. This time I'm through."

She always talked in headlines and her excitement forced him to be casual. "O. K.," he said. "When? Where?"

"Anywhere, I'm through with that skunk, I tell you, I'm through."

She had quarreled with Shrike before and he knew that in return for an ordinary number of kisses, he would have to listen to an extraordinary amount of complaining.

"Do you want to meet me here, in Delehanty's?" he asked.

"No, you come here. We'll be alone and anyway I have to bathe and get dressed."

When he arrived at her place, he would probably find Shrike there with her on his lap. They would both be glad to see him and all three of them would go to the movies where Mary would hold his hand under the seat.

He went back to the bar for another drink, then bought a quart of Scotch and took a cab. Shrike opened the door. Although he had expected to see him, he was embarrassed and tried to cover his confusion by making believe that he was extremely drunk.

"Come in, come in, homebreaker," Shrike said with a laugh. "The Mrs. will be out in a few minutes. She's in the tub."

Shrike took the bottle he was carrying and pulled its cork. Then he got some charged water and made two high-balls.

"Well," Shrike said, lifting his drink, "so you're going in for this kind of stuff, eh? Whisky and the boss's wife."

Miss Lonelyhearts always found it impossible to reply to

him. The answers he wanted to make were too general and began too far back in the history of their relationship.

"You're doing field work, I take it," Shrike said. "Well, don't put this whisky on your expense account. However, we like to see a young man with his heart in his work. You've been going around with yours in your mouth."

Miss Lonelyhearts made a desperate attempt to kid back. "And you," he said, "you're an old meanie who beats his wife."

Shrike laughed, but too long and too loudly, then broke off with an elaborate sigh. "Ah, my lad," he said, "you're wrong. It's Mary who does the beating."

He took a long pull at his highball and sighed again, still more elaborately. "My good friend, I want to have a heart-to-heart talk with you. I adore heart-to-heart talks and nowadays there are so few people with whom one can really talk. Everybody is so hard-boiled. I want to make a clean breast of matters, a nice clean breast. It's better to make a clean breast of matters than to let them fester in the depths of one's soul."

While talking, he kept his face alive with little nods and winks that were evidently supposed to inspire confidence and to prove him a very simple fellow.

"My good friend, your accusation hurts me to the quick. You spiritual lovers think that you alone suffer. But you are mistaken. Although my love is of the flesh flashy, I too suffer. It's suffering that drives me into the arms of the Miss Farkises of this world. Yes, I suffer."

Here the dead pan broke and pain actually crept into his voice. "She's selfish. She's a damned selfish bitch. She was a virgin when I married her and has been fighting ever since to remain one. Sleeping with her is like sleeping with a knife in one's groin."

It was Miss Lonelyhearts' turn to laugh. He put his face close to Shrike's and laughed as hard as he could.

Shrike tried to ignore him by finishing as though the whole thing were a joke.

"She claims that I raped her. Can you imagine Willie Shrike, wee Willie Shrike, raping any one? I'm like you, one of those grateful lovers."

Mary came into the room in her bathrobe. She leaned over Miss Lonelyhearts and said: "Don't talk to that pig. Come with me and bring the whisky."

As he followed her into the bedroom, he heard Shrike slam the front door. She went into a large closet to dress. He sat on the bed.

"What did that swine say to you?"

"He said you were selfish, Mary—sexually selfish."

"Of all the god-damned nerve. Do you know why he lets me go out with other men? To save money. He knows that I let them neck me and when I get home all hot and bothered, why he climbs into my bed and begs for it. The cheap bastard!"

She came out of the closet wearing a black lace slip and began to fix her hair in front of the dressing table. Miss Lonelyhearts bent down to kiss the back of her neck.

"Now, now," she said, acting kittenish, "you'll muss me."

He took a drink from the whisky bottle, then made her a highball. When he brought it to her, she gave him a kiss, a little peck of reward.

"Where'll we eat?" she asked. "Let's go where we can dance. I want to be gay."

They took a cab to a place called El Gaucho. When they entered, the orchestra was playing a Cuban rhumba. A waiter dressed as a South-American cowboy led them to a table. Mary immediately went Spanish and her movements became languorous and full of abandon.

But the romantic atmosphere only heightened his feeling of icy fatness. He tried to fight it by telling himself that it was childish. What had happened to his great understanding heart? Guitars, bright shawls, exotic foods, outlandish costumes—all these things were part of the business of dreams. He had learned not to laugh at the advertisements offering to teach writing, cartooning, engineering, to add inches to the biceps and to develop the bust. He should therefore realize that the people who came to El Gaucho were the same as those who wanted to write and live the life of an artist, wanted to be an engineer and wear leather puttees, wanted to develop a grip that would impress the boss, wanted to cushion Raoul's head on their swollen breasts. They were the same people as those who wrote to Miss Lonelyhearts for help.

But his irritation was too profound for him to soothe it in this way. For the time being, dreams left him cold, no matter how humble they were.

"I like this place," Mary said. "It's a little fakey, I know, but it's gay and I so want to be gay."

She thanked him by offering herself in a series of formal, impersonal gestures. She was wearing a tight, shiny dress that was like glass-covered steel and there was something cleanly mechanical in her pantomime.

"Why do you want to be gay?"

"Every one wants to be gay—unless they're sick."

Was he sick? In a great cold wave, the readers of his column crashed over the music, over the bright shawls and picturesque waiters, over her shining body. To save himself, he asked to see the medal. Like a little girl helping an old man to cross the street, she leaned over for him to look into the neck of her dress. But before he had a chance to see anything, a waiter came up to the table.

"The way to be gay is to make other people gay," Miss Lonelyhearts said. "Sleep with me and I'll be one gay dog."

The defeat in his voice made it easy for her to ignore his request and her mind sagged with his. "I've had a tough time," she said. "From the beginning, I've had a tough time. When I was a child, I saw my mother die. She had cancer of the breast and the pain was terrible. She died leaning over a table."

"Sleep with me," he said.

"No, let's dance."

"I don't want to. Tell me about your mother."

"She died leaning over a table. The pain was so terrible that she climbed out of bed to die."

Mary leaned over to show how her mother had died and he made another attempt to see the medal. He saw that there was a runner on it, but was unable to read the inscription.

"My father was very cruel to her," she continued. "He was a portrait painter, a man of genius, but . . ."

He stopped listening and tried to bring his great understanding heart into action again. Parents are also part of the business of dreams. My father was a Russian prince, my father was a Piute Indian chief, my father was an Australian sheep baron, my father lost all his money in Wall Street, my father was a portrait painter. People like Mary were unable to do without such tales. They told them because they wanted to talk about something besides clothing or business or the movies, because they wanted to talk about something poetic.

When she had finished her story, he said, "You poor kid," and leaned over for another look at the medal. She bent to help him and pulled out the neck of her dress with her fingers. This time he was able to read the inscription: "Awarded by the Boston Latin School for first place in the 100 yd. dash."

It was a small victory, yet it greatly increased his fatigue and he was glad when she suggested leaving. In the cab, he again begged her to sleep with him. She refused. He kneaded her body like a sculptor grown angry with his clay, but there was too much method in his caresses and they both remained cold.

At the door of her apartment, she turned for a kiss and pressed against him. A spark flared up in his groin. He refused to let go and tried to work this spark into a flame. She pushed his mouth away a long wet kiss.

"Listen to me," she said. "We can't stop talking. We must talk. Willie probably heard the elevator and is listening behind the door. You don't know him. If he doesn't hear us talk, he'll know you're kissing me and open the door. It's an old trick of his."

He held her close and tried desperately to keep the spark alive.

"Don't kiss my lips," she begged. "I must talk."

He kissed her throat, then opened her dress and kissed her breasts. She was afraid to resist or to stop talking.

"My mother died of cancer of the breast," she said in a brave voice, like a little girl reciting at a party. "She died leaning over a table. My father was a portrait painter. He

led a very gay life. He mistreated my mother. She had cancer of the breast. She . . ." He tore at her clothes and she
began to mumble and repeat herself. Her dress fell to her
feet and he tore away her underwear until she was naked
under her fur coat. He tried to drag her to the floor.

"Please, please," she begged, "he'll come out and find us."

He stopped her mouth with a long kiss.

"Let me go, honey," she pleaded, "maybe he's not home.
If he isn't, I'll let you in."

He released her. She opened the door and tiptoed in,
carrying her rolled up clothes under her coat. He heard her
switch on the light in the foyer and knew that Shrike had
not been behind the door. Then he heard footsteps and
limped behind a projection of the elevator shaft. The door
opened and Shrike looked into the corridor. He had on
only the top of his pajamas.

MISS LONELYHEARTS

ON A

FIELD TRIP

It was cold and damp in the city room the next day, and Miss Lonelyhearts sat at his desk with his hands in his pockets and his legs pressed together. A desert, he was thinking, not of sand, but of rust and body dirt, surrounded by a back-yard fence on which are posters describing the events of the day. Mother slays five with ax, slays seven, slays nine. . . . Babe slams two, slams three. . . . Inside the fence Desperate, Broken-hearted, Disillusioned-with-tubercular-husband and the rest were gravely forming the letters MISS LONELYHEARTS out of white-washed clam shells, as if decorating the lawn of a rural depot.

He failed to notice Goldsmith's waddling approach until a heavy arm dropped on his neck like the arm of a deadfall. He freed himself with a grunt. His anger amused Goldsmith, who smiled, bunching his fat cheeks like twin rolls of smooth pink toilet paper.

"Well, how's the drunkard?" Goldsmith asked, imitating Shrike.

Miss Lonelyhearts knew that Goldsmith had written the

column for him yesterday, so he hid his annoyance to be grateful.

"No trouble at all," Goldsmith said. "It was a pleasure to read your mail." He took a pink envelope out of his pocket and threw it on the desk. "From an admirer." He winked, letting a thick gray lid down slowly and luxuriously over a moist, rolling eye.

Miss Lonelyhearts picked up the letter.

Dear Miss Lonelyhearts—

I am not very good at writing so I wonder if I could have a talk with you. I am 32 years old but have had a lot of trouble in my life and am unhappily married to a cripple. I need some good advice bad but cant state my case in a letter as I am not good at letters and it would take an expert to state my case. I know your a man and am glad as I dont trust women. You were pointed out to me in Delehantys as the man who does the advice in the paper and the minute I saw you I said you can help me. You had on a blue suit and a gray hat when I came in with my husband who is a cripple.

I dont feel so bad about asking to see you personal because I feel almost like I knew you. So please call me up at Burgess 7-7323 which is my number as I need your advice bad about my married life.

An admirer,
Fay Doyle

He threw the letter into the waste-paper basket with a great show of distaste.

Goldsmith laughed at him. "How now, Dostoievski?" he said. "That's no way to act. Instead of pulling the Russian by recommending suicide, you ought to get the lady with child and increase the potential circulation of the paper."

To drive him away, Miss Lonelyhearts made believe that he was busy. He went over his typewriter and started pounding out his column.

"Life, for most of us, seems a terrible struggle of pain and heartbreak, without hope or joy. Oh, my dear readers, it only seems so. Every man, no matter how poor or humble, can teach himself to use his senses. See the cloud-flecked sky, the foam-decked sea.... Smell the sweet pine and heady privet.... Feel of velvet and of satin.... As the popular song goes, 'The best things in life are free.' Life is ..."

He could not go on with it and turned again to the imagined desert where Desperate, Broken-hearted and the others were still building his name. They had run out of sea shells and were using faded photographs, soiled fans, timetables, playing cards, broken toys, imitation jewelry—junk that memory had made precious, far more precious than anything the sea might yield.

He killed his great understanding heart by laughing, then reached into the waste-paper basket for Mrs. Doyle's letter. Like a pink tent, he set it over the desert. Against the dark mahogany desk top, the cheap paper took on rich flesh tones. He thought of Mrs. Doyle as a tent, hair-covered and veined, and of himself as the skeleton in a water closet, the skull and cross-bones on a scholar's bookplate. When he made the skeleton enter the flesh tent, it flowered at every joint.

But despite these thoughts, he remained as dry and cold as a polished bone and sat trying to discover a moral reason for not calling Mrs. Doyle. If he could only believe in Christ, then adultery would be a sin, then everything would be simple and the letters extremely easy to answer.

The completeness of his failure drove him to the telephone. He left the city room and went into the hall to use the pay station from which all private calls had to be made. The walls of the booth were covered with obscene drawings. He fastened his eyes on two disembodied genitals and gave the operator Burgess 7-7323.

"Is Mrs. Doyle in?"

"Hello, who is it?"

"I want to speak to Mrs. Doyle," he said. "Is this Mrs. Doyle?"

"Yes, that's me." Her voice was hard with fright.

"This is Miss Lonelyhearts."

"Miss who?"

"Miss Lonelyhearts, Miss Lonelyhearts, the man who does the column."

He was about to hang up, when she cooed, "Oh, hello...."

"You said I should call."

"Oh, yes ... what?"

He guessed that she wanted him to do the talking. "When can you see me?"

"Now." She was still cooing and he could almost feel her warm, moisture-laden breath through the earpiece.

"Where?"

"You say."

"I'll tell you what," he said. "Meet me in the park, near the obelisk, in about an hour."

He went back to his desk and finished his column, then started for the park. He sat down on a bench near the obelisk to wait for Mrs. Doyle. Still thinking of tents, he examined the sky and saw that it was canvas-colored and ill-stretched. He examined it like a stupid detective who is searching for a clue to his own exhaustion. When he found nothing, he turned his trained eye on the skyscrapers that menaced the little park from all sides. In their tons of forced rock and tortured steel, he discovered what he thought was a clue.

Americans have dissipated their racial energy in an orgy of stone breaking. In their few years they have broken more stones than did centuries of Egyptians. And they have done their work hysterically, desperately, almost as if they knew that the stones would some day break them.

The detective saw a big woman enter the park and start in his direction. He made a quick catalogue: legs like Indian clubs, breasts like balloons and a brow like a pigeon. Despite her short plaid skirt, red sweater, rabbit-skin jacket and knitted tam-o'-shanter, she looked like a police captain.

He waited for her to speak first.

"Miss Lonelyhearts? Oh, hello . . ."

"Mrs. Doyle?" He stood up and took her arm. It felt like a thigh.

"Where are we going?" she asked, as he began to lead her off.

"For a drink."

"I can't go to Delehanty's. They know me."

"We'll go to my place."

"Ought I?"

He did not have to answer, for she was already on her way. As he followed her up the stairs to his apartment, he watched the action of her massive hams; they were like two enormous grindstones.

He made some highballs and sat down beside her on the bed.

"You must know an awful lot about women from your job," she said with a sigh, putting her hand on his knee.

He had always been the pursuer, but now found a strange pleasure in having the rôles reversed. He drew back when she reached for a kiss. She caught his head and kissed him on his mouth. At first it ticked like a watch, then the tick softened and thickened into a heart throb. It beat louder and more rapidly each second, until he thought that it was going to explode and pulled away with a rude jerk.

"Don't," she begged.

"Don't what?"

"Oh, darling, turn out the light."

He smoked a cigarette, standing in the dark and listening to her undress. She made sea sounds; something flapped like a sail; there was the creak of ropes; then he heard the wave-against-a-wharf smack of rubber on flesh. Her call for him to hurry was a sea-moan, and when he lay beside her, she heaved, tidal, moon-driven.

Some fifteen minutes later, he crawled out of bed like an exhausted swimmer leaving the surf, and dropped down into a large armchair near the window. She went into the bathroom, then came back and sat in his lap.

"I'm ashamed of myself," she said. "You must think I'm a bad woman."

He shook his head no.

"My husband isn't much. He's a cripple like I wrote you, and much older than me." She laughed. "He's all dried up. He hasn't been a husband to me for years. You know, Lucy, my kid, isn't his."

He saw that she expected him to be astonished and did his best to lift his eyebrows.

"It's a long story," she said. "It was on account of Lucy that I had to marry him. I'll bet you must have wondered how it was I came to marry a cripple. It's a long story."

Her voice was as hypnotic as a tom-tom, and as monotonous. Already his mind and body were half asleep.

"It's a long, long story, and that's why I couldn't write it in a letter. I got into trouble when the Doyles lived above us on Center Street. I used to be kind to him and go to the movies with him because he was a cripple, although I was one of the most popular girls on the block. So when I got into trouble, I didn't know what to do and asked him for the money for an abortion. But he didn't have the money, so we got married instead. It all came through my trusting a dirty dago. I thought he was a gent, but when I asked him to marry me, why he spurned me from the door and wouldn't even give me money for an abortion. He said if he gave me the money that would mean it was his fault and I would have something on him. Did you ever hear of such a skunk?"

"No," he said. The life out of which she spoke was even heavier than her body. It was as if a gigantic, living Miss Lonelyhearts letter in the shape of a paper weight had been placed on his brain.

"After the baby was born, I wrote the skunk, but he never wrote back, and about two years ago, I got to thinking how unfair it was for Lucy to have to depend on a cripple and not come into her rights. So I looked his name up in the telephone book and took Lucy to see him. As I told him then, not that I wanted anything for myself, but just that I wanted Lucy to get what was coming to her. Well, after keeping us waiting in the hall over an hour—I was boiling mad, I can tell you, thinking of the wrong he had done me and my child—we were taken into the parlor by the butler. Very quiet and lady-like, because money ain't everything and he's no more a gent than I'm a lady, the dirty wop—I told him he ought to do something for Lucy see'n' he's her father. Well, he had the nerve to say that he had never seen me before and that if I didn't stop bothering him, he'd have me run in. That got me riled and I lit into the bastard and gave him a piece of my mind. A woman came in while we were arguing that I figured was his wife, so I hollered, "He's the father of my child, he's the father of my child." When they went to the 'phone to call a cop, I picked up the kid and beat it.

"And now comes the funniest part of the whole thing. My husband is a queer guy and he always makes believe that he is the father of the kid and even talks to me about *our* child. Well, when we got home, Lucy kept asking me why I said a strange man was her papa. She wanted to know if Doyle wasn't really her papa. I must of been crazy because I told her that she should remember that her real papa was a man named Tony Benelli and that he had wronged me. I told her a lot of other crap like that—too much movies I guess. Well, when Doyle got home the first thing Lucy says to him is that he ain't her papa. That got him sore and he wanted to know what I had told her. I didn't like his high falutin' ways and said, 'The truth.' I guess too that I was kinda sick of see'n' him moon over her. He went for me and hit me one on the cheek. I wouldn't let no man get away with that so I socked back and he swung at me with his stick but missed and fell on the floor and started to cry. The kid was on the floor crying too and that set me off because the next thing I know I'm on the floor bawling too."

She waited for him to comment, but he remained silent until she nudged him into speech with her elbow. "Your husband probably loves you and the kid," he said.

"Maybe so, but I was a pretty girl and could of had my pick. What girl wants to spend her life with a shrimp of a cripple?"

"You're still pretty," he said without knowing why, except that he was frightened.

She rewarded him with a kiss, then dragged him to the bed.

MISS LONELYHEARTS

IN THE

DISMAL SWAMP

Soon after Mrs. Doyle left, Miss Lonelyhearts became physically sick and was unable to leave his room. The first two days of his illness were blotted out by sleep, but on the third day, his imagination began again to work.

He found himself in the window of a pawnshop full of fur coats, diamond rings, watches, shotguns, fishing tackle, mandolins. All these things were the paraphernalia of suffering. A tortured high light twisted on the blade of a gilt knife, a battered horn grunted with pain.

He sat in the window thinking. Man has a tropism for order. Keys in one pocket, change in another. Mandolins are tuned G D A E. The physical world has a tropism for disorder, entropy. Man against Nature . . . the battle of the centuries. Keys yearn to mix with change. Mandolins strive to get out of tune. Every order has within it the germ of destruction. All order is doomed, yet the battle is worth while.

A trumpet, marked to sell for $2.49, gave the call to battle and Miss Lonelyhearts plunged into the fray. First he formed a phallus of old watches and rubber boots, then a heart of umbrellas and trout flies, then a diamond of musical instruments and derby hats, after these a circle, triangle, square, swastika. But nothing proved definitive and he began to make a gigantic cross. When the cross became too large for the pawnshop, he moved it to the shore of the ocean. There every wave added to his stock faster than he could lengthen its arms. His labors were enormous. He staggered from the last wave line to his work, loaded down with marine refuse—bottles, shells, chunks of cork, fish heads, pieces of net.

Drunk with exhaustion, he finally fell asleep. When he awoke, he felt very weak, yet calm.

There was a timid knock on the door. It was open and Betty tiptoed into the room with her arms full of bundles. He made believe that he was asleep.

"Hello," he said suddenly.

Startled, she turned to explain. "I heard you were sick, so I brought some hot soup and other stuff."

He was too tired to be annoyed by her wide-eyed little mother act and let her feed him with a spoon. When he had finished eating, she opened the window and freshened the bed. As soon as the room was in order, she started to leave, but he called her back.

"Don't go, Betty."

She pulled a chair to the side of his bed and sat there without speaking.

"I'm sorry about what happened the other day," he said. "I guess I was sick."

She showed that she accepted his apology by helping him to excuse himself. "It's the Miss Lonelyhearts job. Why don't you give it up?"

"And do what?"

"Work in an advertising agency, or something."

"You don't understand, Betty, I can't quit. And even if I were to quit, it wouldn't make any difference. I wouldn't be able to forget the letters, no matter what I did."

"Maybe I don't understand," she said, "but I think you're making a fool of yourself."

"Perhaps I can make you understand. Let's start from the beginning. A man is hired to give advice to the readers of a newspaper. The job is a circulation stunt and the whole staff considers it a joke. He welcomes the job, for it might lead to a gossip column, and anyway he's tired of being a leg man. He too considers the job a joke, but after several months at it, the joke begins to escape him. He sees that the majority of the letters are profoundly humble pleas for moral and spiritual advice, that they are inarticulate expressions of genuine suffering. He also discovers that his correspondents take him seriously. For the first time in his life, he is forced to examine the values by which he lives. This examination shows him that he is the victim of the joke and not its perpetrator."

Although he had spoken soberly, he saw that Betty still thought him a fool. He closed his eyes.

"You're tired," she said. "I'll go."

"No, I'm not tired. I'm just tired of talking, you talk a while."

She told him about her childhood on a farm and of her love for animals, about country sounds and country smells and of how fresh and clean everything in the country is. She said that he ought to live there and that if he did, he would find that all his troubles were city troubles.

While she was talking, Shrike burst into the room. He was drunk and immediately set up a great shout, as though he believed that Miss Lonelyhearts was too near death to hear distinctly. Betty left without saying good-by.

Shrike had evidently caught some of her farm talk, for he said: "My friend, I agree with Betty, you're an escapist. But I do not agree that the soil is the proper method for you to use."

Miss Lonelyhearts turned his face to the wall and pulled up the covers. But Shrike was unescapable. He raised his voice and talked through the blankets into the back of Miss Lonelyhearts' head.

"There are other methods, and for your edification I shall describe them. But first let us do the escape to the soil, as recommended by Betty:

"You are fed up with the city and its teeming millions. The ways and means of men, as getting and lending and spending, you lay waste your inner world, are too much with you. The bus takes too long, while the subway is always crowded. So what do you do? So you buy a farm and walk behind your horse's moist behind, no collar or tie, plowing your broad swift acres. As you turn up the rich black soil, the wind carries the smell of pine and dung across the fields and the rhythm of an old, old work enters your soul. To this rhythm, you sow and weep and chivy your kine, not kin or kind, between the pregnant rows of corn and taters. Your step becomes the heavy sexual step of a dance-drunk Indian and you tread the seed down into the female earth. You plant, not dragon's teeth, but beans and greens. . . .

"Well, what do you say, my friend, shall it be the soil?"

Miss Lonelyhearts did not answer. He was thinking of how Shrike had accelerated his sickness by teaching him to handle his one escape, Christ, with a thick glove of words.

"I take your silence to mean that you have decided against the soil. I agree with you. Such a life is too dull and laborious. Let us now consider the South Seas:

"You live in a thatch hut with the daughter of the king, a slim young maiden in whose eyes is an ancient wisdom. Her breasts are golden speckled pears, her belly a melon, and her odor is like nothing so much as a jungle fern. In the evening, on the blue lagoon, under the silvery moon, to your love you croon in the soft sylabelew and vocabelew of her langorour tongorour. Your body is golden brown like hers, and tourists have need of the indignant finger of the missionary to point you out. They envy you your breech clout and carefree laugh and little brown bride and fingers instead of forks. But you don't return their envy, and when a beautiful society girl comes to your hut in the night, seeking to learn the secret of your happiness, you send her back to her yacht that hangs on the horizon like a nervous race-horse. And so you dream away the days, fishing, hunting, dancing, swimming, kissing, and picking flowers to twine in your hair. . . .

"Well, my friend, what do you think of the South Seas?"

Miss Lonelyhearts tried to stop him by making believe that he was asleep. But Shrike was not fooled.

"Again silence," he said, "and again you are right. The South Seas are played out and there's little use in imitating Gauguin. But don't be discouraged, we have only scratched the surface of our subject. Let us now examine Hedonism, or take the cash and let the credit go. . . .

"You dedicate your life to the pursuit of pleasure. No overindulgence, mind you, but knowing that your body is a pleasure machine, you treat it carefully in order to get the most out of it. Golf as well as booze, Philadelphia Jack

O'Brien and his chestweights as well as Spanish dancers. Nor do you neglect the pleasures of the mind. You fornicate under pictures by Matisse and Picasso, you drink from Renaissance glassware, and often you spend an evening beside the fireplace with Proust and an apple. Alas, after much good fun, the day comes when you realize that soon you must die. You keep a stiff upper lip and decide to give a last party. You invite all your old mistresses, trainers, artists and boon companions. The guests are dressed in black, the waiters are coons, the table is a coffin carved for you by Eric Gill. You serve caviar and blackberries and licorice candy and coffee without cream. After the dancing girls have finished, you get to your feet and call for silence in order to explain your philosophy of life. 'Life,' you say, 'is a club where they won't stand for squawks, where they deal you only one hand and you must sit in. So even if the cards are cold and marked by the hand of fate, play up, play up like a gentleman and a sport. Get tanked, grab what's on the buffet, use the girls upstairs, but remember, when you throw box cars, take the curtain like a dead game sport, don't squawk.' ...

"I won't even ask you what you think of such an escape. You haven't the money, nor are you stupid enough to manage it. But we come now to one that should suit you much better. ...

"Art! Be an artist or a writer. When you are cold, warm yourself before the flaming tints of Titian, when you are hungry, nourish yourself with great spiritual foods by listening to the noble periods of Bach, the harmonies of Brahms and the thunder of Beethoven. Do you think there is anything in the fact that their names all begin with B? But don't take a chance, smoke a 3 B pipe, and remember these immortal lines: *When to the suddenness of melody the echo parting falls the failing day.* What a rhythm! Tell them to keep their society whores and pressed duck with oranges. For you *l'art vivant,* the living art, as you call it. Tell them that you know that your shoes are broken and that there are pimples on your face, yes, and that you have buck teeth and a club foot, but that you don't care, for to-morrow they are playing Beethoven's last quartets in Carnegie Hall and at home you have Shakespeare's plays in one volume."

After art, Shrike described suicide and drugs. When he had finished with them, he came to what he said was the goal of his lecture.

"My friend, I know of course that neither the soil, nor the South Seas, nor Hedonism, nor art, nor suicide, nor drugs, can mean anything to us. We are not men who swallow camels only to strain at stools. God alone is our escape. The church is our only hope, the First Church of Christ Dentist, where He is worshipped as Preventer of Decay. The church whose symbol is the trinity new-style: Father, Son and Wirehaired Fox Terrier. . . . And so, my good friend, let me dictate a letter to Christ for you:

Dear Miss Lonelyhearts of Miss Lonelyhearts—

I am twenty-six years old and in the newspaper game. Life for me is a desert empty of comfort. I cannot find pleasure in food, drink, or women—nor do the arts give me joy any longer. The Leopard of Discontent walks the streets of my city; the Lion of Discouragement crouches outside the walls of my citadel. All is desolation and a vexation of the spirit. I feel like hell. How can I believe, how can I have faith in this day and age? Is it true that the greatest scientists believe again in you?

I read your column and like it very much. There you once wrote: 'When the salt has lost its savour, who shall savour it again?' Is the answer: 'None but the Saviour?'

Thanking you very much for a quick reply, I remain yours truly,

A Regular Subscriber"

Miss Lonelyhearts

in the

Country

Betty came to see Miss Lonelyhearts the next day and every day thereafter. With her she brought soup and boiled chicken for him to eat.

He knew that she believed he did not want to get well, yet he followed her instructions because he realized that his present sickness was unimportant. It was merely a trick by his body to relieve one more profound.

Whenever he mentioned the letters or Christ, she changed the subject to tell long stories about life on a farm. She seemed to think that if he never talked about these things, his body would get well, that if his body got well everything would be well. He began to realize that there was a definite plan behind her farm talk, but could not guess what it was.

When the first day of spring arrived, he felt better. He had already spent more than a week in bed and was anxious to get out. Betty took him for a walk in the zoo and he was amused by her evident belief in the curative power of animals. She seemed to think that it must steady him to look at a buffalo.

He wanted to go back to work, but she made him get Shrike to extend his sick leave a few days. He was grateful to her and did as she asked. She then told him her plan. Her aunt still owned the farm in Connecticut on which she had been born and they could go there and camp in the house.

She borrowed an old Ford touring car from a friend. They loaded it with food and equipment and started out early one morning. As soon as they reached the outskirts of the city, Betty began to act like an excited child, greeting the trees and grass with delight.

After they had passed through New Haven, they came to Bramford and turned off the State highway on a dirt road that led to Monkstown. The road went through a wild-looking stretch of woods and they saw some red squirrels and a partridge. He had to admit, even to himself, that the pale new leaves, shaped and colored like candle flames, were beautiful and that the air smelt clean and alive.

There was a pond on the farm and they caught sight of it through the trees just before coming to the house. She did not have the key so they had to force the door open. The heavy, musty smell of old furniture and wood rot made them cough. He complained. Betty said that she did not mind because it was not a human smell. She put so much meaning into the word "human" that he laughed and kissed her.

They decided to camp in the kitchen because it was the largest room and the least crowded with old furniture. There were four windows and a door and they opened them all to air the place out.

While he unloaded the car, she swept up and made a fire

in the stove out of a broken chair. The stove looked like a locomotive and was almost as large, but the chimney drew all right and she soon had a fire going. He got some water from the well and put it on the stove to boil. When the water was scalding hot, they used it to clean an old mattress that they had found in one of the bedrooms. Then they put the mattress out in the sun to dry.

It was almost sundown before Betty would let him stop working. He sat smoking a cigarette, while she prepared supper. They had beans, eggs, bread, fruit and drank two cups of coffee apiece.

After they had finished eating, there was still some light left and they went down to look at the pond. They sat close together with their backs against a big oak and watched a heron hunt frogs. Just as they were about to start back, two deer and a fawn came down to the water on the opposite side of the pond. The flies were bothering them and they went into the water and began to feed on the lily pads. Betty accidentally made a noise and the deer floundered back into the woods.

When they returned to the house, it was quite dark. They lit the kerosene lamp that they had brought with them, then dragged the mattress into the kitchen and made their bed on the floor next to the stove.

Before going to bed, they went out on the kitchen porch to smoke a last cigarette. It was very cold and he had to go back for a blanket. They sat close together with the blanket wrapped around them.

There were plenty of stars. A screech owl made a horrible racket somewhere in the woods and when it quit, a loon began down on the pond. The crickets made almost as much noise as the loon.

Even with the blanket around them it was cold. They went inside and made a big fire in the stove, using pieces of a hardwood table to make the fire last. They each ate an apple, then put on their pajamas and went to bed. He fondled her, but when she said that she was a virgin, he let her alone and went to sleep.

He woke up with the sun in his eyes. Betty was already busy at the stove. She sent him down to the pond to wash and when he got back, breakfast was ready. It consisted of eggs, ham, potatoes, fried apples, bread and coffee.

After breakfast, she worked at making the place more comfortable and he drove to Monkstown for some fresh fruit and the newspapers. He stopped for gas at the Aw-Kum-On Garage and told the attendant about the deer. The man said that there was still plenty of deer at the pond because no yids ever went there. He said it wasn't the hunters who drove out the deer, but the yids.

He got back to the house in time for lunch and, after eating, they went for a walk in the woods. It was very sad under the trees. Although spring was well advanced, in the deep shade there was nothing but death—rotten leaves, gray and white fungi, and over everything a funereal hush.

Later it grew very hot and they decided to go for a swim. They went in naked. The water was so cold that they could only stay in for a short time. They ran back to the house and took a quick drink of gin, then sat in a sunny spot on the kitchen porch.

Betty was unable to sit still for long. There was nothing to do in the house, so she began to wash the underwear she had worn on the trip up. After she had finished, she rigged a line between two trees.

He sat on the porch and watched her work. She had her

hair tied up in a checked handkerchief, otherwise she was completely naked. She looked a little fat, but when she lifted something to the line, all the fat disappeared. Her raised arms pulled her breasts up until they were like pink-tipped thumbs.

There was no wind to disturb the pull of the earth. The new green leaves hung straight down and shone in the hot sun like an army of little metal shields. Somewhere in the woods a thrush was singing. Its sound was like that of a flute choked with saliva.

Betty stopped with her arms high to listen to the bird. When it was quiet, she turned towards him with a guilty laugh. He blew her a kiss. She caught it with a gesture that was childishly sexual. He vaulted the porch rail and ran to kiss her. As they went down, he smelled a mixture of sweat, soap and crushed grass.

Miss Lonelyhearts
Returns

Several days later, they started to drive back to the city. When they reached the Bronx slums, Miss Lonelyhearts knew that Betty had failed to cure him and that he had been right when he had said that he could never forget the letters. He felt better, knowing this, because he had begun to think himself a faker and a fool.

Crowds of people moved through the street with a dream-like violence. As he looked at their broken hands and torn mouths he was overwhelmed by the desire to help them, and because this desire was sincere, he was happy despite the feeling of guilt which accompanied it.

He saw a man who appeared to be on the verge of death stagger into a movie theater that was showing a picture called *Blonde Beauty*. He saw a ragged woman with an enormous goiter pick a love story magazine out of a garbage can and seem very excited by her find.

Prodded by his conscience, he began to generalize. Men have always fought their misery with dreams. Although dreams were once powerful, they have been made puerile by the movies, radio and newspapers. Among many betrayals, this one is the worst.

The thing that made his share in it particularly bad was that he was capable of dreaming the Christ dream. He felt that he had failed at it, not so much because of Shrike's jokes or his own self-doubt, but because of his lack of humility.

He finally got to bed. Before falling asleep, he vowed to make a sincere attempt to be humble. In the morning, when he started for his office, he renewed his vow.

Fortunately for him, Shrike was not in the city room and his humility was spared an immediate trial. He went straight to his desk and began to open letters. When he had opened about a dozen, he felt sick and decided to do his column for that day without reading any of them. He did not want to test himself too severely.

The typewriter was uncovered and he put a sheet of paper into the roller.

"Christ died for you.

"He died nailed to a tree for you. His gift to you is suffering and it is only through suffering that you can know Him. Cherish this gift, for . . ."

He snatched the paper out of the machine. With him, even the word Christ was a vanity. After staring at the pile of letters on his desk for a long time, he looked out the window. A slow spring rain was changing the dusty tar roofs below him to shiny patent leather. The water made everything slippery and he could find no support for either his eyes or his feelings.

Turning back to his desk, he picked up a bulky letter in a dirty envelope. He read it for the same reason that an animal tears at a wounded foot: to hurt the pain.

Dear Miss Lonelyhearts—

Being an admirer of your column because you give such good advice to people in trouble as that is what I am in also I would appreciate very much your advising me what to do after I tell you my troubles.

During the war I was told if I wanted to do my bit I should marry the man I was engaged to as he was going away to help Uncle Sam and to make a long story short I was married to him. After the war was over he still had to remain in the army for one more year as he signed for it and naturally I went to work as while doing this patriotic stunt he had only $18 to his name. I worked for three years steady and then had to stay home because I became a mother and in the meantime of those years my husband would get a job and then would tire of it or want to roam. It was all right before the baby came because then I could work steady and then bills were paid but when I stopped everything went sliding backward. Then two years went by and a baby boy was added to our union. My girl will be eight and my boy six years of age.

I made up my mind after I had the second child that in spite of my health as I was hit by an auto while carrying the first I would get some work to do but debts collected so rapidly it almost took a derick to lift them let alone a sick woman. I went to work evenings why my husband would be home so as somebody could watch the baby and I did this until the baby was three years old when I thought of taking in a man who had been boarding with his sister as she moved to Rochester and he had to look for a new place. Well my husband agreed as he figured the $15 dollars per he paid us would make it easier for him as this man was a widower with two children and as my husband knew him for twelve years being real pals then going out together etc. After the boarder was with us for about a year my husband didn't come home one night and then two nights etc. I listed him in the missing persons and after two and a half months I was told to go to Grove St. which I did and he was arrested because he refused to support me and my kids. When he served three months of the six the judge asked me to give him another chance which like a fool I did and when he got home he beat me up so I had to spend over $30 dollars in the dentist afterwards.

He got a pension from the army and naturaly I was the one to take it to the store and cash it as he was so lazy I always had to sign his name and of course put per my name and through wanting to pay the landlord because he wanted to put us out I signed his check as usual but forgot to put per my name and for this to get even with me because he did three months time he sent to Washington for the copy of the check so I could be arrested for forgery but as the butcher knew about me signing the checks etc nothing was done to me.

He threatened my life many times saying no one solved the Mrs. Mills murder and the same will happen to you and many times when making beds I would find under his pillow a hammer, scissors, knife, stone lifter etc and when I asked him what the idea was he would make believe he knew nothing about it or say the children put them there and then a few months went buy and I was going to my work as usual as the boarder had to stay home that day due to the fact the material for his boss did not arrive and he could not go to work as he is a piece worker. I always made a habit of setting the breakfast and cooking the food the night before so I could stay in bed until seven as at that time my son was in the Kings County hospital with a disease which my husband gave me that he got while fighting for Uncle Sam and I had to be at the clinic for the needle to. So while I was in bed unbeknown to me my husband sent the boarder out for a paper and when he came back my husband was gone. So later when I came from my room I was told that my husband had gone out. I fixed the childs breakfast and ate my own then went to the washtub to do the weeks wash and while the boarder was reading the paper at twelve o'clock noon my mother came over to mind the baby as I had a chance to go out and make a little money doing house work. Things were a little out of order beds not dressed and things out of place and a little sweeping had to be done as I was washing all morning and I didn't have a chance to do it so I thought to do it then while my mother was in the house with her to help me so that I could finish quickly. Hurrying at break neck speed to get finished I swept through the rooms to make sure everything was spick and span so when my husband came home he couldn't have anything to say. We had three beds and I was on the last which was a double bed when stooping to put the broom under the bed to get at the lint and the dust when lo and behold I saw a face like the mask of a devil with only the whites of the eyes showing and hands clenched to choke anyone and then I saw it move and I was so frighted that almost till night I was hystirical and I was paralised from my waist down. I thought I would never be able to walk again. A doctor was called for me by my mother and he said the man ought to be put in an asylum to do a thing like that. It was my husband lieing under the bed from seven in the morning until almost half past one o'clock lieing in his own dirt instead of going to the bath room when he had to be dirtied himself waiting to fright me.

So as I could not trust him I would not sleep with him and as I told the boarder to find a new place because I thought maybe he was jealous of something I slept in the boarders bed in an other room. Some nights I would wake up and find him standing by my bed laughing like a crazy man or walking around stripped etc.

I bought a new sowing machine as I do some sowing for other people to make both ends meet and one night while I was out delivering my work I got back to find the house cleaned out and he had pawned my sowing machine and also all the other pawnables in the house. Ever since he frighted me I have been so nervous during the night when I get up for the children that he would be standing behind a curtain and either jump out at me or put his hand on me before I could light the light. Well as I had to see that I could not make him work steady and that I had to be mother and housekeeper and wage earner etc and I could not let my nerves get the best of me as I lost a good job once on account of having bad nerves I simply moved away from him and anyway there was nothing much left in the house. But he pleaded with me for another chance so I thought seeing he is the father of my children I will and then he did more crazy things to many to write and I left him again. Four times we got together and four times I left. Please Miss Lonelyhearts believe me just for the childrens sake is the bunk and pardon me because I dont know how you are fixed but all I know is that in over three years I got $200 dollars from him altogether.

About four months ago I handed him a warrant for his arrest for non support and he tore it up and left the house and I haven't seen him since and as I had pneumonia and my little girl had the flu I was put in financial embarasment with the doctor and we had to go to the ward and when we came out of the hospital I had to ask the border to come to live with us again as he was a sure $15 dollars a week and if anything happened to me he would be there to take care of the children. But he tries to make me be bad and as there is nobody in the house when he comes home drunk on Saturday night I dont know what to do but so far I didnt let him. Where my husband is I dont know but I received a vile letter from him where he even accused his inocent children of things and sarcasticaly asked about the star boarder.

Dear Miss Lonelyhearts please dont be angry at me for writing such a long letter and taking up so much of your time in reading it but if I ever write all the things which happened to me living with him it would fill a book and please forgive me for saying some nasty things as I had to give you an idea of what is going on in my home. Every woman is intitiled to a home isn't she? So Miss Lonelyhearts please put a few lines in your column when you refer to this letter so I will know you are helping me. Shall I take my husband back? How can I support my children?

Thanking you for anything you can advise me in I remain your truly—

Broad Shoulders

P.S. Dear Miss Lonelyhearts dont think I am broad shouldered but that is the way I feel about life and me I mean.

Miss Lonelyhearts

and the

Cripple

Miss Lonelyhearts dodged Betty because she made him feel ridiculous. He was still trying to cling to his humility, and the farther he got below self-laughter, the easier it was for him to practice it. When Betty telephoned, he refused to answer and after he had twice failed to call her back, she left him alone.

One day, about a week after he had returned from the country, Goldsmith asked him out for a drink. When he accepted, he made himself so humble that Goldsmith was frightened and almost suggested a doctor.

They found Shrike in Delehanty's and joined him at the bar. Goldsmith tried to whisper something to him about Miss Lonelyhearts' condition, but he was drunk and refused to listen. He caught only part of what Goldsmith was trying to say.

"I must differ with you, my good Goldsmith," Shrike said. "Don't call sick those who have faith. They are the well. It is you who are sick."

Goldsmith did not reply and Shrike turned to Miss Lonelyhearts. "Come, tell us, brother, how it was that you first came to believe. Was it music in a church, or the death of a loved one, or, mayhap, some wise old priest?"

The familiar jokes no longer had any effect on Miss Lonelyhearts. He smiled at Shrike as the saints are supposed to have smiled at those about to martyr them.

"Ah, but how stupid of me," Shrike continued. "It was the letters, of course. Did I myself not say that the Miss Lonelyhearts are the priests of twentieth-century America?"

Goldsmith laughed, and Shrike, in order to keep him laughing, used an old trick; he appeared to be offended. "Goldsmith, you are the nasty product of this unbelieving age. You cannot believe, you can only laugh. You take everything with a bag of salt and forget that salt is the enemy of fire as well as of ice. Be warned, the salt you use is not Attic salt, it is coarse butcher's salt. It doesn't preserve; it kills."

The bartender who was standing close by, broke in to address Miss Lonelyhearts. "Pardon me, sir, but there's a gent here named Doyle who wants to meet you. He says you know his wife."

Before Miss Lonelyhearts could reply, he beckoned to someone standing at the other end of the bar. The signal was answered by a little cripple, who immediately started in their direction. He used a cane and dragged one of his feet behind him in a box-shaped shoe with a four-inch sole. As he hobbled along, he made many waste motions, like those of a partially destroyed insect.

The bartender introduced the cripple as Mr. Peter Doyle. Doyle was very excited and shook hands twice all around, then with a wave that was meant to be sporting, called for a round of drinks.

Before lifting his glass, Shrike carefully inspected the cripple. When he had finished, he winked at Miss Lonelyhearts and said, "Here's to humanity." He patted Doyle on the back. "Mankind, mankind . . ." he sighed, wagging his head sadly. "What is man that . . ."

The bartender broke in again on behalf of his friend and tried to change the conversation to familiar ground. "Mr. Doyle inspects meters for the gas company."

"And an excellent job it must be," Shrike said. "He should be able to give us the benefit of a different viewpoint. We newspapermen are limited in many ways and I like to hear both sides of a case."

Doyle had been staring at Miss Lonelyhearts as though searching for something, but he now turned to Shrike and tried to be agreeable. "You know what people say, Mr. Shrike?"

"No, my good man, what is it that people say?"

"Everybody's got a frigidaire nowadays, and they say that we meter inspectors take the place of the iceman in the stories." He tried, rather diffidently, to leer.

"What!" Shrike roared at him. "I can see, sir, that you are not the man for us. You can know nothing about humanity; you are humanity. I leave you to Miss Lonelyhearts." He called to Goldsmith and stalked away.

The cripple was confused and angry. "Your friend is a nut," he said. Miss Lonelyhearts was still smiling, but the character of his smile had changed. It had become full of sympathy and a little sad.

The new smile was for Doyle and he knew it. He smiled back gratefully.

"Oh, I forgot," Doyle said, "the wife asked me, if I bumped into you, to ask you to our house to eat. That's why I made Jake introduce us."

Miss Lonelyhearts was busy with his smile and accepted without thinking of the evening he had spent with Mrs. Doyle. The cripple felt honored and shook hands for a third time. It was evidently his only social gesture.

After a few more drinks, when Doyle said that he was tired, Miss Lonelyhearts suggested that they go into the back room. They found a table and sat opposite each other.

The cripple had a very strange face. His eyes failed to balance; his mouth was not under his nose; his forehead was square and bony; and his round chin was like a forehead in miniature. He looked like one of those composite photographs used by screen magazines in guessing contests.

They sat staring at each other until the strain of wordless communication began to excite them both. Doyle made vague, needless adjustments to his clothing. Miss Lonelyhearts found it very difficult to keep his smile steady.

When the cripple finally labored into speech, Miss Lonelyhearts was unable to understand him. He listened hard for a few minutes and realized that Doyle was making no attempt to be understood. He was giving birth to groups of words that lived inside of him as things, a jumble of the retorts he had meant to make when insulted and the private curses against fate that experience had taught him to swallow.

Like a priest, Miss Lonelyhearts turned his face slightly away. He watched the play of the cripple's hands. At first they conveyed nothing but excitement, then gradually they became pictorial. They lagged behind to illustrate a matter with which he was already finished, or ran ahead to illustrate something he had not yet begun to talk about. As he grew more articulate, his hands stopped trying to aid his speech and began to dart in and out of his clothing. One of them suddenly emerged from a pocket of his coat, dragged some sheets of letter paper. He forced these on Miss Lonelyhearts.

Dear Miss Lonelyhearts—

I am kind of ashamed to write you because a man like me dont take stock in things like that but my wife told me you were a man and not some dopey woman so I thought I would write to you after reading your answer to Disillusioned. I am a cripple 41 yrs of age which I have been all my life and I have never let myself get blue until lately when I have been feeling lousy all the time on account of not getting anywhere and asking myself what is it all for. You have a education so I figured may be you no. What I want to no is why I go around pulling my leg up and down stairs reading meters for the gas company for a stinking $22.50 per while the bosses ride around in swell cars living off the fat of the land. Dont think I am a greasy red. I read where they shoot cripples in Russia because they cant work but I can work better than any park bum and support a wife and child to. But thats not what I am writing you about. What I want to no is what is it all for my pulling my god damed leg along the streets and down in stinking cellars with it all the time hurting fit to burst so that near quitting time I am crazy with pain and when I get home all I hear is money money which aint no home for a man like me. What I want to no is what in hell is the use day after day with a foot like mine when you have to go around pulling and scrambling for a lousy three squares with a toothache in it that comes from using the foot so much. The doctor told me I ought to rest it for six months but who will pay me when I am resting it. But that aint what I mean either because you might tell me to change my job and where could I get another one I am lucky to have one at all. It aint the job that I am complaining about but what I want to no is what is the whole stinking business for.

Please write me an answer not in the paper because my wife reads your stuff and I dont want her to no I wrote to you because I always said the papers is crap but I figured maybe you no something about it because you have read a lot of books and I never finished high.

Yours truly,
Peter Doyle

While Miss Lonelyhearts was puzzling out the crabbed writing, Doyle's damp hand accidentally touched his under the table. He jerked away, but then drove his hand back and forced it to clasp the cripple's. After finishing the letter, he did not let go, but pressed it firmly with all the love he could manage. At first the cripple covered his embarrassment by disguising the meaning of the clasp with a handshake, but he soon gave in to it and they sat silently hand in hand.

Miss Lonelyhearts
Pays a Visit

They left the speakeasy together, both very drunk and very busy: Doyle with the wrongs he had suffered and Miss Lonelyhearts with the triumphant thing that his humility had become.

They took a cab. As they entered the street in which Doyle lived, he began to curse his wife and his crippled foot. He called on Christ to blast them both.

Miss Lonelyhearts was very happy and inside of his head he was also calling on Christ. But his call was not a curse, it was the shape of his joy.

When the cab drew up to the curb, Miss Lonelyhearts helped his companion out and led him into the house. They made a great deal of noise with the front door and Mrs. Doyle came into the hall. At the sight of her the cripple started to curse again.

She greeted Miss Lonelyhearts, then took hold of her husband and shook the breath out of him. When he was quiet, she dragged him into their apartment. Miss Lonelyhearts followed and as he passed her in the dark foyer, she goosed him and laughed.

After washing their hands, they sat down to eat. Mrs. Doyle had had her supper earlier in the evening and she waited on them. The first thing she put on the table was a quart bottle of guinea red.

When they had reached their coffee, she sat down next to Miss Lonelyhearts. He could feel her knee pressing his under the table, but he paid no attention to her and only broke his beatific smile to drink. The heavy food had dulled him and he was trying desperately to feel again what he had felt while holding hands with the cripple in the speakeasy.

She put her thigh under his, but when he still failed to respond, she got up abruptly and went into the parlor. They followed a few minutes later and found her mixing ginger-ale highballs.

They all drank silently. Doyle looked sleepy and his wife was just beginning to get drunk. Miss Lonelyhearts made no attempt to be sociable. He was busy trying to find a message. When he did speak it would have to be in the form of a message.

After the third highball, Mrs. Doyle began to wink quite openly at Miss Lonelyhearts, but he still refused to pay any attention to her. The cripple, however, was greatly disturbed by her signals. He began to fidget and mumble under his breath.

The vague noises he was making annoyed Mrs. Doyle. "What in hell are you talking about?" she demanded.

The cripple started a sigh that ended in a groan and then, as though ashamed of himself, said, "Ain't I the pimp, to bring home a guy for my wife?" He darted a quick look at Miss Lonelyhearts and laughed apologetically.

Mrs. Doyle was furious. She rolled a newspaper into a club and struck her husband on the mouth with it. He surprised her by playing the fool. He growled like a dog and caught the paper in his teeth. When she let go of her end, he dropped to his hands and knees and continued the imitation on the floor.

Miss Lonelyhearts tried to get the cripple to stand up and bent to lift him; but, as he did so, Doyle tore open Miss Lonelyhearts' fly, then rolled over on his back, laughing wildly.

His wife kicked him and turned away with a snort of contempt.

The cripple soon laughed himself out, and they all returned to their seats. Doyle and his wife sat staring at each other, while Miss Lonelyhearts again began to search for a message.

The silence bothered Mrs. Doyle. When she could stand it no longer, she went to the sideboard to make another round of drinks. But the bottle was empty. She asked her husband to go to the corner drug store for some gin. He refused with a single, curt nod of his head.

She tried to argue with him. He ignored her and she lost her temper. "Get some gin!" she yelled. "Get some gin, you bastard!"

Miss Lonelyhearts stood up. He had not yet found his message, but he had to say something. "Please don't fight," he pleaded. "He loves you, Mrs. Doyle; that's why he acts like that. Be kind to him."

She grunted with annoyance and left the room. They could hear her slamming things around in the kitchen.

Miss Lonelyhearts went over to the cripple and smiled at him with the same smile he had used in the speakeasy.

The cripple returned the smile and stuck out his hand. Miss Lonelyhearts clasped it, and they stood this way, smiling and holding hands, until Mrs. Doyle re-entered the room.ß

"What a sweet pair of fairies you guys are," she said.

The cripple pulled his hand away and made as though to strike his wife. Miss Lonelyhearts realized that now was the time to give his message. It was now or never.

"You have a big, strong body, Mrs. Doyle. Holding your husband in your arms, you can warm him and give him life. You can take the chill out of his bones. He drags his days out in areaways and cellars, carrying a heavy load of weariness and pain. You can substitute a dream of yourself for this load. A buoyant dream that will be like a dynamo in him. You can do this by letting him conquer you in your bed. He will repay you by flowering and becoming ardent over you. . . ."

She was too astonished to laugh, and the cripple turned his face away as though embarrassed.

With the first few words Miss Lonelyhearts had known that he would be ridiculous. By avoiding God, he had failed to tap the force in his heart and had merely written a column for his paper.

He tried again by becoming hysterical. "Christ is love," he screamed at them. It was a stage scream, but he kept on. "Christ is the black fruit that hangs on the crosstree. Man was lost by eating of the bidden fruit. He shall be saved by eating of the bidden fruit. The black Christ-fruit, the love fruit . . ."

This time he had failed still more miserably. He had substituted the rhetoric of Shrike for that of Miss Lonelyhearts. He felt like an empty bottle, shiny and sterile.

He closed his eyes. When he heard the cripple say, "I love you," he opened them and saw him kissing his wife. He knew that the cripple was doing this, not because of the things he had said, but out of loyalty.

"All right, you nut," she said, queening it over her husband. "I forgive you, but go to the drug store for some gin."

Without looking at Miss Lonelyhearts, the cripple took his hat and left. When he had gone, Mrs. Doyle smiled. "You were a scream with your fly open," she said. "I thought I'd die laughing."

He did not answer.

"Boy, is he jealous," she went on. "All I have to do is point to some big guy and say, 'Gee, I'd love to have him love me up.' It drives him nuts."

Her voice was low and thick and it was plain that she was trying to excite him. When she went to the radio to tune in on a jazz orchestra, she waved her behind at him like a flag.

He said that he was too tired to dance. After doing a few obscene steps in front of him, she sat down in his lap. He tried to fend her off, but she kept pressing her open mouth against his and when he turned away, she nuzzled his cheek. He felt like an empty bottle that is being slowly filled with warm, dirty water.

When she opened the neck of her dress and tried to force his head between her breasts, he parted his knees with a quick jerk that slipped her to the floor. She tried to pull him down on top of her. He struck out blindly and hit her in the face. She screamed and he hit her again and again. He kept hitting her until she stopped trying to hold him, then he ran out of the house.

Miss Lonelyhearts
Attends a Party

Miss Lonelyhearts had gone to bed again. This time his bed was surely taking him somewhere, and with great speed. He had only to ride it quietly. He had already been riding for three days.

Before climbing aboard, he had prepared for the journey by jamming the telephone bell and purchasing several enormous cans of crackers. He now lay on the bed, eating crackers, drinking water and smoking cigarettes.

He thought of how calm he was. His calm was so perfect that he could not destroy it even by being conscious of it. In three days he had gone very far. It grew dark in the room. He got out of bed, washed his teeth, urinated, then turned out the light and went to sleep. He fell asleep without even a sigh and slept the sleep of the wise and the innocent. Without dreaming, he was aware of fireflies and the slop of oceans.

Later a train rolled into a station where he was a reclining statue holding a stopped clock, a coach rumbled into the yard of an inn where he was sitting over a guitar, cap in hand, shedding the rain with his hump.

He awoke. The noise of both arrivals had combined to become a knocking on the door. He climbed out of bed. Although he was completely naked, he went to the door without covering himself. Five people rushed in, two of whom were women. The women shrieked when they saw him and jumped back into the hall.

The three men held their ground. Miss Lonelyhearts recognized Shrike among them and saw that he, as well as the others, was very drunk. Shrike said that one of the women was his wife and wanted to fight Miss Lonelyhearts for insulting her.

Miss Lonelyhearts stood quietly in the center of the room. Shrike dashed against him, but fell back, as a wave that dashes against an ancient rock, smooth with experience, falls back. There was no second wave.

Instead Shrike became jovial. He slapped Miss Lonelyhearts on the back. "Put on a pair of pants, my friend," he said, "we're going to a party."

Miss Lonelyhearts picked up a can of crackers.

"Come on, my son," Shrike urged. "It's solitary drinking that makes drunkards."

Miss Lonelyhearts carefully examined each cracker before popping it into his mouth.

"Don't be a spoil-sport," Shrike said with a great deal of irritation. He was a gull trying to lay an egg in the smooth flank of a rock, a screaming, clumsy gull. "There's a game we want to play and we need you to play it.—'Everyman his own Miss Lonelyhearts.' I invented it, and we can't play without you."

Shrike pulled a large batch of letters out of his pockets and waved them in front of Miss Lonelyhearts. He recognized them; they were from his office file.

The rock remained calm and solid. Although Miss Lonelyhearts did not doubt that it could withstand any test, he was willing to have it tried. He began to dress.

They went downstairs, and all six of them piled into one cab. Mary Shrike sat on his lap, but despite her drunken wriggling the rock remained perfect.

The party was in Shrike's apartment. A roar went up when Miss Lonelyhearts entered and the crowd surged forward. He stood firm and they slipped back in a futile curl. He smiled. He had turned more than a dozen drunkards. He had turned them without effort or thought. As he stood smiling, a little wave crept up out of the general welter and splashed at his feet for attention. It was Betty.

"What's the matter with you?" she asked. "Are you sick again?"

He did not answer.

When every one was seated, Shrike prepared to start the game. He distributed paper and pencils, then led Miss Lonelyhearts to the center of the room and began his spiel.

"Ladies and gentlemen," he said, imitating the voice and gestures of a circus barker. "We have with us to-night a man whom you all know and admire. Miss Lonelyhearts, he of the singing heart—a still more swollen Mussolini of the soul.

"He has come here to-night to help you with your moral and spiritual problems, to provide you with a slogan, a cause, an absolute value and a *raison d'être*.

"Some of you, perhaps, consider yourself too far gone for help. You are afraid that even Miss Lonelyhearts, no matter how fierce his torch, will be unable to set you on fire. You are afraid that even when exposed to his bright flame, you will only smolder and give off a bad smell. Be of good heart, for I know that you will burst into flame. Miss Lonelyhearts is sure to prevail."

Shrike pulled out the batch of letters and waved them above his head.

"We will proceed systematically," he said. "First, each of you will do his best to answer one of these letters, then, from your answers, Miss Lonelyhearts will diagnose your moral ills. Afterwards he will lead you in the way of attainment."

Shrike went among his guests and distributed the letters as a magician does cards. He talked continuously and read a part of each letter before giving it away.

"Here's one from an old woman whose son died last week. She is seventy years old and sells pencils for a living. She has no stockings and wears heavy boots on her torn and bleeding feet. She has rheum in her eyes. Have you room in your heart for her?

"This one is a jim-dandy. A young boy wants a violin. It looks simple; all you have to do is get the kid one. But then you discover that he had dictated the letter to his little sister. He is paralyzed and can't even feed himself. He has a toy violin and hugs it to his chest, imitating the sound of playing with his mouth. How pathetic? However, one can learn much from this parable. Label the boy Labor, the violin Capital, and so on . . ."

Miss Lonelyhearts stood it with the utmost serenity; he was not even interested. What goes on in the sea is of no interest to the rock.

When all the letters had been distributed, Shrike gave

one to Miss Lonelyhearts. He took it, but after holding it for a while, he dropped it to the floor without reading it.

Shrike was not quiet for a second.

"You are plunging into a world of misery and suffering, peopled by creatures who are strangers to everything but disease and policemen. Harried by one, they are hurried by the other...

"Pain, pain, pain, the dull, sordid, gnawing, chronic pain of heart and brain. The pain that only a great spiritual liniment can relieve...."

When Miss Lonelyhearts saw Betty get up to go, he followed her out of the apartment. She too should see the rock he had become.

Shrike did not miss him until he discovered the letter on the floor. He picked it up, tried to find Miss Lonelyhearts, then addressed the gathering again.

"The master has disappeared," he announced, "but do not despair. I am still with you. I am his disciple and I shall lead you in the way of attainment. First let me read you this letter which is addressed directly to the master."

He took the letter out of its envelope, as though he had not read it previously, and began: " 'What kind of a dirty skunk are you? When I got home with the gin, I found my wife crying on the floor and the house full of neighbors. She said that you tried to rape her you dirty skunk and they wanted to get the police but I said that I'd do the job myself you ...'

"My, oh my, I really can't bring myself to utter such vile language. I'll skip the swearing and go on. 'So that's what all your fine speeches come to, you bastard, you ought to have your brains blown out.' It's signed, 'Doyle.'

"Well, well, so the master is another Rasputin. How this

shakes one's faith! But I can't believe it. I won't believe it.
The master can do no wrong. My faith is unshaken. This is
only one more attempt against him by the devil. He has
spent his life struggling with the arch fiend for our sakes,
and he shall triumph. I mean Miss Lonelyhearts, not the
devil.

"The gospel according to Shrike. Let me tell you about
his life. It unrolls before me like a scroll. First, in the dawn
of childhood, radiant with pure innocence, like a rain-
washed star, he wends his weary way to the University of
Hard Knocks. Next, a youth, he dashes into the night from
the bed of his first whore. And then, the man, the man Miss
Lonelyhearts—struggling valiantly to realize a high ideal,
his course shaped by a proud aim. But, alas! cold and scorn-
ful, the world heaps obstacle after obstacle in his path;
deems he the goal at hand, a voice of thunder bids him
'Halt!' 'Let each hindrance be thy ladder,' thinks he.
'Higher, even higher, mount!' And so he climbs, rung by
weary rung, and so he urges himself on, breathless with
hallowed fire. And so . . ."

Miss Lonelyhearts

and the

Party Dress

When Miss Lonelyhearts left Shrike's apartment, he found Betty in the hall waiting for the elevator. She had on a light-blue dress that was very much a party dress. She dressed for things, he realized.

Even the rock was touched by this realization. No; it was not the rock that was touched. The rock was still perfect. It was his mind that was touched, the instrument with which he knew the rock.

He approached Betty with a smile, for his mind was free and clear. The things that muddied it had precipitated out into the rock.

But she did not smile back. "What are you grinning at?" she snapped.

"Oh, I'm sorry," he said. "I didn't mean anything."

They entered the elevator together. When they reached the street, he took her arm although she tried to jerk away.

"Won't you have a soda, please?" he begged. The party dress had given his simplified mind its cue and he delighted in the boy-and-girl argument that followed.

"No; I'm going home."

"Oh, come on," he said, pulling her towards a soda fountain. As she went, she unconsciously exaggerated her little-girl-in-a-party-dress air.

They both had strawberry sodas. They sucked the pink drops up through straws, she pouting at his smile, neither one of them conscious of being cute.

"Why are you mad at me, Betty? I didn't do anything. It was Shrike's idea and he did all the talking."

"Because you are a fool."

"I've quit the Miss Lonelyhearts job. I haven't been in the office for almost a week."

"What are you going to do?"

"I'm going to look for a job in an advertising agency."

He was not deliberately lying. He was only trying to say what she wanted to hear. The party dress was so gay and charming, light blue with a frothy lace collar flecked with pink, like the collar of her soda.

"You ought to see Bill Wheelright about a job. He owns an agency—he's a swell guy. . . . He's in love with me."

"I couldn't work for a rival."

She screwed up her nose and they both laughed.

He was still laughing when he noticed that something had gone wrong with her laugh. She was crying.

He felt for the rock. It was still there; neither laughter nor tears could affect the rock. It was oblivious to wind or rain.

"Oh . . ." she sobbed. "I'm a fool." She ran out of the store.

He followed and caught her. But her sobs grew worse and he hailed a taxi and forced her to get in.

She began to talk under her sobs. She was pregnant. She was going to have a baby.

He put the rock forward and waited with complete poise for her to stop crying. When she was quiet, he asked her to marry him.

"No," she said. "I'm going to have an abortion."

"Please marry me." He pleaded just as he had pleaded with her to have a soda.

He begged the party dress to marry him, saying all the things it expected to hear, all the things that went with strawberry sodas and farms in Connecticut. He was just what the party dress wanted him to be: simple and sweet, whimsical and poetic, a trifle collegiate yet very masculine.

By the time they arrived at her house, they were discussing their life after marriage. Where they would live and in how many rooms. Whether they could afford to have the child. How they would rehabilitate the farm in Connecticut. What kind of furniture they both liked.

She agreed to have the child. He won that point. In return, he agreed to see Bill Wheelright about a job. With a great deal of laughter, they decided to have three beds in their bedroom. Twin beds for sleep, very prim and puritanical, and between them a love bed, an ornate double bed with cupids, nymphs and Pans.

He did not feel guilty. He did not feel. The rock was a solidification of his feeling, his conscience, his sense of reality, his self-knowledge. He could have planned anything. A castle in Spain and love on a balcony or a pirate trip and love on a tropical island.

When her door closed behind him, he smiled. The rock had been thoroughly tested and had been found perfect. He had only to climb aboard the bed again.

Miss Lonelyhearts
Has a
Religious Experience

After a long night and morning, towards noon, Miss Lonelyhearts welcomed the arrival of fever. It promised heat and mentally unmotivated violence. The promise was soon fulfilled; the rock became a furnace.

He fastened his eyes on the Christ that hung on the wall opposite his bed. As he stared at it, it became a bright fly, spinning with quick grace on a background of blood velvet sprinkled with tiny nerve stars.

Everything else in the room was dead—chairs, table, pencils, clothes, books. He thought of this black world of things as a fish. And he was right, for it suddenly rose to the bright bait on the wall. It rose with a splash of music and he saw its shining silver belly.

Christ is life and light.

"Christ! Christ!" This shout echoed through the innermost cells of his body.

He moved his head to a cooler spot on the pillow and the vein in his forehead became less swollen. He felt clean and fresh. His heart was a rose and in his skull another rose bloomed.

The room was full of grace. A sweet, clean grace, not washed clean, but clean as the innersides of the inner petals of a newly forced rosebud.

Delight was also in the room. It was like a gentle wind, and his nerves rippled under it like small blue flowers in a pasture.

He was conscious of two rhythms that were slowly becoming one. When they became one, his identification with God was complete. His heart was the one heart, the heart of God. And his brain was likewise God's.

God said, "Will you accept it, now?"

And he replied, "I accept, I accept."

He immediately began to plan a new life and his future conduct as Miss Lonelyhearts. He submitted drafts of his column to God and God approved them. God approved his every thought.

Suddenly the door bell rang. He climbed out of bed and went into the hall to see who was coming. It was Doyle, the cripple, and he was slowly working his way up the stairs.

God had sent him so that Miss Lonelyhearts could perform a miracle and be certain of his conversion. It was a sign. He would embrace the cripple and the cripple would be made whole again, even as he, a spiritual cripple, had been made whole.

He rushed down the stairs to meet Doyle with his arms spread for the miracle.

Doyle was carrying something wrapped in a newspaper. When he saw Miss Lonelyhearts, he put his hand inside the package and stopped. He shouted some kind of a warning, but Miss Lonelyhearts continued his charge. He did not understand the cripple's shout and heard it as a cry for help from Desperate, Harold S. Catholic-mother, Broken-hearted, Broad-shoulders, Sick-of-it-all, Disillusioned-with-tubercular-husband. He was running to succor them with love.

The cripple turned to escape, but he was too close and Miss Lonelyhearts caught him.

While they were struggling, Betty came in through the street door. She called to them to stop and started up the stairs. The cripple saw her cutting off his escape and tried to get rid of the package. He pulled his hand out. The gun inside the package exploded and Miss Lonelyhearts fell, dragging the cripple with him. They both rolled part of the way down the stairs.

THE DAY
OF THE
LOCUST

1

Around quitting time, Tod Hackett heard a great din on the road outside his office. The groan of leather mingled with the jangle of iron and over all beat the tattoo of a thousand hooves. He hurried to the window.

An army of cavalry and foot was passing. It moved like a mob; its lines broken, as though fleeing from some terrible defeat. The dolmans of the hussars, the heavy shakos of the guards, Hanoverian light horse, with their flat leather caps and flowing red plumes, were all jumbled together in bobbing disorder. Behind the cavalry came the infantry, a wild sea of waving sabretaches, sloped muskets, crossed shoulder belts and swinging cartridge boxes. Tod recognized the scarlet infantry of England with their white shoulder pads, the black infantry of the Duke of Brunswick, the French grenadiers with their enormous white gaiters, the Scotch with bare knees under plaid skirts.

While he watched, a little fat man, wearing a cork sun-helmet, polo shirt and knickers, darted around the corner of the building in pursuit of the army.

"Stage Nine—you bastards—Stage Nine!" he screamed through a small megaphone.

The cavalry put spur to their horses and the infantry broke into a dogtrot. The little man in the cork hat ran after them, shaking his fist and cursing.

Tod watched until they had disappeared, behind half a Mississippi steamboat, then put away his pencils and drawing board, and left the office. On the sidewalk outside the studio he stood for a moment trying to decide whether to walk home or take a streetcar. He had been in Hollywood less than three months and still found it a very exciting place, but he was lazy and didn't like to walk. He decided to take the streetcar as far as Vine Street and walk the rest of the way.

A talent scout for National Films had brought Tod to the Coast after seeing some of his drawings in an exhibit of undergraduate work at the Yale School of Fine Arts. He had been hired by telegram. If the scout had met Tod, he probably wouldn't have sent him to Hollywood to learn set and costume designing. His large sprawling body, his slow blue eyes and sloppy grin made him seem completely without talent, almost doltish in fact.

Yet, despite his appearance, he was really a very complicated young man with a whole set of personalities, one inside the other like a nest of Chinese boxes. And "The Burning of Los Angeles," a picture he was soon to paint, definitely proved he had talent.

He left the car at Vine Street. As he walked along, he examined the evening crowd. A great many of the people wore sports clothes which were not really sports clothes. Their sweaters, knickers, slacks, blue flannel jackets with brass buttons were fancy dress. The fat lady in the yachting cap was going shopping, not boating; the man in the Norfolk jacket and Tyrolean hat was returning, not from a mountain, but an insurance office; and the girl in slacks and sneaks with a bandanna around her head had just left a switchboard, not a tennis court.

Scattered among these masquerades were people of a different type. Their clothing was somber and badly cut, bought from mail-order houses. While the others moved rapidly, darting into stores and cocktail bars, they loitered on the corners or stood with their backs to the shop windows and stared at everyone who passed. When their stare was returned, their eyes filled with hatred. At this time Tod knew very little about them except that they had come to California to die.

He was determined to learn much more. They were the people he felt he must paint. He would never again do a fat red barn, old stone wall or sturdy Nantucket fisherman. From the moment he had seen them, he had known that, despite his race, training and heritage, neither Winslow Homer nor Thomas Ryder could be his masters and he turned to Goya and Daumier.

He had learned this just in time. During his last year in art school, he had begun to think that he might give up painting completely. The pleasures he received from the problems of composition and color had decreased as his facility had increased and he had realized that he was going the way of all his classmates, toward illustration or mere handsomeness. When the Hollywood job had come along, he had grabbed it despite the arguments of his friends who were certain that he was selling out and would never paint again.

He reached the end of Vine Street and began the climb into Pinyon Canyon. Night had started to fall.

The edges of the trees burned with a pale violet light and their centers gradually turned from deep purple to black. The same violet piping, like a Neon tube, outlined the tops of the ugly, hump-backed hills and they were almost beautiful.

But not even the soft wash of dusk could help the houses. Only dynamite would be of any use against the Mexican ranch houses, Samoan huts, Mediterranean villas, Egyptian and Japanese temples, Swiss chalets, Tudor cottages, and every possible combination of these styles that lined the slopes of the canyon.

When he noticed that they were all of plaster, lath and paper, he was charitable and blamed their shape on the materials used. Steel, stone and brick curb a builder's fancy a little, forcing him to distribute his stresses and weights and to keep his corners plumb, but plaster and paper know no law, not even that of gravity.

On the corner of La Huerta Road was a miniature Rhine castle with tarpaper turrets pierced for archers. Next to it was a highly colored shack with domes and minarets out of the *Arabian Nights*. Again he was charitable. Both houses were comic, but he didn't laugh. Their desire to startle was so eager and guileless.

It is hard to laugh at the need for beauty and romance, no matter how tasteless, even horrible, the results of that are. But it is easy to sigh. Few things are sadder than the truly monstrous.

2

The house he lived in was a nondescript affair called the San Bernardino Arms. It was an oblong three stories high, the back and sides of which were of plain, unpainted stucco, broken by even rows of unadorned windows. The façade was the color of diluted mustard and its windows, all double, were framed by pink Moorish columns which supported turnip-shaped lintels.

His room was on the third floor, but he paused for a moment on the landing of the second. It was on that floor that Faye Greener lived, in 208. When someone laughed in one of the apartments he started guiltily and continued upstairs.

As he opened his door a card fluttered to the floor. "Honest Abe Kusich," it said in large type, then underneath in smaller italics were several endorsements, printed to look like press notices.

'... the Lloyds of Hollywood'—Stanley Rose.

'Abe's word is better than Morgan's bonds'—Gail Brenshaw.

On the other side was a penciled message:

"Kingpin fourth, Solitair sixth. You can make some real dough on those nags."

After opening the window, he took off his jacket and lay down on the bed. Through the window he could see a square of enameled sky and a spray of eucalyptus. A light breeze stirred its long, narrow leaves, making them show first their green side, then their silver one.

He began to think of "Honest Abe Kusich" in order not to think of Faye Greener. He felt comfortable and wanted to remain that way.

Abe was an important figure in a set of lithographs called "The Dancers" on which Tod was working. He was one of the dancers. Faye Greener was another and her father, Harry, still another. They changed with each plate, but the group of uneasy people who formed their audience remained the same. They stood staring at the performers in just the way that they stared at the masqueraders on Vine Street. It was their stare that drove Abe and the others to spin crazily and leap into the air with twisted backs like hooked trout.

Despite the sincere indignation that Abe's grotesque depravity aroused in him, he welcomed his company. The little man excited him and in that way made him feel certain of his need to paint.

He had first met Abe when he was living on Ivar Street, in a hotel called the Chateau Mirabella. Another name for Ivar Street was "Lysol Alley," and the Chateau was mainly inhabited by hustlers, their managers, trainers and advance agents.

In the morning its halls reeked of antiseptic. Tod didn't like this odor. Moreover, the rent was high because it included police protection, a service for which he had no need. He wanted to move, but inertia and the fact that he didn't know where to go kept him in the Chateau until he met Abe. The meeting was accidental.

He was on the way to his room late one night when he saw what he supposed was a pile of soiled laundry lying in front of the door across the hall from his own. Just as he was passing it, the bundle moved and made a peculiar noise. He struck a match, thinking it might be a dog wrapped in a blanket. When the light flared up, he saw it was a tiny man.

The match went out and he hastily lit another. It was a male dwarf rolled up in a woman's flannel bathrobe. The round thing at the end was his slightly hydrocephalic head. A slow, choked snore bubbled from it.

The hall was cold and draughty. Tod decided to wake the man and stirred him with his toe. He groaned and opened his eyes.

"You oughtn't to sleep there."

"The hell you say," said the dwarf, closing his eyes again.

"You'll catch cold."

This friendly observation angered the little man still more.

"I want my clothes!" he bellowed.

The bottom of the door next to which he was lying filled with light. Tod decided to take a chance and knock. A few seconds later a woman opened it part way.

"What the hell do you want?" she demanded.

"There's a friend of yours out here who ..."

Neither of them let him finish.

"So what!" she barked, slamming the door.

"Give me my clothes, you bitch!" roared the dwarf.

She opened the door again and began to hurl things into the hall. A jacket and trousers, a shirt, socks, shoes and underwear, a tie and hat followed each other through the air in rapid succession. With each article went a special curse.

Tod whistled with amazement.

"Some gal!"

"You bet," said the dwarf. "A lollapalooza—all slut and a yard wide."

He laughed at his own joke, using a high-pitched cackle more dwarflike than anything that had come from him so far, then struggled to his feet and arranged the voluminous robe so that he could walk without tripping. Tod helped him gather his scattered clothing.

"Say, mister," he asked, "could I dress in your place?"

Tod let him into his bathroom. While waiting for him to reappear, he couldn't help imagining what had happened in the woman's apartment. He began to feel sorry for having interfered. But when the dwarf came out wearing his hat, Tod felt better.

The little man's hat fixed almost everything. That year Tyrolean hats were being worn a great deal along Hollywood Boulevard and the dwarf's was a fine specimen. It was the proper magic green color and had a high, conical crown. There should have been a brass buckle on the front, but otherwise it was quite perfect.

The rest of his outfit didn't go well with the hat. Instead of shoes with long points and a leather apron, he wore a blue, double-breasted suit and a black shirt with a yellow tie. Instead of a crooked thorn stick, he carried a rolled copy of the *Daily Running Horse.*

"That's what I get for fooling with four-bit broads," he said by way of greeting.

Tod nodded and tried to concentrate on the green hat. His ready acquiescence seemed to irritate the little man.

"No quiff can give Abe Kusich the fingeroo and get away with it," he said bitterly. "Not when I can get her leg broke for twenty bucks and I got twenty."

He took out a thick billfold and shook it at Tod.

"So she thinks she can give me the fingeroo, hah? Well, let me tell . . ."

Tod broke in hastily.

"You're right, Mr. Kusich."

The dwarf came over to where Tod was sitting and for a moment Tod thought he was going to climb into his lap, but he only asked his name and shook hands. The little man had a powerful grip.

"Let me tell you something, Hackett, if you hadn't come along, I'da broke in the door. That dame thinks she can give me the fingeroo, but she's got another thinkola coming. But thanks anyway."

"Forget it."

"I don't forget nothing. I remember. I remember those who do me dirt and those who do me favors."

He wrinkled his brow and was silent for a moment.

"Listen," he finally said, "seeing as you helped me, I got to return it. I don't want anybody going around saying Abe Kusich owes him anything. So I'll tell you what. I'll give you a good one for the fifth at Caliente. You put a fiver on its nose and it'll get you twenty smackeroos. What I'm telling you is strictly correct."

Tod didn't know how to answer and his hesitation offended the little man.

"Would I give you a bum steer?" he demanded, scowling. "Would I?"

Tod walked toward the door to get rid of him.

"No," he said.

"Then why won't you bet, hah?"

"What's the name of the horse?" Tod asked, hoping to calm him.

The dwarf had followed him to the door, pulling the bathrobe after him by one sleeve. Hat and all, he came to a foot below Tod's belt.

"Tragopan. He's a certain, sure winner. I know the guy who owns him and he gave me the office."

"Is he a Greek?" Tod asked.

He was being pleasant in order to hide the attempt he was making to maneuver the dwarf through the door.

"Yeh, he's a Greek. Do you know him?"

"No."

"No?"

"No," said Tod with finality.

"Keep your drawers on," ordered the dwarf, "all I want to know is how you know he's a Greek if you don't know him?"

His eyes narrowed with suspicion and he clenched his fists.

Tod smiled to placate him.

"I just guessed it."

"You did?"

The dwarf hunched his shoulders as though he were going to pull a gun or throw a punch. Tod backed off and tried to explain.

"I guessed he was a Greek because Tragopan is a Greek word that means pheasant."

The dwarf was far from satisfied.

"How do you know what it means? You ain't a Greek?"

"No, but I know a few Greek words."

"So you're a wise guy, hah, a know-it-all."

He took a short step forward, moving on his toes, and Tod got set to block a punch.

"A college man, hah? Well, let me tell . . ."

His foot caught in the wrapper and he fell forward on his hands. He forgot Tod and cursed the bathrobe, then got started on the woman again.

"So she thinks she can give me the fingeroo."

He kept poking himself in the chest with his thumbs.

"Who gave her forty bucks for an abortion? Who? And another ten to go to the country for a rest that time. To a ranch I sent her. And who got her fiddle out of hock that time in Santa Monica? Who?"

"That's right," Tod said, getting ready to give him a quick shove through the door.

But he didn't have to shove him. The little man suddenly darted out of the room and ran down the hall, dragging the bathrobe after him.

A few days later, Tod went into a stationery store on Vine Street to buy a magazine. While he was looking through the rack, he felt a tug at the bottom of his jacket. It was Abe Kusich, the dwarf, again.

"How's things?" he demanded.

Tod was surprised to find that he was just as truculent as he had been the other night. Later, when he got to know him better, he discovered that Abe's pugnacity was often a joke. When he used it on his friends, they played with him like one does with a growling puppy, staving off his mad rushes and then baiting him to rush again.

"Fair enough," Tod said, "but I think I'll move."

He had spent most of Sunday looking for a place to live and was full of the subject. The moment he mentioned it, however, he knew that he had made a mistake. He tried to end the matter by turning away, but the little man blocked him. He evidently considered himself an expert on the housing situation. After naming and discarding a dozen possibilities without a word from Tod, he finally hit on the San Bernardino Arms.

"That's the place for you, the San Berdoo. I live there, so I ought to know. The owner's strictly from hunger. Come on, I'll get you fixed up swell."

"I don't know, I . . ." Tod began.

The dwarf bridled instantly, and appeared to be mortally offended.

"I suppose it ain't good enough for you. Well, let me tell you something, you . . ."

Tod allowed himself to be bullied and went with the dwarf to Pinyon Canyon. The rooms in the San Berdoo were small and not very clean. He rented one without hesitation, however, when he saw Faye Greener in the hall.

3

Tod had fallen asleep. When he woke again, it was after eight o'clock. He took a bath and shaved, then dressed in front of the bureau mirror. He tried to watch his fingers as he fixed his collar and tie, but his eyes kept straying to the photograph that was pushed into the upper corner of the frame.

It was a picture of Faye Greener, a still from a two-reel farce in which she had worked as an extra. She had given him the photograph willingly enough, had even autographed it in a large, wild hand, "Affectionately yours, Faye Greener," but she refused his friendship, or, rather, insisted on keeping it impersonal. She had told him why. He had nothing to offer her, neither money nor looks, and she could only love a handsome man and would only let a wealthy man love her. Tod was a "good-hearted man," and she liked "good-hearted men," but only as friends. She wasn't hard-boiled. It was just that she put love on a special plane, where a man without money or looks couldn't move.

Tod grunted with annoyance as he turned to the photograph. In it she was wearing a harem costume, full Turkish trousers, breastplates and a monkey jacket, and lay stretched out on a silken divan. One hand held a beer bottle and the other a pewter stein.

He had gone all the way to Glendale to see her in that movie. It was about an American drummer who gets lost in the seraglio of a Damascus merchant and has a lot of fun with the female inmates. Faye played one of the dancing girls. She had only one line to speak, "Oh, Mr. Smith!" and spoke it badly.

She was a tall girl with wide, straight shoulders and long, swordlike legs. Her neck was long, too, and columnar. Her face was much fuller than the rest of her body would lead you to expect and much larger. It was a moon face, wide at the cheek bones and narrow at chin and brow. She wore her "platinum" hair long, letting it fall almost to her shoulders in back, but kept it away from her face and ears with a narrow blue ribbon that went under it and was tied on top of her head with a little bow.

She was supposed to look drunk and she did, but not with alcohol. She lay stretched out on the divan with her arms and legs spread, as though welcoming a lover, and her lips were parted in a heavy, sullen smile. She was supposed to look inviting, but the invitation wasn't to pleasure.

Tod lit a cigarette and inhaled with a nervous gasp. He started to fool with his tie again, but had to go back to the photograph.

Her invitation wasn't to pleasure, but to struggle, hard and sharp, closer to murder than to love. If you threw yourself on her, it would be like throwing yourself from the parapet of a skyscraper. You would do it with a scream. You couldn't expect to rise again. Your teeth would be driven into your skull like nails into a pine board and your back would be broken. You wouldn't even have time to sweat or close your eyes.

He managed to laugh at his language, but it wasn't a real laugh and nothing was destroyed by it.

If she would only let him, he would be glad to throw himself, no matter what the cost. But she wouldn't have him. She didn't love him and he couldn't further her career. She wasn't sentimental and she had no need for tenderness, even if he were capable of it.

When he had finished dressing, he hurried out of the room. He had promised to go to a party at Claude Estee's.

4

Claude was a successful screen writer who lived in a big house that was an exact reproduction of the old Dupuy mansion near Biloxi, Mississippi. When Tod came up the walk between the boxwood hedges, he greeted him from the enormous, two-story porch by doing the impersonation that went with the Southern colonial architecture. He teetered back and forth on his heels like a Civil War colonel and made believe he had a large belly.

He had no belly at all. He was a dried-up little man with the rubbed features and stooped shoulders of a postal clerk. The shiny mohair coat and nondescript trousers of that official would have become him, but he was dressed, as always, elaborately. In the buttonhole of his brown jacket was a lemon flower. His trousers were of reddish Harris tweed with a hound tooth check and on his feet were a pair of magnificent, rust-colored blüchers. His shirt was ivory flannel and his knitted tie a red that was almost black.

While Tod mounted the steps to reach his outstretched hand, he shouted to the butler.

"Here, you black rascal! A mint julep."

A Chinese servant came running with a Scotch and soda.

After talking to Tod for a moment, Claude started him in the direction of Alice, his wife, who was at the other end of the porch.

"Don't run off," he whispered. "We're going to a sporting house."

Alice was sitting in a wicker swing with a woman named Mrs. Joan Schwartzen. When she asked him if he was playing any tennis, Mrs. Schwartzen interrupted her.

"How silly, batting an inoffensive ball across something that ought to be used to catch fish on account of millions are starving for a bite of herring."

"Joan's a female tennis champ," Alice explained.

Mrs. Schwartzen was a big girl with large hands and feet and square, bony shoulders. She had a pretty, eighteen-year-old face and a thirty-five-year-old neck that was veined and sinewy. Her deep sunburn, ruby colored with a slight blue tint, kept the contrast between her face and neck from being too startling.

"Well, I wish we were going to a brothel this minute," she said. "I adore them."

She turned to Tod and fluttered her eyelids.

"Don't you, Mr. Hackett?"

"That's right, Joan darling," Alice answered for him. "Nothing like a bagnio to set a fellow up. Hair of the dog that bit you."

"How dare you insult me!"

She stood up and took Tod's arm.

"Convoy me over there."

She pointed to the group of men with whom Claude was standing.

"For God's sake, convoy her," Alice said. "She thinks they're telling dirty stories."

Mrs. Schwartzen pushed right among them, dragging Tod after her.

"Are you talking smut?" she asked. "I adore smut."

They all laughed politely.

"No, shop," said someone.

"I don't believe it. I can tell from the beast in your voices. Go ahead, do say something obscene."

This time no one laughed.

Tod tried to disengage her arm, but she kept a firm grip on it. There was a moment of awkward silence, then the man she had interrupted tried to make a fresh start.

"The picture business is too humble," he said. "We ought to resent people like Coombes."

"That's right," said another man. "Guys like that come out here, make a lot of money, grouse all the time about the place, flop on their assignments, then go back East and tell dialect stories about producers they've never met."

"My God," Mrs. Schwartzen said to Tod in a loud, stagey whisper, "they *are* talking shop."

"Let's look for the man with the drinks," Tod said.

"No. Take me into the garden. Have you seen what's in the swimming pool?"

She pulled him along.

The air of the garden was heavy with the odor of mimosa and honeysuckle. Through a slit in the blue serge sky poked a grained moon that looked like an enormous bone button. A little flagstone path, made narrow by its border of oleander, led to the edge of the sunken pool. On the bottom, near the deep end, he could see a heavy, black mass of some kind.

"What is it?" he asked.

She kicked a switch that was hidden at the base of a shrub and a row of submerged floodlights illuminated the green water. The thing was a dead horse, or, rather, a life-size, realistic reproduction of one. Its legs stuck up stiff and straight and it had an enormous, distended belly. Its hammerhead lay twisted to one side and from its mouth, which was set in an agonized grin, hung a heavy, black tongue.

"Isn't it marvelous!" exclaimed Mrs. Schwartzen, clapping her hands and jumping up and down excitedly like a little girl.

"What's it made of?"

"Then you weren't fooled? How impolite! It's rubber, of course. It cost lots of money."

"But why?"

"To amuse. We were looking at the pool one day and somebody, Jerry Appis, I think, said that it needed a dead horse on the bottom, so Alice got one. Don't you think it looks cute?"

"Very."

"You're just an old meanie. Think how happy the Estees must feel, showing it to people and listening to their merriment and their oh's and ah's of unconfined delight."

She stood on the edge of the pool and "ohed and ahed" rapidly several times in succession.

"Is it still there?" someone called.

Tod turned and saw two women and a man coming down the path.

"I think its belly's going to burst," Mrs. Schwartzen shouted to them gleefully.

"Goody," said the man, hurrying to look.

"But it's only full of air," said one of the women.

Mrs. Schwartzen made believe she was going to cry.

"You're just like that mean Mr. Hackett. You just won't let me cherish my illusions."

Tod was half way to the house when she called after him. He waved but kept going.

The men with Claude were still talking shop.

"But how are you going to get rid of the illiterate mockies that run it? They've got a strangle hold on the industry. Maybe they're intellectual stumblebums, but they're damn good business men. Or at least they know how to go into receivership and come up with a gold watch in their teeth."

"They ought to put some of the millions they make back into the business again. Like Rockefeller does with his Foundation. People used to hate the Rockefellers, but now instead of hollering about their ill-gotten oil dough, everybody praises them for what the Foundation does. It's a swell stunt and pictures could do the same thing. Have a Cinema Foundation and make contributions to Science and Art. You know, give the racket a front."

Tod took Claude to one side to say good night, but he wouldn't let him go. He led him into the library and mixed two double Scotches. They sat down on the couch facing the fireplace.

"You haven't been to Audrey Jenning's place?" Claude asked.

"No, but I've heard tell of it."

"Then you've got to come along."

"I don't like pro-sport."

"We won't indulge in any. We're just going to see a movie."

"I get depressed."

"Not at Jenning's you won't. She makes a vice attractive

by skillful packaging. Her dive's a triumph of industrial design."

Tod liked to hear him talk. He was master of an involved comic rhetoric that permitted him to express his moral indignation and still keep his reputation for worldliness and wit.

Tod fed him another lead. "I don't care how much cellophane she wraps it in," he said—"nautch joints are depressing, like all places for deposit, banks, mail boxes, tombs, vending machines."

"Love is like a vending machine, eh? Not bad. You insert a coin and press home the lever. There's some mechanical activity inside the bowels of the device. You receive a small sweet, frown at yourself in the dirty mirror, adjust your hat, take a firm grip on your umbrella and walk away, trying to look as though nothing had happened. It's good, but it's not for pictures."

Tod played straight again.

"That's not it. I've been chasing a girl and it's like carrying something a little too large to conceal in your pocket, like a briefcase or a small valise. It's uncomfortable."

"I know, I know. It's always uncomfortable. First your right hand gets tired, then your left. You put the valise down and sit on it, but people are surprised and stop to stare at you, so you move on. You hide it behind a tree and hurry away, but someone finds it and runs after you to return it. It's a small valise when you leave home in the morning, cheap and with a bad handle, but by evening it's a trunk with brass corners and many foreign labels. I know. It's good, but it won't film. You've got to remember your audience. What about the barber in Purdue? He's been cutting hair all day and he's tired. He doesn't want to see some dope carrying a valise or fooling with a nickel machine. What the barber wants is amour and glamor."

The last part was for himself and he sighed heavily. He was about to begin again when the Chinese servant came in and said that the others were ready to leave for Mrs. Jenning's.

5

They started out in several cars. Tod rode in the front of the one Claude drove and as they went down Sunset Boulevard he described Mrs. Jenning for him. She had been a fairly prominent actress in the days of silent films, but sound made it impossible for her to get work. Instead of becoming an extra or a bit player like many other old stars, she had shown excellent business sense and had opened a callhouse. She wasn't vicious. Far from it. She ran her business just as other women run lending libraries, shrewdly and with taste.

None of the girls lived on the premises. You telephoned and she sent a girl over. The charge was thirty dollars for a single night of sport and Mrs. Jenning kept fifteen of it. Some people might think that fifty per cent is a high brokerage fee, but she really earned every cent of it. There was a big overhead. She maintained a beautiful house for the girls to wait in and a car and a chauffeur to deliver them to the clients.

Then, too, she had to move in the kind of society where

she could make the right contacts. After all, not every man can afford thirty dollars. She permitted her girls to service only men of wealth and position, not to say taste and discretion. She was so particular that she insisted on meeting the prospective sportsman before servicing him. She had often said, and truthfully, that she would not let a girl of hers go to a man with whom she herself would not be willing to sleep.

And she was really cultured. All the most distinguished visitors considered it quite a lark to meet her. They were disappointed, however, when they discovered how refined she was. They wanted to talk about certain lively matters of universal interest, but she insisted on discussing Gertrude Stein and Juan Gris. No matter how hard the distinguished visitor tried, and some had been known to go to really great lengths, he could never find a flaw in her refinement or make a breach in her culture.

Claude was still using his peculiar rhetoric on Mrs. Jenning when she came to the door of her house to greet them.

"It's so nice to see you again," she said. "I was telling Mrs. Prince at tea only yesterday—the Estees are my favorite couple."

She was a handsome woman, smooth and buttery, with fair hair and a red complexion.

She led them into a small drawing room whose color scheme was violet, gray and rose. The Venetian blinds were rose, as was the ceiling, and the walls were covered with a pale gray paper that had a tiny, widely spaced flower design in violet. On one wall hung a silver screen, the kind that rolls up, and against the opposite wall, on each side of a cherrywood table, was a row of chairs covered with rose and gray, glazed chintz bound in violet piping. There was a small projection machine on the table and a young man in evening dress was fumbling with it.

She waved them to their seats. A waiter then came in and asked what they wanted to drink. When their orders had been taken and filled, she flipped the light switch and the young man started his machine. It whirred merrily, but he had trouble in getting it focused.

"What are we going to see first?" Mrs. Schwartzen asked.

"Le Predicament de Marie."

"That sounds ducky."

"It's charming, utterly charming," said Mrs. Jenning.

"Yes," said the cameraman, who was still having trouble. "I love *Le Predicament de Marie.* It has a marvelous quality that is too exciting."

There was a long delay, during which he fussed desperately with his machine. Mrs. Schwartzen started to whistle and stamp her feet and the others joined in. They imitated a rowdy audience in the days of the nickelodeon.

"Get a move on, slow poke."

"What's your hurry? Here's your hat."

"Get a horse!"

"Get out and get under!"

The young man finally found the screen with his light beam and the film began.

LE PREDICAMENT DE MARIE

ou

LA BONNE DISTRAITE

Marie, the "bonne," was a buxom young girl in a tight-fitting black silk uniform with very short skirts. On her head was a tiny lace cap. In the first scene, she was shown serving dinner to a middle-class family in an oak-paneled dining room full of heavy, carved furniture. The family was very respectable and consisted of a bearded, frock-coated father, a mother with a whalebone collar and a cameo brooch, a tall, thin son with a long mustache and almost no chin and a little girl wearing a large bow in her hair and a crucifix on a gold chain around her neck.

After some low comedy with father's beard and the soup, the actors settled down seriously to their theme. It was evident that while the whole family desired Marie, she only desired the young girl. Using his napkin to hide his activities, the old man pinched Marie, the son tried to look down the neck of her dress and the mother patted her knee. Marie, for her part, surreptitiously fondled the child.

The scene changed to Marie's room. She undressed and got into a chiffon negligee, leaving on only her black silk stockings and high-heeled shoes. She was making an elaborate night toilet when the child entered. Marie took her on her lap and started to kiss her. There was a knock on the door. Consternation. She hid the child in the closet and let in the bearded father. He was suspicious and she had to accept his advances. He was embracing her when there was another knock. Again consternation and tableau. This time it was the mustachioed son. Marie hid the father under the bed. No sooner had the son begun to grow warm than there was another knock. Marie made him climb into a large blanket chest. The new caller was the lady of the house. She, too, was just settling down to work when there was another knock.

Who could it be? A telegram? A policeman? Frantically Marie counted the different hiding places. The whole family was present. She tiptoed to the door and listened.

"Who can it be that wishes to enter now?" read the title card.

And there the machine stuck. The young man in evening dress became as frantic as Marie. When he got it running again, there was a flash of light and the film whizzed through the apparatus until it had all run out.

"I'm sorry, extremely," he said. "I'll have to rewind."

"It's a frameup," someone yelled.

"Fake!"

"Cheat!"

"The old teaser routine!"

They stamped their feet and whistled.

Under cover of the mock riot, Tod sneaked out. He wanted to get some fresh air. The waiter, whom he found loitering in the hall, showed him to the patio in back of the house.

On his return, he peeked into the different rooms. In one of them he found a large number of miniature dogs in a curio cabinet. There were glass pointers, silver beagles, porcelain schnauzers, stone dachshunds, aluminum bull-dogs, onyx whippets, china bassets, wooden spaniels. Every recognized breed was represented and almost every material that could be sculptured, cast or carved.

While he was admiring the little figures, he heard a girl singing. He thought he recognized her voice and peeked into the hall. It was Mary Dove, one of Faye Greener's best friends.

Perhaps Faye also worked for Mrs. Jenning. If so, for thirty dollars . . .

He went back to see the rest of the film.

6

Tod's hope that he could end his trouble by paying a small fee didn't last long. When he got Claude to ask Mrs. Jenning about Faye, that lady said she had never heard of the girl. Claude then asked her to inquire through Mary Dove. A few days later she phoned him to say there was nothing doing. The girl wasn't available.

Tod wasn't really disappointed. He didn't want Faye that way, not at least while he still had a chance some other way. Lately, he had begun to think he had a good one. Harry, her father, was sick and that gave him an excuse for hanging around their apartment. He ran errands and kept the old man company. To repay his kindness, she permitted him the intimacies of a family friend. He hoped to deepen her gratitude and make it serious.

Apart from this purpose, he was interested in Harry and enjoyed visiting him. The old man was a clown and Tod had all the painter's usual love of clowns. But what was more important, he felt that his clownship was a clue to the people who stared (a painter's clue, that is—a clue in the form of a symbol), just as Faye's dreams were another.

He sat near Harry's bed and listened to his stories by the hour. Forty years in vaudeville and burlesque had provided him with an infinite number of them. As he put it, his life had consisted of a lightning series of "nip-ups," "high-gruesomes," "flying-W's" and "hundred-and-eights" done to escape a barrage of "exploding stoves." An "exploding stove" was any catastrophe, natural or human, from a flood in Medicine Hat, Wyoming, to an angry policeman in Moose Factory, Ontario.

When Harry had first begun his stage career, he had probably restricted his clowning to the boards, but now he clowned continuously. It was his sole method of defense. Most people, he had discovered, won't go out of their way to punish a clown.

He used a set of elegant gestures to accent the comedy of his bent, hopeless figure and wore a special costume, dressing like a banker, a cheap, unconvincing, imitation banker. The costume consisted of a greasy derby with an unusually high crown, a wing collar and polka dot four-in-hand, a shiny double-breasted jacket and gray-striped trousers. His outfit fooled no one, but then he didn't intend it to fool anyone. His slyness was of a different sort.

On the stage he was a complete failure and knew it. Yet he claimed to have once come very close to success. To prove how close, he made Tod read an old clipping from the theatrical section of the Sunday *Times*.

"BEDRAGGLED HARLEQUIN," it was headed.

"The commedia dell'arte is not dead, but lives on in Brooklyn, or was living there last week on the stage of the

Oglethorpe Theatre in the person of one Harry Greener. Mr. Greener is of a troupe called 'The Flying Lings,' who, by the time this reaches you, have probably moved on to Mystic, Connecticut, or some other place more fitting than the borough of large families. If you have the time and really love the theatre, by all means seek out the Lings wherever they may be.

"Mr. Greener, the bedraggled Harlequin of our caption, is not bedraggled but clean, neat and sweet when he first comes on. By the time the Lings, four muscular Orientals, finish with him, however, he is plenty bedraggled. He is tattered and bloody, but still sweet.

"When Mr. Greener enters, the trumpets are properly silent. Mama Ling is spinning a plate on the end of a stick held in her mouth, Papa Ling is doing cartwheels, Sister Ling is juggling fans and Sonny Ling is hanging from the proscenium arch by his pigtail. As he inspects his strenuous colleagues, Mr. Greener tries to hide his confusion under some much too obvious worldliness. He ventures to tickle Sister and receives a powerful kick in the belly in return for this innocent attention. Having been kicked, he is on familiar ground and begins to tell a dull joke. Father Ling sneaks up behind him and tosses him to Brother, who looks the other way. Mr. Greener lands on the back of his neck. He shows his mettle by finishing his dull story from a recumbent position. When he stands up, the audience, which failed to laugh at his joke, laughs at his limp, so he continues lame for the rest of the act.

"Mr. Greener begins another story, even longer and duller than his first. Just before he arrives at the gag line, the orchestra blares loudly and drowns him out. He is very patient and very brave. He begins again, but the orchestra will not let him finish. The pain that almost, not quite, thank God, crumples his stiff little figure would be unbearable if it were not obviously make-believe. It is gloriously funny.

"The finale is superb. While the Ling Family flies through the air, Mr. Greener, held to the ground by his sense of reality and his knowledge of gravitation, tries hard to make the audience think that he is neither surprised nor worried by the rocketing Orientals. It's familiar stuff, his hands signal, but his face denies this. As time goes on and no one is hurt, he regains his assurance. The acrobats ignore him, so he ignores the acrobats. His is the final victory; the applause is for him.

"My first thought was that some producer should put Mr. Greener into a big revue against a background of beautiful girls and glittering curtains. But my second was that this would be a mistake. I am afraid that Mr. Greener, like certain humble field plants which die when transferred to richer soil, had better be left to bloom in vaudeville against a background of ventriloquists and lady bicycle riders."

Harry had more than a dozen copies of this article, several on rag paper. After trying to get a job by inserting a small advertisement in *Variety* ("... 'some producer should put Mr. Greener into a big revue ...' The *Times*"), he had come to Hollywood, thinking to earn a living playing comedy bits in films. There proved to be little demand for his talents, however. As he himself put it, he "stank from hunger." To supplement his meager income from the studios, he peddled silver polish which he made in the bathroom of the apartment out of chalk, soap and yellow axle grease. When Faye wasn't at Central Casting, she took him around on his peddling trips in her Model T Ford. It was on their last expedition together that he had fallen sick.

It was on this trip that Faye acquired a new suitor by the name of Homer Simpson. About a week after Harry had taken to his bed, Tod met Homer for the first time. He was keeping the old man company when their conversation was interrupted by a light knock on the apartment door. Tod answered it and found a man standing in the hall with flowers for Faye and a bottle of port wine for her father.

Tod examined him eagerly. He didn't mean to be rude but at first glance this man seemed an exact model for the kind of person who comes to California to die, perfect in every detail down to fever eyes and unruly hands.

"My name is Homer Simpson," the man gasped, then shifted uneasily and patted his perfectly dry forehead with a folded handkerchief.

"Won't you come in?" Tod asked.

He shook his head heavily and thrust the wine and flowers at Tod. Before Tod could say anything, he had lumbered off.

Tod saw that he was mistaken. Homer Simpson was only physically the type. The men he meant were not shy.

He took the gifts in to Harry, who didn't seem at all surprised. He said Homer was one of his grateful customers.

"That Miracle Polish of mine sure does fetch 'em."

Later, when Faye came home and heard the story, she was very much amused. They both told Tod how they had happened to meet Homer, interrupting themselves and each other every few seconds to laugh.

The next thing Tod saw Homer staring at the apartment house from the shadow of a date palm on the opposite side of the street. He watched him for a few minutes, then called out a friendly greeting. Without replying, Homer ran away. On the next day and the one after, Tod again saw him lurking near the palm tree. He finally caught him by approaching the tree silently from the rear.

"Hello, Mr. Simpson," Tod said softly. "The Greeners were very grateful for your gift."

This time Simpson didn't move, perhaps because Tod had him backed against the tree.

"That's fine," he blurted out. "I was passing . . . I live up the street."

Tod managed to keep their conversation going for several minutes before he escaped again.

The next time Tod was able to approach him without the stalk. From then on, he responded very quickly to his advances. Sympathy, even of the most obvious sort, made him articulate, almost garrulous.

7

Tod was right about one thing at least. Like most of the people he was interested in, Homer was a Middle-Westerner. He came from a little town near Des Moines, Iowa, called Wayneville, where he had worked for twenty years in a hotel.

One day, while sitting in the park in the rain, he had caught cold and his cold developed into pneumonia. When he came out of the hospital, he found that the hotel had hired a new bookkeeper. They offered to take him on again, but his doctor advised him to go to California for a rest. The doctor had an authoritative manner, so Homer left Wayneville for the Coast.

After living for a week in a railroad hotel in Los Angeles, he rented a cottage in Pinyon Canyon. It was only the second house the real estate agent showed him, but he took it because he was tired and because the agent was a bully.

He rather liked the way the cottage was located. It was the last house in the canyon and the hills rose directly behind the garage. They were covered with lupines, Canterbury bells, poppies, and several varieties of large yellow daisy. There were also some scrub pines, Joshua and eucalyptus trees. The agent told him that he would see doves and plumed quail, but during all the time he lived there, he saw only a few large, black velvet spiders and a lizard. He grew very fond of the lizard.

The house was cheap because it was hard to rent. Most of the people who took cottages in the neighborhood wanted them to be "Spanish" and this one, so the agent claimed, was "Irish." Homer thought that the place looked kind of queer, but the agent insisted that it was cute.

The house was queer. It had an enormous and very crooked stone chimney, little dormer windows with big hoods and a thatched roof that came down very low on both sides of the front door. This door was of gumwood painted like fumed oak and it hung on enormous hinges. Although made by machine, the hinges had been carefully stamped to appear hand-forged. The same kind of care and skill had been used to make the roof thatching, which was not really straw but heavy fireproof paper colored and ribbed to look like straw.

The prevailing taste had been followed in the living room. It was "Spanish." The walls were pale orange flecked with pink and on them hung several silk armorial banners in red and gold. A big galleon stood on the mantelpiece. Its hull was plaster, its sails paper and its rigging wire. In the fireplace was a variety of cactus in gaily colored Mexican pots. Some of the plants were made of rubber and cork; others were real.

The room was lit by wall fixtures in the shape of galleons with pointed amber bulbs projecting from their decks. The table held a lamp with a paper shade, oiled to look like parchment, that had several more galleons painted on it. On each side of the windows red velvet draperies hung from black, double-headed spears.

The furniture consisted of a heavy couch that had fat monks for legs and was covered with faded red damask, and three swollen armchairs, also red. In the center of the room was a very long mahogany table. It was of the trestle type and studded with large-headed bronze nails. Beside each of the chairs was a small end table, the same color and design as the big one, but with a colored tile let into the top.

In the two small bedrooms still another style had been used. This the agent had called "New England." There was a spool bed made of iron grained like wood, a Windsor chair of the kind frequently seen in tea shops, and a Governor Winthrop dresser painted to look like unpainted pine. On the floor was a small hooked rug. On the wall facing the dresser was a colored etching of a snowbound Connecticut farmhouse, complete with wolf. Both of these rooms were exactly alike in every detail. Even the pictures were duplicates.

There was also a bathroom and a kitchen.

8

It took Homer only a few minutes to get settled in his new home. He unpacked his trunk, hung his two suits, both dark gray, in the closet of one of his bedrooms and put his shirts and underclothes into the dresser drawers. He made no attempt to rearrange the furniture.

After an aimless tour of the house and the yard, he sat down on the couch in the living room. He sat as though waiting for someone in the lobby of a hotel. He remained that way for almost half an hour without moving anything but his hands, then got up and went into the bedroom and sat down on the edge of the bed.

Although it was still early in the afternoon, he felt very sleepy. He was afraid to stretch out and go to sleep. Not because he had bad dreams, but because it was so hard for him to wake again. When he fell asleep, he was always afraid that he would never get up.

But his fear wasn't as strong as his need. He got his alarm clock and set it for seven o'clock, then lay down with it next to his ear. Two hours later, it seemed like seconds to him, the alarm went off. The bell rang for a full minute before he began to work laboriously toward consciousness. The struggle was a hard one. He groaned. His head trembled and his feet shot out. Finally his eyes opened, then widened. Once more the victory was his.

He lay stretched out on the bed, collecting his senses and testing the different parts of his body. Every part was awake but his hands. They still slept. He was not surprised. They demanded special attention, had always demanded it. When he had been a child, he used to stick pins into them and once had even thrust them into a fire. Now he used only cold water.

He got out of bed in sections, like a poorly made automaton, and carried his hands into the bathroom. He turned on the cold water. When the basin was full, he plunged his hands in up to the wrists. They lay quietly on the bottom like a pair of strange aquatic animals. When they were thoroughly chilled and began to crawl about, he lifted them out and hid them in a towel.

He was cold. He ran hot water into the tub and began to undress, fumbling with the buttons of his clothing as though he were undressing a stranger. He was naked before the tub was full enough to get in and he sat down on a stool to wait. He kept his enormous hands folded quietly on his belly. Although absolutely still, they seemed curbed rather than resting.

Except for his hands, which belonged on a piece of monumental sculpture, and his small head, he was well proportioned. His muscles were large and round and he had a full, heavy chest. Yet there was something wrong. For all his size and shape, he looked neither strong nor fertile. He was like one of Picasso's great sterile athletes, who brood hopelessly on pink sand, staring at veined marble waves.

When the tub was full, he got in and sank down in the hot water. He grunted his comfort. But in another moment he would begin to remember, in just another moment. He tried to fool his memory by overwhelming it with tears and brought up the sobs that were always lurking uneasily in his chest. He cried softly at first, then harder. The sound he made was like that of a dog lapping gruel. He concentrated on how miserable and lonely he was, but it didn't work. The thing he was trying so desperately to avoid kept crowding into his mind.

One day when he was working in the hotel, a guest called Romola Martin had spoken to him in the elevator.

"Mr. Simpson, you're Mr. Simpson, the bookkeeper?"

"Yes."

"I'm in six-eleven."

She was small and childlike, with a quick, nervous manner. In her arms she coddled a package which obviously contained a square gin bottle.

"Yes," said Homer again, working against his natural instinct to be friendly. He knew that Miss Martin owed several weeks' rent and had heard the room clerk say she was a drunkard.

"Oh! . . ." the girl went on coquettishly, making obvious their difference in size, "I'm sorry you're worried about your bill, I . . ."

The intimacy of her tone embarrassed Homer.

"You'll have to speak to the manager," he rapped out, turning away.

He was trembling when he reached his office.

How bold the creature was! She was drunk, of course,

but not so drunk that she didn't know what she was doing. He hurriedly labeled his excitement disgust.

Soon afterwards the manager called and asked him to bring in Miss Martin's credit card. When he went into the manager's office, he found Miss Carlisle, the room clerk, there. Homer listened to what the manager was saying to her.

"You roomed six-eleven?"

"I did, yes sir."

"Why? She's obvious enough, isn't she?"

"Not when she's sober."

"Never mind that. We don't want her kind in this hotel."

"I'm sorry."

The manager turned to Homer and took the credit card he was holding.

"She owed thirty-one dollars," Homer said.

"She'll have to pay up and get out. I don't want her kind around here." He smiled. "Especially when they run up bills. Get her on the phone for me."

Homer asked the telephone operator for six-eleven and after a short time was told that the room didn't answer.

"She's in the house," he said. "I saw her in the elevator."

"I'll have the housekeeper look."

Homer was working on his books some minutes later when his phone rang. It was the manager again. He said that six-eleven had been reported in by the housekeeper and asked Homer to take her a bill.

"Tell her to pay up or get out," he said.

His first thought was to ask that Miss Carlisle be sent because he was busy, but he didn't dare to suggest it. While making out the bill, he began to realize how excited he was.

It was terrifying. Little waves of sensation moved along his nerves and the base of his tongue tingled.

When he got off at the sixth floor, he felt almost gay. His step was buoyant and he had completely forgotten his troublesome hands. He stopped at six-eleven and made as though to knock, then suddenly took fright and lowered his fist without touching the door.

He couldn't go through with it. They would have to send Miss Carlisle.

The housekeeper, who had been watching from the end of the hall, came up before he could escape.

"She doesn't answer," Homer said hurriedly.

"Did you knock hard enough? That slut is in there."

Before Homer could reply, she pounded on the door.

"Open up!" she shouted.

Homer heard someone move inside, then the door opened a few inches.

"Who is it, please?" a light voice asked.

"Mr. Simpson, the bookkeeper," he gasped.

"Come in, please."

The door opened a little wider and Homer went in without daring to look around at the housekeeper. He stumbled to the center of the room and stopped. At first he was conscious only of the heavy odor of alcohol and stale tobacco, but then underneath he smelled a metallic perfume. His eyes moved in a slow circle. On the floor was a litter of clothing, newspapers, magazines and bottles. Miss Martin was huddled up on a corner of the bed. She was wearing a man's black silk dressing gown with light-blue cuffs and lapel facings. Her close-cropped hair was the color and texture of straw and she looked like a little boy.

Her youthfulness was heightened by her blue button eyes, pink button nose and red button mouth.

Homer was too busy with his growing excitement to speak or even think. He closed his eyes to tend it better, nursing carefully what he felt. He had to be careful, for if he went too fast, it might wither and then he would be cold again. It continued to grow.

"Go away, please, I'm drunk," Miss Martin said.

Homer neither moved nor spoke.

She suddenly began to sob. The coarse, broken sounds she made seemed to come from her stomach. She buried her face in her hands and pounded the floor with her feet.

Homer's feelings were so intense that his head bobbed stiffly on his neck like that of a toy Chinese dragon.

"I'm broke. I haven't any money. I haven't a dime. I'm broke, I tell you."

Homer pulled out his wallet and moved on the girl as though to strike her with it.

She cowered away from him and her sobs grew stronger.

He dropped the wallet in her lap and stood over her, not knowing what else to do. When she saw the wallet, she smiled, but continued sobbing.

"Sit down," she said.

He sat down on the bed beside her.

"You strange man," she said coyly. "I could kiss you for being so nice."

He caught her in his arms and hugged her. His suddenness frightened her and she tried to pull away, but he held on and began awkwardly to caress her. He was completely unconscious of what he was doing. He knew only that what he felt was marvelously sweet and that he had to make the sweetness carry through to the poor, sobbing woman.

Miss Martin's sobs grew less and soon stopped altogether. He could feel her fidget and gather strength.

The telephone rang.

"Don't answer it," she said, beginning to sob once more.

He pushed her away gently and stumbled to the telephone. It was Miss Carlisle.

"Are you all right?" she asked, "or shall we send for the cops?"

"All right," he said, hanging up.

It was all over. He couldn't go back to the bed.

Miss Martin laughed at his look of acute distress.

"Bring the gin, you enormous cow," she shouted gaily. "It's under the table."

He saw her stretch herself out in a way that couldn't be mistaken. He ran out of the room.

Now in California, he was crying because he had never seen Miss Martin again. The next day the manager had told him that he had done a good job and that she had paid up and checked out.

Homer tried to find her. There were two other hotels in Wayneville, small run-down houses, and he inquired at both of them. He also asked in the few rooming places, but with no success. She had left town.

He settled back into his regular routine, working ten hours, eating two, sleeping the rest. Then he caught cold and had been advised to come to California. He could easily afford not to work for a while. His father had left him about six thousand dollars and during the twenty years he had kept books in the hotel, he had saved at least ten more.

9

He got out of the tub, dried himself hurriedly with a rough towel, then went into the bedroom to dress. He felt even more stupid and washed out than usual. It was always like that. His emotions surged up in an enormous wave, curving and rearing, higher and higher, until it seemed as though the wave must carry everything before it. But the crash never came. Something always happened at the very top of the crest and the wave collapsed to run back like water down a drain, leaving, at the most, only the refuse of feeling.

It took him a long time to get all his clothing on. He stopped to rest after each garment with a desperation far out of proportion to the effort involved.

There was nothing to eat in the house and he had to go down to Hollywood Boulevard for food. He thought of waiting until morning, but then, although he was not hungry, decided against waiting. It was only eight o'clock and the trip would kill some time. If he just sat around, the temptation to go to sleep again would become irresistible.

The night was warm and very still. He started down hill, walking on the outer edge of the pavement. He hurried between lamp-posts, where the shadows were heaviest, and came to a full stop for a moment at every circle of light. By the time he reached the boulevard, he was fighting the desire to run. He stopped for several minutes on the corner to get his bearings. As he stood there, poised for flight, his fear made him seem almost graceful.

When several other people passed without paying any attention to him, he quieted down. He adjusted the collar of his coat and prepared to cross the street. Before he could take two steps someone called to him.

"Hey, you, mister."

It was a beggar who had spotted him from the shadow of a doorway. With the infallible instinct of his kind, he knew that Homer would be easy.

"Can you spare a nickle?"

"No," Homer said without conviction.

The beggar laughed and repeated his question, threateningly.

"A nickel, mister!"

He poked his hand into Homer's face.

Homer fumbled in his change pocket and dropped several coins on the sidewalk. While the man scrambled for them, he made his escape across the street.

The SunGold Market into which he turned was a large, brilliantly lit place. All the fixtures were chromium and the floors and walls were lined with white tile. Colored spotlights played on the showcases and counters, heightening the natural hues of the different foods. The oranges were bathed in red, the lemons in yellow, the fish in pale green, the steaks in rose and the eggs in ivory.

Homer went directly to the canned goods department and bought a can of mushroom soup and another of sardines. These and a half a pound of soda crackers would be enough for his supper.

Out on the street again with his parcel, he started to walk home. When he reached the corner that led to Pinyon Canyon and saw how steep and black the hill looked, he turned back along the lighted boulevard. He thought of waiting until someone else started up the hill, but finally took a taxicab.

10

Although Homer had nothing to do but prepare his scanty meals, he was not bored. Except for the Romola Martin incident and perhaps one or two other widely spaced events, the forty years of his life had been entirely without variety or excitement. As a bookkeeper, he had worked mechanically, totaling figures and making entries with the same impersonal detachment that he now opened cans of soup and made his bed.

Someone watching him go about his little cottage might have thought him sleep-walking or partially blind. His hands seemed to have a life and a will of their own. It was they who pulled the sheets tight and shaped the pillows.

One day, while opening a can of salmon for lunch, his thumb received a nasty cut. Although the wound must have hurt, the calm, slightly querulous expression he usually wore did not change. The wounded hand writhed about on the kitchen table until it was carried to the sink by its mate and bathed tenderly in hot water.

When not keeping house, he sat in the back yard, called

the patio by the real estate agent, in an old broken deck chair. He went out to it immediately after breakfast to bake himself in the sun. In one of the closets he had found a tattered book and he held it in his lap without looking at it.

There was a much better view to be had in any direction other than the one he faced. By moving his chair in a quarter circle he could have seen a large part of the canyon twisting down to the city below. He never thought of making this shift. From where he sat, he saw the closed door of the garage and a patch of its shabby, tarpaper roof. In the foreground was a sooty, brick incinerator and a pile of rusty cans. A little to the right of them were the remains of a cactus garden in which a few ragged, tortured plants still survived.

One of these, a clump of thick, paddlelike blades, covered with ugly needles, was in bloom. From the tip of several of its topmost blades protruded a bright yellow flower, somewhat like a thistle blossom but coarser. No matter how hard the wind blew, its petals never trembled.

A lizard lived in a hole near the base of this plant. It was about five inches long and had a wedge-shaped head from which darted a fine, forked tongue. It earned a hard living catching the flies that strayed over to the cactus from the pile of cans.

The lizard was self-conscious and irritable, and Homer found it very amusing to watch. Whenever one of its elaborate stalks was foiled, it would shift about uneasily on its short legs and puff out its throat. Its coloring matched the cactus perfectly, but when it moved over to the cans where the flies were thick, it stood out very plainly. It would sit on the cactus by the hour without moving, then become impatient and start for the cans. The flies would spot it immediately and after several misses, it would sneak back sheepishly to its original post.

Homer was on the side of the flies. Whenever one of them, swinging too widely, would pass the cactus, he prayed silently for it to keep on going or turn back. If it lighted, he watched the lizard begin its stalk and held his breath until it had killed, hoping all the while that something would warn the fly. But no matter how much he wanted the fly to escape, he never thought of interfering, and was careful not to budge or make the slightest noise. Occasionally the lizard would miscalculate. When that happened Homer would laugh happily.

Between the sun, the lizard and the house, he was fairly well occupied. But whether he was happy or not it is hard to say. Probably he was neither, just as a plant is neither. He had memories to disturb him and a plant hasn't, but after the first bad night his memories were quiet.

11

He had been living this way for almost a month, when, one day, just as he was about to prepare his lunch, the door bell rang. He opened it and found a man standing on the step with a sample case in one hand and a derby hat in the other. Homer hurriedly shut the door again.

The bell continued to ring. He put his head out of the window nearest the door to order the fellow away, but the man bowed very politely and begged for a drink of water. Homer saw that he was old and tired and thought that he looked harmless. He got a bottle of water from the icebox, then opened the door and asked him in.

"The name, sir, is Harry Greener," the man announced in sing-song, stressing every other syllable.

Homer handed him a glass of water. He swallowed it quickly, then poured himself another.

"Much obliged," he said with an elaborate bow. "That was indeed refreshing."

Homer was astonished when he bowed again, did several

quick jig steps, then let his derby hat roll down his arm. It fell to the floor. He stooped to retrieve it, straightening up with a jerk as though he had been kicked, then rubbed the seat of his trousers ruefully.

Homer understood that this was to amuse, so he laughed.

Harry thanked him by bowing again, but something went wrong. The exertion had been too much for him. His face blanched and he fumbled with his collar.

"A momentary indisposition," he murmured, wondering himself whether he was acting or sick.

"Sit down," Homer said.

But Harry wasn't through with his performance. He assumed a gallant smile and took a few unsteady steps toward the couch, then tripped himself. He examined the carpet indignantly, made believe he had found the object that had tripped him and kicked it away. He then limped to the couch and sat down with a whistling sigh like air escaping from a toy balloon.

Homer poured more water. Harry tried to stand up, but Homer pressed him back and made him drink sitting. He drank this glass as he had the other two, in quick gulps, then wiped his mouth with his handkerchief, imitating a man with a big mustache who had just drunk a glass of foamy beer.

"You are indeed kind, sir," he said. "Never fear, some day I'll repay you a thousandfold."

Homer clucked.

From his pocket Harry brought out a small can and held it out for him to take.

"Compliments of the house," he announced. " 'Tis a

box of Miracle Solvent, the modern polish par excellence, the polish without peer or parallel, used by all the movie stars . . ."

He broke off his spiel with a trilling laugh.

Homer took the can.

"Thank you," he said, trying to appear grateful. "How much is it?"

"The ordinary price, the retail price, is fifty cents, but you can have it for the extraordinary price of a quarter, the wholesale price, the price I pay at the factory."

"A quarter?" asked Homer, habit for the moment having got the better of his timidity. "I can buy one twice that size for a quarter in the store."

Harry knew his man.

"Take it, take it for nothing," he said contemptuously.

Homer was tricked into protesting.

"I guess maybe this is a much better polish."

"No," said Harry, as though he were spurning a bribe. "Keep your money. I don't want it."

He laughed, this time bitterly.

Homer pulled out some change and offered it.

"Take it, please. You need it, I'm sure. I'll have two cans."

Harry had his man where he wanted him. He began to practice a variety of laughs, all of them theatrical, like a musician tuning up before a concert. He finally found the right one and let himself go. It was a victim's laugh.

"Please stop," Homer said.

But Harry couldn't stop. He was really sick. The last block that held him poised over the runway of self-pity had been knocked away and he was sliding down the chute, gaining momentum all the time. He jumped to his feet and began doing Harry Greener, poor Harry, honest Harry, well-meaning, humble, deserving, a good husband, a model father, a faithful Christian, a loyal friend.

Homer didn't appreciate the performance in the least. He was terrified and wondered whether to phone the police. But he did nothing. He just held up his hand for Harry to stop.

At the end of his pantomime, Harry stood with his head thrown back, clutching his throat, as though waiting for the curtain to fall. Homer poured him still another glass of water. But Harry wasn't finished. He bowed, sweeping his hat to his heart, then began again. He didn't get very far this time and had to gasp painfully for breath. Suddenly, like a mechanical toy that had been overwound, something snapped inside of him and he began to spin through his entire repertoire. The effort was purely muscular, like the dance of a paralytic. He jigged, juggled his hat, made believe he had been kicked, tripped, and shook hands with himself. He went through it all in one dizzy spasm, then reeled to the couch and collapsed.

He lay on the couch with his eyes closed and his chest heaving. He was even more surprised than Homer. He had put on his performance four or five times already that day and nothing like this had happened. He was really sick.

"You've had a fit," Homer said when Harry opened his eyes.

As the minutes passed, Harry began to feel better and his confidence returned. He pushed all thought of sickness out of his mind and even went so far as to congratulate himself on having given the finest performance of his career. He should be able to get five dollars out of the big dope who was leaning over him.

"Have you any spirits in the house?" he asked weakly.

The grocer had sent Homer a bottle of port wine on approval and he went to get it. He filled a tumbler half full and handed it to Harry, who drank it in small sips, making the faces that usually go with medicine.

Speaking slowly, as though in great pain, he then asked Homer to bring in his sample case.

"It's on the doorstep. Somebody might steal it. The greater part of my small capital in invested in those cans of polish."

When Homer stepped outside to obey, he saw a girl near the curb. It was Faye Greener. She was looking at the house.

"Is my father in there?" she called out.

"Mr. Greener?"

She stamped her foot.

"Tell him to get a move on, damn it. I don't want to stay here all day."

"He's sick."

The girl turned away without giving any sign that she either heard or cared.

Homer took the sample case back into the house with him. He found Harry pouring himself another drink.

"Pretty fair stuff," he said, smacking his lips over it. "Pretty fair, all right, all right. Might I be so bold as to ask what you pay for a . . ."

Homer cut him short. He didn't approve of people who drank and wanted to get rid of him.

"Your daughter's outside," he said with as much firmness as he could muster. "She wants you."

Harry collapsed on the couch and began to breathe heavily. He was acting again.

"Don't tell her," he gasped. "Don't tell her how sick her old daddy is. She must never know."

Homer was shocked by his hypocrisy.

"You're better," he said as coldly as he could. "Why don't you go home?"

Harry smiled to show how offended and hurt he was by the heartless attitude of his host. When Homer said nothing, his smile became one expressing boundless courage. He got carefully to his feet, stood erect for a minute, then began to sway weakly and tumbled back on the couch.

"I'm faint," he groaned.

Once again he was surprised and frightened. He was faint.

"Get my daughter," he gasped.

Homer found her standing at the curb with her back to the house. When he called her, she whirled and came running toward him. He watched her for a second, then went in, leaving the door unlatched.

Faye burst into the room. She ignored Homer and went straight to the couch.

"Now what in hell's the matter?" she exploded.

"Darling daughter," he said. "I have been badly taken, and this gentleman has been kind enough to let me rest for a moment."

"He had a fit or something," Homer said.

She whirled around on him so suddenly that he was startled.

"How do you do?" she said, holding her hand forward and high up.

He shook it gingerly.

"Charmed," she said, when he mumbled something.

She spun around once more.

"It's my heart," Harry said. "I can't stand up."

The little performance he put on to sell polish was familiar to her and she knew that this wasn't part of it. When she turned to face Homer again, she looked quite tragic. Her head, instead of being held far back, now drooped forward.

"Please let him rest there," she said.

"Yes, of course."

Homer motioned her toward a chair, then got her a match for her cigarette. He tried not to stare at her, but his good manners were wasted. Faye enjoyed being stared at.

He thought her extremely beautiful, but what affected him still more was her vitality. She was taut and vibrant. She was as shiny as a new spoon.

Although she was seventeen, she was dressed like a child of twelve in a white cotton dress with a blue sailor collar. Her long legs were bare and she had blue sandals on her feet.

"I'm so sorry," she said when Homer looked at her father again.

He made a motion with his hand to show that it was nothing.

"He has a vile heart, poor dear," she went on. "I've begged and begged him to go to a specialist, but you men are all alike."

"Yes, he ought to go to a doctor," Homer said.

Her odd mannerisms and artificial voice puzzled him.

"What time is it?" she asked.

"About one o'clock."

She stood up suddenly and buried both her hands in her hair at the sides of her head, making it bunch at the top in a shiny ball.

"Oh," she gasped prettily, "and I had a luncheon date."

Still holding her hair, so that her snug dress twisted even

tighter and Homer could see her dainty, arched ribs and little, dimpled belly. This elaborate gesture, like all her others, was so completely meaningless, almost formal, that she seemed a dancer rather than an affected actress.

"Do you like salmon salad?" Homer ventured to ask.

"Salmon sal-ahde?"

She seemed to be repeating the question to her stomach. The answer was yes.

"With plenty of mayonnaise, huh? I adore it."

"I was going to have some for lunch. I'll finish making it."

"Let me help."

They looked at Harry, who appeared to be asleep, then went into the kitchen. While he opened a can of salmon, she climbed on a chair and straddled it with her arms folded across the top of its back and rested her chin on her arms. Whenever he looked at her, she smiled intimately and tossed her pale, glittering hair first forward, then back.

Homer was excited and his hands worked quickly. He soon had a large bowl of salad ready. He set the table with his best cloth and his best silver and china.

"It makes me hungry just to look," she said.

The way she said this seemed to mean that it was Homer who made her hungry and he beamed at her. But before he had a chance to sit down, she was already eating. She buttered a slice of bread, covered the butter with sugar and took a big bite. Then she quickly smeared a gob of mayonnaise on the salmon and went to work. Just as he was about to sit down, she asked for something to drink. He poured her a glass of milk and stood watching her like a waiter. He was unaware of her rudeness.

As soon as she had gobbled up her salad, he brought her a large red apple. She ate the fruit more slowly, nibbling daintily, her smallest finger curled away from the rest of her hand. When she had finished it, she went back to the living room and Homer followed her.

Harry still lay as they had left him, stretched out on the sofa. The heavy noon-day sun hit directly on his face, beating down on him like a club. He hardly felt its blows, however. He was busy with the stabbing pain in his chest. He was so busy with himself that he had even stopped trying to plan how to get money out of the big dope.

Homer drew the window curtain to shade his face. Harry didn't even notice. He was thinking about death. Faye bent over him. He saw, from under his partially closed eyelids, that she expected him to make a reassuring gesture. He refused. He examined the tragic expression that she had assumed and didn't like it. In a serious moment like this, her ham sorrow was insulting.

"Speak to me, Daddy," she begged.

She was baiting him without being aware of it.

"What the hell is this," he snarled, "a Tom show?"

His sudden fury scared her and she straightened up with a jerk. He didn't want to laugh, but a short bark escaped before he could stop it. He waited anxiously to see what would happen. When it didn't hurt he laughed again. He kept on, timidly at first, then with growing assurance. He laughed with his eyes closed and the sweat pouring down his brow. Faye knew only one way to stop him and that was to do something he hated as much as she hated his laughter. She began to sing.

> "Jeepers Creepers!
> Where'd ya get those peepers? . . ."

She trucked, jerking her buttocks and shaking her head from side to side.

Homer was amazed. He felt that the scene he was witnessing had been rehearsed. He was right. Their bitterest quarrels often took this form; he laughing, she singing.

> *"Jeepers Creepers!*
> *Where'd ya get those eyes?*
> *Gosh, all git up!*
> *How'd they get so lit up?*
> *Gosh all git . . ."*

When Harry stopped, she stopped and flung herself into a chair. But Harry was only gathering strength for a final effort. He began again. This new laugh was not critical; it was horrible. When she was a child, he used to punish her with it. It was his masterpiece. There was a director who always called on him to give it when he was shooting a scene in an insane asylum or a haunted castle.

It began with a sharp, metallic crackle, like burning sticks, then gradually increased in volume until it became a rapid bark, then fell away again to an obscene chuckle. After a slight pause, it climbed until it was the nicker of a horse, then still higher to become a machinelike screech.

Faye listened helplessly with her head cocked on one side. Suddenly, she too laughed, not willingly, but fighting the sound.

"You bastard!" she yelled.

She leaped to the couch, grabbed him by the shoulders and tried to shake him quiet.

He kept laughing.

Homer moved as though he meant to pull her away, but he lost courage and was afraid to touch her. She was so naked under her skimpy dress.

"Miss Greener," he pleaded, making his big hands dance at the end of his arms. "Please, please . . ."

Harry couldn't stop laughing now. He pressed his belly with his hands, but the noise poured out of him. It had begun to hurt again.

Swinging her hand as though it held a hammer, she brought her fist down hard on his mouth. She hit him only once. He relaxed and was quiet.

"I had to do it," she said to Homer when he took her arm and led her away.

He guided her to a chair in the kitchen and shut the door. She continued to sob for a long time. He stood behind her chair, helplessly, watching the rhythmical heave of her shoulders. Several times his hands moved forward to comfort her, but he succeeded in curbing them.

When she was through crying, he handed her a napkin and she dried her face. The cloth was badly stained by her rouge and mascara.

"I've spoilt it," she said, keeping her face averted. "I'm very sorry."

"It was dirty," Homer said.

She took a compact from her pocket and looked at herself in its tiny mirror.

"I'm a fright."

She asked if she could use the bathroom and he showed her where it was. He then tiptoed into the living room to see Harry. The old man's breathing was noisy but regular and he seemed to be sleeping quietly. Homer put a cushion under his head without disturbing him and went back into the kitchen. He lit the stove and put the coffeepot on the flame, then sat down to wait for the girl to return. He heard her go into the living room. A few seconds later she came into the kitchen.

She hesitated apologetically in the doorway.

"Won't you have some coffee?"

Without waiting for her to reply, he poured a cup and moved the sugar and cream so that she could reach them.

"I had to do it," she said. "I just had to."

"That's all right."

To show her that it wasn't necessary to apologize, he busied himself at the sink.

"No, I had to," she insisted. "He laughs that way just to drive me wild. I can't stand it. I simply can't."

"Yes."

"He's crazy. We Greeners are all crazy."

She made this last statement as though there were merit in being crazy.

"He's pretty sick," Homer said, apologizing for her. "Maybe he had a sunstroke."

"No, he's crazy."

He put a plate of gingersnaps on the table and she ate them with her second cup of coffee. The dainty crunching sound she made chewing fascinated him.

When she remained quiet for several minutes, he turned from the sink to see if anything was wrong. She was smoking a cigarette and seemed lost in thought.

He tried to be gay.

"What are you thinking?" he said awkwardly, then felt foolish.

She sighed to show how dark and foreboding her thoughts were, but didn't reply.

"I'll bet you would like some candy," Homer said. "There isn't any in the house, but I could call the drugstore and they'd send it right over. Or some ice cream?"

"No, thanks, please."

"It's no trouble."

"My father isn't really a peddler," she said, abruptly. "He's an actor. I'm an actress. My mother was also an actress, a dancer. The theatre is in our blood."

"I haven't seen many shows. I . . ."

He broke off because he saw that she wasn't interested.

"I'm going to be a star some day," she announced as though daring him to contradict her.

"I'm sure you . . ."

"It's my life. It's the only thing in the whole world that I want."

"It's good to know what you want. I used to be a bookkeeper in a hotel, but . . ."

"If I'm not, I'll commit suicide."

She stood up and put her hands to her hair, opened her eyes wide and frowned.

"I don't go to shows very often," he apologized, pushing the gingersnaps toward her. "The lights hurt my eyes."

She laughed and took a cracker.

"I'll get fat."

"Oh, no."

"They say fat women are going to be popular next year. Do you think so? I don't. It's just publicity for Mae West."

He agreed with her.

She talked on and on, endlessly, about herself and about the picture business. He watched her, but didn't listen, and whenever she repeated a question in order to get a reply, he nodded his head without saying anything.

His hands began to bother him. He rubbed them against the edge of the table to relieve their itch, but it only stimulated them. When he clasped them behind his back, the strain became intolerable. They were hot and swollen. Using the dishes as an excuse, he held them under the cold water tap of the sink.

Faye was still talking when Harry appeared in the doorway. He leaned weakly against the door jamb. His nose was very red, but the rest of his face was drained white and he seemed to have grown too small for his clothing. He was smiling, however.

To Homer's amazement, they greeted each other as though nothing had happened.

"You okay now, Pop?"

"Fine and dandy, baby. Right as rain, fit as a fiddle and lively as a flea, as the feller says."

The nasal twang he used in imitation of a country yokel made Homer smile.

"Do you want something to eat?" he asked. "A glass of milk, maybe?"

"I could do with a snack."

Faye helped him over to the table. He tried to disguise how weak he was by doing an exaggerated Negro shuffle.

Homer opened a can of sardines and sliced some bread. Harry smacked his lips over the food, but ate slowly and with an effort.

"That hit the spot, all righty right," he said when he had finished.

He leaned back and fished a crumpled cigar butt out of his vest pocket. Faye lit it for him and he playfully blew a puff of smoke in her face.

"We'd better go, Daddy," she said.

"In a jiffy, child."

He turned to Homer.

"Nice place you've got here. Married?"

Faye tried to interfere.

"Dad!"

He ignored her.

"Bachelor, eh?"

"Yes."

"Well, well, a young fellow like you."

"I'm here for my health," Homer found it necessary to say.

"Don't answer his questions," Faye broke in.

"Now, now, daughter, I'm just being friendly like. I don't mean no harm."

He was still using an exaggerated backwoods accent. He spat dry into an imaginary spittoon and made believe he was shifting a cud of tobacco from cheek to cheek.

Homer thought his mimicry funny.

"I'd be lonesome and scared living alone in a big house like this," Harry went on. "Don't you ever get lonesome?"

Homer looked at Faye for his answer. She was frowning with annoyance.

"No," he said, to prevent Harry from repeating the uncomfortable question.

"No? Well, that's fine."

He blew several smoke rings at the ceiling and watched their behavior judiciously.

"Did you ever think of taking boarders?" he asked. "Some nice, sociable folks, I mean. It'll bring in a little extra money and make things more homey."

Homer was indignant, but underneath his indignation

lurked another idea, a very exciting one. He didn't know what to say.

Faye misunderstood his agitation.

"Cut it out, Dad," she exclaimed before Homer could reply. "You've been a big enough nuisance already."

"Just chinning," he protested innocently. "Just chewing the fat."

"Well, then, let's get going," she snapped.

"There's plenty of time," Homer said.

He wanted to add something stronger, but didn't have the courage. His hands were braver. When Faye shook good-by, they clutched and refused to let go.

Faye laughed at their warm insistence.

"Thanks a million, Mr. Simpson," she said. "You've been very kind. Thanks for the lunch and for helping Daddy."

"We're very grateful," Harry chimed in. "You've done a Christian deed this day. God will reward you."

He had suddenly become very pious.

"Please look us up," Faye said. "We live close-by in the San Berdoo Apartments, about five blocks down the canyon. It's the big yellow house."

When Harry stood, he had to lean against the table for support. Faye and Homer each took him by the arm and helped him into the street. Homer held him erect, while Faye went to get their Ford which was parked across the street.

"We're forgetting your order of Miracle Salve," Harry said, "the polish without peer or parallel."

Homer found a dollar and slipped it into his hand. He hid the money quickly and tried to become businesslike.

"I'll leave the goods tomorrow."

"Yes, that'll be fine," Homer said. "I really need some silver polish."

Harry was angry because it hurt him to be patronized by a sucker. He made an attempt to re-establish what he considered to be their proper relationship by bowing ironically, but didn't get very far with the gesture and began to fumble with his Adam's apple. Homer helped him into the car and he slumped down in the seat beside Faye.

They drove off. She turned to wave, but Harry didn't even look back.

12

Homer spent the rest of the afternoon in the broken deck chair. The lizard was on the cactus, but he took little interest in its hunting. His hands kept his thoughts busy. They trembled and jerked, as though troubled by dreams. To hold them still, he clasped them together. Their fingers twined like a tangle of thighs in miniature. He snatched them apart and sat on them.

When the days passed and he couldn't forget Faye, he began to grow frightened. He somehow knew that his only defense was chastity, that it served him, like the shell of a tortoise, as both spine and armor. He couldn't shed it even in thought. If he did, he would be destroyed.

He was right. There are men who can lust with parts of themselves. Only their brain or their hearts burn and then not completely. There are others, still more fortunate, who are like the filaments of an incandescent lamp. They burn fiercely, yet nothing is destroyed. But in Homer's case it would be like dropping a spark into a barn full of hay. He had escaped in the Romola Martin incident, but he wouldn't escape again. Then, for one thing, he had had his job in the hotel, a daily all-day task that protected him by tiring him, but now he had nothing.

His thoughts frightened him and he bolted into the house, hoping to leave them behind like a hat. He ran into his bedroom and threw himself down on the bed. He was simple enough to believe that people don't think while asleep.

In his troubled state, even this delusion was denied him and he was unable to fall asleep. He closed his eyes and tried to make himself drowsy. The approach to sleep which had once been automatic had somehow become a long, shining tunnel. Sleep was at the far end of it, a soft bit of shadow in the hard glare. He couldn't run, only crawl toward the black patch. Just as he was about to give up, habit came to his rescue. It collapsed the shining tunnel and hurled him into the shadow.

When he awoke it was without a struggle. He tried to fall asleep once more, but this time couldn't even find the tunnel. He was thoroughly awake. He tried to think of how very tired he was, but he wasn't tired. He felt more alive than he had at any time since Romola Martin.

Outside a few birds still sang intermittently, starting and breaking off, as though sorry to acknowledge the end of another day. He thought that he heard the lisp of silk against silk, but it was only the wind playing in the trees. How empty the house was! He tried to fill it by singing.

> *"Oh, say can you see,*
> *By the dawn's early light . . ."*

It was the only song he knew. He thought of buying a victrola or a radio. He knew, however, that he would buy neither. This fact made him very sad. It was a pleasant sadness, very sweet and calm.

But he couldn't let well enough alone. He was impatient and began to prod at his sadness, hoping to make it acute and so still more pleasant. He had been getting pamphlets in the mail from a travel bureau and he thought of the trips he would never take. Mexico was only a few hundred miles away. Boats left daily for Hawaii.

His sadness turned to anguish before he knew it and became sour. He was miserable again. He began to cry.

Only those who still have hope can benefit from tears. When they finish, they feel better. But to those without hope, like Homer, whose anguish is basic and permanent, no good comes from crying. Nothing changes for them. They usually know this, but still can't help crying.

Homer was lucky. He cried himself to sleep.

But he awoke again in the morning with Faye uppermost in his mind. He bathed, ate breakfast and sat in his deck chair. In the afternoon, he decided to go for a walk. There was only one way for him to go and that led past the San Bernardino Apartments.

Some time during his long sleep, he had given up the battle. When he came to the apartment house, he peered into the amber-lit hallway and read the Greener card on the letter box, then turned and went home. On the next night, he repeated the trip, carrying a gift of flowers and wine.

13

Harry Greener's condition didn't improve. He remained in bed, staring at the ceiling with his hands folded on his chest.

Tod went to see him almost every night. There were usually other guests. Sometimes Abe Kusich, sometimes Anna and Annabelle Lee, a sister act of the nineteen-tens, more often the four Gingos, a family of performing Eskimos from Point Barrow, Alaska.

If Harry were asleep or there were visitors, Faye usually invited Tod into her room for a talk. His interest in her grew despite the things she said and he continued to find her very exciting. Had any other girl been so affected, he would have thought her intolerable. Faye's affectations, however, were so completely artificial that he found them charming.

Being with her was like being backstage during an amateurish, ridiculous play. From in front, the stupid lines and grotesque situations would have made him squirm with annoyance, but because he saw the perspiring stagehands and the wires that held up the tawdry summerhouse with its tangle of paper flowers, he accepted everything and was anxious for it to succeed.

He found still another way to excuse her. He believed that while she often recognized the falseness of an attitude, she persisted in it because she didn't know how to be simpler or more honest. She was an actress who had learned from bad models in a bad school.

Yet Faye did have some critical ability, almost enough to recognize the ridiculous. He had often seen her laugh at herself. What was more, he had even seen her laugh at her dreams.

One evening they talked about what she did with herself when she wasn't working as an extra. She told him that she often spent the whole day making up stories. She laughed as she said it. When he questioned her, she described her method quite willingly.

She would get some music on the radio, then lie down on her bed and shut her eyes. She had a large assortment of stories to choose from. After getting herself in the right mood, she would go over them in her mind, as though they were a pack of cards, discarding one after another until she found the one that suited. On some days, she would run through the whole pack without making a choice. When that happened, she would either go to Vine Street for an ice cream soda or, if she was broke, thumb over the pack again and force herself to choose.

While she admitted that her method was too mechanical for the best results and that it was better to slip into a dream naturally, she said that any dream was better than no dream and beggars couldn't be choosers. She hadn't exactly said this, but he was able to understand it from what she did say. He thought it important that she smiled while telling him, not with embarrassment, but critically. However, her critical powers ended there. She only smiled at the mechanics.

The first time he had ever heard one of her dreams was late at night in her bedroom. About half an hour earlier, she had knocked on his door and had asked him to come and help her with Harry because she thought he was dying. His noisy breathing, which she had taken for the death rattle, had awakened her and she was badly frightened. Tod put on his bathrobe and followed her downstairs. When he got to the apartment, Harry had managed to clear his throat and his breathing had become quiet again.

She invited him into her room for a smoke. She sat on the bed and he sat beside her. She was wearing an old beach robe of white toweling over her pajamas and it was very becoming.

He wanted to beg her for a kiss but was afraid, not because she would refuse, but because she would insist on making it meaningless. To flatter her, he commented on her appearance. He did a bad job of it. He was incapable of direct flattery and got bogged down in a much too roundabout observation. She didn't listen and he broke off feeling like an idiot.

"I've got a swell idea," she said suddenly. "An idea how we can make some real money."

He made another attempt to flatter her. This time by assuming an attitude of serious interest.

"You're educated," she said. "Well, I've got some swell ideas for pictures. All you got to do is write them up and then we'll sell them to the studios."

He agreed and she described her plan. It was very vague

until she came to what she considered would be its results, then she went into concrete details. As soon as they had sold one story, she would give him another. They would make loads and loads of money. Of course she wouldn't give up acting, even if she was a big success as a writer, because acting was her life.

He realized as she went on that she was manufacturing another dream to add to her already very thick pack. When she finally got through spending the money, he asked her to tell him the idea he was to "write up," keeping all trace of irony out of his voice.

On the wall of the room beyond the foot of her bed was a large photograph that must have once been used in the lobby of a theatre to advertise a Tarzan picture. It showed a beautiful young man with magnificent muscles, wearing only a narrow loin cloth, who was ardently squeezing a slim girl in a torn riding habit. They stood in a jungle clearing and all around the pair writhed great vines loaded with fat orchids. When she told her story, he knew that this photograph had a lot to do with inspiring it.

A young girl is cruising on her father's yacht in the South Seas. She is engaged to marry a Russian count, who is tall, thin and old, but with beautiful manners. He is on the yacht, too, and keeps begging her to name the day. But she is spoiled and won't do it. Maybe she became engaged to him in order to spite another man. She becomes interested in a young sailor who is far below her in station, but very handsome. She flirts with him because she is bored. The sailor refuses to be toyed with no matter how much money she's got and tells her that he only takes orders from the captain and to go back to her foreigner. She gets sore as hell and threatens to have him fired, but he only laughs at her.

How can he be fired in the middle of the ocean? She falls in love with him, although maybe she doesn't realize it herself, because he is the first man who has ever said no to one of her whims and because he is so handsome. Then there is a big storm and the yacht is wrecked near an island. Everybody is drowned, but she manages to swim to shore. She makes herself a hut of boughs and lives on fish and fruit. It's the tropics. One morning, while she is bathing naked in a brook, a big snake grabs her. She struggles but the snake is too strong for her and it looks like curtains. But the sailor, who has been watching her from behind some bushes, leaps to her rescue. He fights the snake for her and wins.

Tod was to go on from there. He asked her how she thought the picture should end, but she seemed to have lost interest. He insisted on hearing, however.

"Well, he marries her, of course, and they're rescued. First they're rescued and then they're married, I mean. Maybe he turns out to be a rich boy who is being a sailor just for the adventure of it, or something like that. You can work it out easy enough."

"It's sure-fire," Tod said earnestly, staring at her wet lips and the tiny point of her tongue which she kept moving between them.

"I've got just hundreds and hundreds more."

He didn't say anything and her manner changed. While telling the story, she had been full of surface animation and her hands and face were alive with little illustrative grimaces and gestures. But now her excitement narrowed and became deeper and its play internal. He guessed that she must be thumbing over her pack and that she would soon select another card to show him.

He had often seen her like this, but had never before understood it. All these little stories, these little daydreams of hers, were what gave such extraordinary color and mystery to her movements. She seemed always to be struggling in their soft grasp as though she were trying to run in a swamp. As he watched her, he felt sure that her lips must taste of blood and salt and that there must be a delicious weakness in her legs. His impulse wasn't to aid her to get free, but to throw her down in the soft, warm mud and to keep her there.

He expressed some of his desire by a grunt. If he only had the courage to throw himself on her. Nothing less violent than rape would do. The sensation he felt was like that he got when holding an egg in his hand. Not that she was fragile or even seemed fragile. It wasn't that. It was her completeness, her egglike self-sufficiency, that made him want to crush her.

But he did nothing and she began to talk again.

"I've got another swell idea that I want to tell you. Maybe you had better write this one up first. It's a back-stage story and they're making a lot of them this year."

She told him about a young chorus girl who gets her big chance when the star of the show falls sick. It was a familiar version of the Cinderella theme, but her technique was much different from the one she had used for the South Sea tale. Although the events she described were miraculous, her description of them was realistic. The effect was similar to that obtained by the artists of the Middle Ages, who, when doing a subject like the raising of Lazarus from the dead or Christ walking on water, were careful to keep all the details intensely realistic. She, like them, seemed to think that fantasy could be made plausible by a humdrum technique.

"I like that one, too," he said when she had finished.

"Think them over and do the one that has the best chance."

She was dismissing him and if he didn't act at once the opportunity would be gone. He started to lean toward her, but she caught his meaning and stood up. She took his arm with affectionate brusqueness—they were now business partners—and guided him to the door.

In the hall, when she thanked him for coming down and apologized for having disturbed him, he tried again. She seemed to melt a little and he reached for her. She kissed him willingly enough, but when he tried to extend the caress, she tore free.

"Whoa there, palsy-walsy," she laughed. "Mama spank."

He started for the stairs.

"Good-by now," she called after him, then laughed again.

He barely heard her. He was thinking of the drawings he had made of her and of the new one he would do as soon as he got to his room.

In "The Burning of Los Angeles" Faye is the naked girl in the left foreground being chased by the group of men and women who have separated from the main body of the mob. One of the women is about to hurl a rock at her to bring her down. She is running with her eyes closed and a strange half-smile on her lips. Despite the dreamy repose of her face, her body is straining to hurl her along at top speed. The only explanation for this contrast is that she is enjoying the release that wild flight gives in much the same way that a game bird must when, after hiding for several tense minutes, it bursts from cover in complete, unthinking panic.

14

Tod had other and more successful rivals than Homer Simpson. One of the most important was a young man called Earle Shoop.

Earle was a cowboy from a small town in Arizona. He worked occasionally in horse-operas and spent the rest of his time in front of a saddlery store on Sunset Boulevard. In the window of this store was an enormous Mexican saddle covered with carved silver, and around it was arranged a large collection of torture instruments. Among other things there were fancy, braided quirts, spurs with great spiked wheels, and double bits that looked as though they could break a horse's jaw without trouble. Across the back of the window ran a low shelf on which was a row of boots, some black, some red and some a pale yellow. All of the boots had scalloped tops and very high heels.

Earle always stood with his back to the window, his eyes fixed on a sign on the roof of a one-story building across the street that read: "Malted Milks Too Thick For a Straw." Regularly, twice every hour, he pulled a sack of tobacco and a sheaf of papers from his shirt pocket and rolled a cigarette. Then he tightened the cloth of his trousers by lifting his knee and struck a match along the underside of his thigh.

He was over six feet tall. The big Stetson hat he wore added five inches more to his height and the heels of his boots still another three. His polelike appearance was further exaggerated by the narrowness of his shoulders and by his lack of either hips or buttocks. The years he had spent in the saddle had not made him bowlegged. In fact, his legs were so straight that his dungarees, bleached a very light blue by the sun and much washing, hung down without a wrinkle, as though they were empty.

Tod could see why Faye thought him handsome. He had a two-dimensional face that a talented child might have drawn with a ruler and a compass. His chin was perfectly round and his eyes, which were wide apart, were also round. His thin mouth ran at right angles to his straight, perpendicular nose. His reddish tan complexion was the same color from hairline to throat, as though washed in by an expert, and it completed his resemblance to a mechanical drawing.

Tod had told Faye that Earle was a dull fool. She agreed laughing, but then said that he was "criminally handsome," an expression she had picked up in the chatter column of a trade paper.

Meeting her on the stairs one night, Tod asked if she would go to dinner with him.

"I can't. I've got a date. But you can come along."

"With Earle?"

"Yes, with Earle," she repeated, mimicking his annoyance.

"No, thanks."

She misunderstood, perhaps on purpose, and said, "He'll treat this time."

Earle was always broke and whenever Tod went with them he was the one who paid.

"That isn't it, and you damn well know it."

"Oh, isn't it?" she asked archly, then, absolutely sure of herself, added, "Meet us at Hodge's around five."

Hodge's was the saddlery store. When Tod got there, he found Earle Shoop at his usual post, just standing and just looking at the sign across the street. He had on his ten-gallon hat and his high-heeled boots. Neatly folded over his left arm was a dark gray jacket. His shirt was navy-blue cotton with large polka dots, each the size of a dime. The sleeves of his shirt were not rolled, but pulled to the middle of his forearm and held there by a pair of fancy, rose armbands. His hands were the same clean reddish tan as his face.

"Lo, thar," was the way he returned Tod's salute.

Tod found his Western accent amusing. The first time he had heard it, he had replied, "Lo, thar, stranger," and had been surprised to discover that Earle didn't know he was being kidded. Even when Tod talked about "cayuses," "mean hombres" and "rustlers," Earl took him seriously.

"Howdy, partner," Tod said.

Next to Earle was another Westerner in a big hat and boots, sitting on his heels and chewing vigorously on a little twig. Close behind him was a battered paper valise held together by heavy rope tied with professional-looking knots.

Soon after Tod arrived a third man came along. He made a thorough examination of the merchandise in the window, then turned and began to stare across the street like the other two.

He was middle-aged and looked like an exercise boy from a racing stable. His face was completely covered with a fine mesh of wrinkles, as though he had been sleeping with it pressed against a roll of rabbit wire. He was very shabby and had probably sold his big hat, but he still had his boots.

"Lo, boys," he said.

"Lo, Hink," said the man with the paper valise.

Tod didn't know whether he was included in the greeting, but took a chance and replied.

"Howdy."

Hink prodded the valise with his toe.

"Goin' some place, Calvin?" he asked.

"Azusa, there's a rodeo."

"Who's running it?"

"A fellow calls himself 'Badlands Jack.' "

"That grifter! . . . You goin', Earle?"

"Nope."

"I gotta eat," said Calvin.

Hink carefully considered all the information he had received before speaking again.

"Mono's makin' a new Buck Stevens," he said. "Will Ferris told me they'd use more than forty riders."

Calvin turned and looked up at Earle.

"Still got the piebald vest?" he asked slyly.

"Why?"

"It'll cinch you a job as a road agent."

Tod understood that this was a joke of some sort because Calvin and Hink chuckled and slapped their thighs loudly while Earle frowned.

There was another long silence, then Calvin spoke again.

"Ain't your old man still got some cows?" he asked Earle.

But Earle was wary this time and refused to answer.

Calvin winked at Tod, slowly and elaborately, contorting one whole side of his face.

"That's right, Earle," Hink said. "Your old man's still got some stock. Why don't you go home?"

They couldn't get a rise out of Earle, so Calvin answered the question.

"He dassint. He got caught in a sheep car with a pair of rubber boots on."

It was another joke. Calvin and Hink slapped their thighs and laughed, but Tod could see that they were waiting for something else. Earle, suddenly, without even shifting his weight, shot his foot out and kicked Calvin solidly in the rump. This was the real point of the joke. They were delighted by Earle's fury. Tod also laughed. The way Earle had gone from apathy to action without the usual transition was funny. The seriousness of his violence was even funnier.

A little while later, Faye drove by in her battered Ford touring car and pulled into the curb some twenty feet away. Calvin and Hink waved, but Earle didn't budge. He took his time, as befitted his dignity. Not until she tooted her horn did he move. Tod followed a short distance behind him.

"Hi, cowboy," said Faye gaily.

"Lo, honey," he drawled, removing his hat carefully and replacing it with even greater care.

Faye smiled at Tod and motioned for them both to climb in. Tod got in the back. Earle unfolded the jacket he was carrying, slapped it a few times to remove the wrinkles, then put it on and adjusted its collar and shaped the roll of its lapels. He then climbed in beside Faye.

She started the car with a jerk. When she reached LaBrea, she turned right to Hollywood Boulevard and then left along it. Tod could see that she was watching Earle out of the corner of her eye and that he was preparing to speak.

"Get going," she said, trying to hurry him. "What is it?"

"Looka here, honey, I ain't got any dough for supper."

She was very much put out.

"But I told Tod we'd treat him. He's treated us enough times."

"That's all right," Tod interposed. "Next time'll do. I've got plenty of money."

"No, damn it," she said without looking around. "I'm sick of it."

She pulled into the curb and slammed on the brakes.

"It's always the same story," she said to Earle.

He adjusted his hat, his collar and his sleeves, then spoke.

"We've got some grub at camp."

"Beans, I suppose."

"Nope."

She prodded him.

"Well, what've you got?"

"Mig and me's set some traps."

Faye laughed.

"Rat traps, eh? We're going to eat rats."

Earle didn't say anything.

"Listen, you big, strong, silent dope," she said, "either make sense, or God damn it, get out of this car."

"They're quail traps," he said without the slightest change in his wooden, formal manner.

She ignored his explanation.

"Talking to you is like pulling teeth. You wear me out."

Tod knew that there was no hope for him in this quarrel. He had heard it all before.

"I didn't mean nothing," Earle said. "I was only funning. I wouldn't feed you rats."

She slammed off the emergency brake and started the car again. At Zacarias Street, she turned into the hills. After climbing steadily for a quarter of a mile, she reached a dirt road and followed it to its end. They all climbed out, Earle helping Faye.

"Give me a kiss," she said, smiling her forgiveness.

He took his hat off ceremoniously and placed it on the hood of the car, then wrapped his long arms around her. They paid no attention to Tod, who was standing off to one side watching them. He saw Earle close his eyes and pucker up his lips like a little boy. But there was nothing boyish about what he did to her. When she had had as much as she wanted, she pushed him away.

"You, too?" she called gaily to Tod, who had turned his back.

"Oh, some other time," he replied, imitating her casualness.

She laughed, then took out a compact and began to fix her mouth. When she was ready, they started along a little path that was a continuation of the dirt road. Earle led, Faye came next and Tod brought up the rear.

It was full spring. The path ran along the bottom of a narrow canyon and wherever weeds could get a purchase in its steep banks they flowered in purple, blue and yellow.

Orange poppies bordered the path. Their petals were wrinkled like crepe and their leaves were heavy with talcumlike dust.

They climbed until they reached another canyon. This one was sterile, but its bare ground and jagged rocks were even more brilliantly colored than the flowers of the first. The path was silver, grained with streaks of rose-gray, and the walls of the canyon were turquoise, mauve, chocolate and lavender. The air itself was vibrant pink.

They stopped to watch a hummingbird chase a bluejay. The jay flashed by squawking with its tiny enemy on its tail like a ruby bullet. The gaudy birds burst the colored air into a thousand glittering particles like metal confetti.

When they came out of this canyon, they saw below them a little green valley thick with trees, mostly eucalyptus, with here and there a poplar and one enormous black live-oak. Sliding and stumbling down a dry wash, they made for the valley.

Tod saw a man watching their approach from the edge of the wood. Faye also saw him and waved.

"Hi, Mig!" she shouted.

"Chinita!" he called back.

She ran the last ten yards of the slope and the man caught her in his arms.

He was toffee-colored with large Armenian eyes and pouting black lips. His head was a mass of tight, ordered curls. He wore a long-haired sweater, called a "gorilla" in and around Los Angeles, with nothing under it. His soiled duck trousers were held up by a red bandanna handkerchief. On his feet were a pair of tattered tennis sneakers.

They moved on to the camp which was located in a clearing in the center of the wood. It consisted of little more than a ramshackle hut patched with tin signs that had been stolen from the highway and a stove without legs or bottom set on some rocks. Near the hut was a row of chicken coops.

Earle started a fire under the stove while Faye sat down on a box and watched him. Tod went over to look at the chickens. There was one old hen and a half a dozen game cocks. A great deal of pains had been taken in making the coops, which were of grooved boards, carefully matched and joined. Their floors were freshly spread with peat moss.

The Mexican came over and began to talk about the cocks. He was very proud of them.

"That's Hermano, five times winner. He's one of Street's Butcher Boys. Pepe and El Negro are still stags. I fight them next week in San Pedro. That's Villa, he's a blinker, but still good. And that one's Zapata, twice winner, a Tassel Dom he is. And that's Jujutla. My champ."

He opened the coop and lifted the bird out for Tod.

"A murderer is what the guy is. Speedy and how!"

The cock's plumage was green, bronze and copper. Its beak was lemon and its legs orange.

"He's beautiful," Tod said.

"I'll say."

Mig tossed the bird back into the coop and they went back to join the others at the fire.

"When do we eat?" Faye asked.

Miguel tested the stove by spitting on it. He next found a large iron skillet and began to scour it with sand. Earle gave Faye a knife and some potatoes to peel, then picked up a burlap sack.

"I'll get the birds," he said.

Tod went along with him. They followed a narrow path that looked as though it had been used by sheep until they came to a tiny field covered with high, tufted grass. Earle stopped behind a gum bush and held up his hand to warn Tod.

A mocking bird was singing near by. Its song was like pebbles being dropped one by one from a height into a pool of water. Then a quail began to call, using two soft guttural notes. Another quail answered and the birds talked back and forth. Their call was not like the cheerful whistle of the Eastern bobwhite. It was full of melancholy and weariness, yet marvelously sweet. Still another quail joined the duet. This one called from near the center of the field. It was a trapped bird, but the sound it made had no anxiety in it, only sadness, impersonal and without hope.

When Earle was satisfied that no one was there to spy on his poaching, he went to the trap. It was a wire basket about the size of a washtub with a small door in the top. He stooped over and began to fumble with the door. Five birds ran wildly along the inner edge and threw themselves at the wire. One of them, a cock, had a dainty plume on his head that curled forward almost to his beak.

Earle caught the birds one at a time and pulled their heads off before dropping them into his sack. Then he started back. As he walked along, he held the sack under his left arm. He lifted the birds out with his right hand and plucked them one at a time. Their feathers fell to the ground, point first, weighed down by the tiny drop of blood that trembled on the tips of their quills.

The sun went down before they reached the camp again. It grew chilly and Tod was glad of the fire. Faye shared her seat on the box with him and they both leaned forward into the heat.

Mig brought a jug of tequila from the hut. He filled a peanut butter jar for Faye and passed the jug to Tod. The liquor smelled like rotten fruit, but he liked the taste. When he had had enough, Earle took it and then Miguel. They continued to pass it from hand to hand.

Earle tried to show Faye how plump the game was, but she wouldn't look. He gutted the birds, then began cutting them into quarters with a pair of heavy tin shears. Faye held her hands over her ears in order not to hear the soft click made by the blades as they cut through flesh and bone. Earle wiped the pieces with a rag and dropped them into the skillet where a large piece of lard was already sputtering.

For all her squeamishness, Faye ate as heartily as the men did. There was no coffee and they finished with tequila. They smoked and kept the jug moving. Faye tossed away the peanut butter jar and drank like the others, throwing her head back and tilting the jug.

Tod could sense her growing excitement. The box on which they were sitting was so small that their backs touched and he could feel how hot she was and how restless. Her neck and face had turned from ivory to rose. She kept reaching for his cigarettes.

Earle's features were hidden in the shadow of his big hat, but the Mexican sat full in the light of the fire. His skin glowed and the oil in his black curls sparkled. He kept smiling at Faye in a manner that Tod didn't like. The more he drank, the less he liked it.

Faye kept crowding Tod, so he left the box to sit on the ground where he could watch her better. She was smiling back at the Mexican. She seemed to know what he was thinking and to be thinking the same thing. Earle, too, became aware of what was passing between them. Tod heard him curse softly and saw him lean forward into the light and pick up a thick piece of firewood.

Mig laughed guiltily and began to sing.

> *"Las palmeras lloran por tu ausencia,*
> *Las laguna se seco—ay!*
> *La cerca de alambre que estaba en*
> *El patio tambien se cayo!"*

His voice was a plaintive tenor and it turned the revolutionary song into a sentimental lament, sweet and cloying. Faye joined in when he began another stanza. She didn't know the words, but she was able to carry the melody and to harmonize.

> *"Pues mi madre las cuidaba, ay!*
> *Toditito se acabo—ay!"*

Their voices touched in the thin, still air to form a minor chord and it was as though their bodies had touched. The song was transformed again. The melody remained the same, but the rhythm broke and its beat became ragged. It was a rumba now.

Earle shifted uneasily and played with his stick. Tod saw her look at him and saw that she was afraid, but instead of becoming wary, she grew still more reckless. She took a long pull at the jug and stood up. She put one hand on each of her buttocks and began to dance.

Mig seemed to have completely forgotten Earle. He clapped his hands, cupping them to make a hollow, drum-like sound, and put all he felt into his voice. He had changed to a more fitting song.

> *"Tony's wife,*
> *The boys in Havana love Tony's wife . . ."*

Faye had her hands clasped behind her head now and she rolled her hips to the broken beat. She was doing the "bump."

> *"Tony's wife,*
> *They're fightin' their duels about Tony's wife . . ."*

Perhaps Tod had been mistaken about Earle. He was using his club on the back of the skillet, using it to bang out the rhythm.

The Mexican stood up, still singing, and joined her in the dance. They approached each other with short mincing steps. She held her skirt up and out with her thumbs and forefingers and he did the same with his trousers. They met head on, blue-black against pale-gold, and used their heads to pivot, then danced back to back with their buttocks touching, their knees bent and wide apart. While Faye shook her breasts and her head, holding the rest of her body rigid, he struck the soft ground heavily with his feet and circled her. They faced each other again and made believe they were cradling their behinds in a shawl.

Earle pounded the skillet harder and harder until it rang like an anvil. Suddenly he, too, jumped up and began to dance. He did a crude hoe-down. He leaped into the air and knocked his heels together. He whooped. But he couldn't become part of their dance. Its rhythm was like a smooth glass wall between him and the dancers. No matter how loudly he whooped or threw himself around, he was unable to disturb the precision with which they retreated and advanced, separated and came together again.

Tod saw the blow before it fell. He saw Earle raise his stick and bring it down on the Mexican's head. He heard the crack and saw the Mexican go to his knees still dancing, his body unwilling or unable to acknowledge the interruption.

Faye had her back to Mig when he fell, but she didn't turn to look. She ran. She flashed by Tod. He reached for her ankle to pull her down, but missed. He scrambled to his feet and ran after her.

If he caught her now, she wouldn't escape. He could hear her on the hill a little way ahead of him. He shouted to her, a deep, agonized bellow, like that a hound makes when it strike a fresh line after hours of cold trailing. Already he could feel how it would be when he pulled her to the ground.

But the going was heavy and the stones and sand moved under his feet. He fell prone with his face in a clump of wild mustard that smelled of the rain and sun, clean, fresh and sharp. He rolled over on his back and stared up at the sky. The violent exercise had driven most of the heat out of his blood, but enough remained to make him tingle pleasantly. He felt comfortably relaxed, even happy.

Somewhere farther up the hill a bird began to sing. He listened. At first the low, rich music sounded like water dripping on something hollow, the bottom of a silver pot perhaps, then like a stick dragged slowly over the string of a harp. He lay quietly, listening.

When the bird grew silent, he made an effort to put Faye out of his mind and began to think about the series of cartoons he was making for his canvas of Los Angeles on fire. He was going to show the city burning at high noon, so that the flames would have to compete with the desert sun and thereby appear less fearful, more like bright flags flying from roofs and windows than a terrible holocaust. He wanted the city to have quite a gala air as it burned, to appear almost gay. And the people who set it on fire would be a holiday crowd.

The bird began to sing again. When it stopped, Faye was forgotten and he only wondered if he weren't exaggerating the importance of the people who come to California to die. Maybe they weren't really desperate enough to set a single city on fire, let alone the whole country. Maybe they were only the pick of America's madmen and not at all typical of the rest of the land.

He told himself that it didn't make any difference because he was an artist, not a prophet. His work would not be judged by the accuracy with which it foretold a future event but by its merit as painting. Nevertheless, he refused to give up the role of Jeremiah. He changed "pick of America's madmen" to "cream" and felt almost certain that the milk from which it had been skimmed was just as rich in violence. The Angelenos would be first, but their comrades all over the country would follow. There would be civil war.

He was amused by the strong feeling of satisfaction this

dire conclusion gave him. Were all prophets of doom and destruction such happy men?

He stood up without trying to answer. When he reached the dirt road at the top of the canyon, Faye and the car were gone.

15

"She went to the pictures with that Simpson guy," Harry told him when he called to see her the next night.

He sat down to wait for her. The old man was very ill and lay on the bed with extreme care as though it were a narrow shelf from which he might fall if he moved.

"What are they making on your lot?" he asked slowly, rolling his eyes toward Tod without budging his head.

" 'Manifest Destiny,' 'Sweet and Low Down,' 'Waterloo,' 'The Great Divide,' 'Begging Your . . .' "

" 'The Great Divide'—" Harry said, interrupting eagerly. "I remember that vehicle."

Tod realized he shouldn't have got him started, but there was nothing he could do about it now. He had to let him run down like a clock.

"When it opened I was playing the Irving in a little number called 'Enter Two Gents,' a trifle, but entertainment, real entertainment. I played a Jew comic, a Ben Welch effect, derby and big pants—'Pat, dey hoffered me a chob in de Heagle Laundreh' . . . 'Faith now, Ikey, and did you take it?' . . . 'No, who vants to vash heagles?' Joe Parvos played straight for me in a cop's suit. Well, the night 'The Great Divide' opened, Joe was laying up with a whisker in the old Fifth Avenue when the stove exploded. It was the broad's husband who blew the whistle. He was . . ."

He hadn't run down. He had stopped and was squeezing his left side with both hands.

Tod leaned over anxiously.

"Some water?"

Harry framed the word "no" with his lips, then groaned skillfully. It was a second-act curtain groan, so phony that Tod had to hide a smile. And yet, the old man's pallor hadn't come from a box.

Harry groaned again, modulating from pain to exhaustion, then closed his eyes. Tod saw how skillfully he got the maximum effect out of his agonized profile by using the pillow to set it off. He also noticed that Harry, like many actors, had very little back or top to his head. It was almost all face, like a mask, with deep furrows between the eyes, across the forehead and on either side of the nose and mouth, plowed there by years of broad grinning and heavy frowning. Because of them, he could never express anything either subtly or exactly. They wouldn't permit degrees of feeling, only the furthest degree.

Tod began to wonder if it might not be true that actors suffer less than other people. He thought about this for a while, then decided that he was wrong. Feeling is of the heart and nerves and the crudeness of its expression has nothing to do with its intensity. Harry suffered as keenly as anyone, despite the theatricality of his groans and grimaces.

He seemed to enjoy suffering. But not all kinds, certainly not sickness. Like many people, he only enjoyed the sort that was self-inflicted. His favorite method was to bare his soul to strangers in barrooms. He would make believe he was drunk, and stumble over to where some strangers were sitting. He usually began by reciting a poem.

> *"Let me sit down for a moment,*
> *I have a stone in my shoe.*
> *I was once blithe and happy,*
> *I was once young like you."*

If his audience shouted, "scram, bum!" he only smiled humbly and went on with his act.

> *"Have pity, folks, on my gray hair . . ."*

The bartender or someone else had to stop him by force, otherwise he would go on no matter what was said to him. Once he got started everyone in the bar usually listened, for he gave a great performance. He roared and whispered, commanded and cajoled. He imitated the whimper of a little girl crying for her vanished mother, as well as the different dialects of the many cruel managers he had known. He even did the off-stage noises, twittering like birds to herald the dawn of Love and yelping like a pack of bloodhounds when describing how an Evil Fate ever pursued him.

He made his audience see him start out in his youth to play Shakespeare in the auditorium of the Cambridge Latin School, full of glorious dreams, burning with ambition. Follow him, as still a mere stripling, he starved in a Broadway rooming house, an idealist who desired only to share his art with the world. Stand with him, as, in the prime of manhood, he married a beautiful dancer, a headliner on the Gus Sun time. Be close behind him as, one night, he returned home unexpectedly to find her in the arms of a head usher. Forgive, as he forgave, out of the goodness of his heart and the greatness of his love. Then laugh, tasting the bitter gall, when the very next night he found her in the arms of a booking agent. Again he forgave her and again she sinned. Even then he didn't cast her out, no, though she jeered, mocked and even struck him repeatedly with an umbrella. But she ran off with a foreigner, a swarthy magician fellow. Behind she left memories and their baby daughter. He made his audience shadow him still as misfortune followed misfortune and, a middle-aged man, he haunted the booking offices, only a ghost of his former self. He who had hoped to play Hamlet, Lear, Othello, must needs become the Co. in an act called Nat Plumstone & Co., light quips and breezy patter. He made them dog his dragging feet as, an aged and trembling old man, he . . .

Faye came in quietly. Tod started to greet her, but she put her finger to her lips for him to be silent and motioned toward the bed.

The old man was asleep. Tod thought his worn, dry skin looked like eroded ground. The few beads of sweat that glistened on his forehead and temples carried no promise of relief. It might rot, like rain that comes too late to a field, but could never refresh.

They both tiptoed out of the room.

In the hall he asked if she had had a good time with Homer.

"That dope!" she exclaimed, making a wry face. "He's strictly home-cooking."

Tod started to ask some more questions, but she dismissed him with a curt, "I'm tired, honey."

16

The next afternoon, Tod was on his way upstairs when he saw a crowd in front of the door of the Greeners' apartment. They were excited and talked in whispers.

"What's happened?" he asked.

"Harry's dead."

He tried the door of the apartment. It wasn't locked, so he went in. The corpse lay stretched out on the bed, completely covered with a blanket. From Faye's room came the sound of crying. He knocked softly on her door. She opened it for him, then turned without saying a word, and stumbled to her bed. She was sobbing into a face towel.

He stood in the doorway, without knowing what to do or say. Finally, he went over to the bed and tried to comfort her. He patted her shoulder.

"You poor kid."

She was wearing a tattered, black lace negligee that had large rents in it. When he leaned over her, he noticed that her skin gave off a warm, sweet odor, like that of buckwheat in flower.

He turned away and lit a cigarette. There was a knock on the door. When he opened it, Mary Dove rushed past him to take Faye in her arms.

Mary also told Faye to be brave. She phrased it differently than he had done, however, and made it sound a lot more convincing.

"Show some guts, kid. Come on now, show some guts."

Faye shoved her away and stood up. She took a few wild steps, then sat down on the bed again.

"I killed him," she groaned.

Mary and he both denied this emphatically.

"I killed him, I tell you! I did! I did!"

She began to call herself names. Mary wanted to stop her, but Tod told her not to. Faye had begun to act and he felt that if they didn't interfere she would manage to escape for herself.

"She'll talk herself quiet," he said.

In a voice heavy with self-accusation, she began to tell what had happened. She had come home from the studio and found Harry in bed. She asked him how he was, but didn't wait for an answer. Instead, she turned her back on him to examine herself in the wall mirror. While fixing her face, she told him that she had seen Ben Murphy and that Ben had said that if Harry were feeling better he might be able to use him in a Bowery sequence. She had been surprised when he didn't shout as he always did when Ben's name was mentioned. He was jealous of Ben and always shouted, "To hell with that bastard; I knew him when he cleaned spittoons in a nigger barroom."

She realized that he must be pretty sick. She didn't turn around because she noticed what looked like the beginning of a pimple. It was only a speck of dirt and she wiped it off, but then she had to do her face all over again. While she was working at it, she told him that she could get a job as a dress extra if she had a new evening gown. Just to kid him, she looked tough and said, "If you can't buy me an evening gown, I'll find someone who can."

When he didn't say anything, she got sore and began to sing, "Jeepers Creepers." He didn't tell her to shut up, so she knew something must be wrong. She ran over to the couch. He was dead.

As soon as she had finished telling all this, she began to sob in a lower key, almost a coo, and rocked herself back and forth.

"Poor papa... Poor darling..."

The fun they used to have together when she was little. No matter how hard up he was, he always brought her dolls and candy, and no matter how tired, he always played with her. She used to ride piggy-back and they would roll on the floor and laugh and laugh.

Mary's sobs made Faye speed up her own and they both began to get out of hand.

There was a knock on the door. Tod answered it and found Mrs. Johnson, the janitress. Faye shook her head for him not to let her in.

"Come back later," Tod said.

He shut the door in her face. A minute later it opened again and Mrs. Johnson entered boldly. She had used a pass-key.

"Get out," he said.

She tried to push past him, but he held her until Faye told him to let her go.

He disliked Mrs. Johnson intensely. She was an officious, bustling woman with a face like a baked apple, soft and blotched. Later he found out that her hobby was funerals. Her preoccupation with them wasn't morbid; it was formal. She was interested in the arrangement of the flowers, the order of the procession, the clothing and deportment of the mourners.

She went straight to Faye and stopped her sobs with a firm, "Now, Miss Greener."

There was so much authority in her voice and manner that she succeeded where Mary and Tod had failed.

Faye looked up at her respectfully.

"First, my dear," Mrs. Johnson said, counting one with the thumb of her right hand on the index finger of her left, "first, I want you to understand that my sole desire in this matter is to help you."

She looked hard at Mary, then at Tod.

"I don't get anything out of it, and it's just a lot of trouble."

"Yes," Faye said.

"All right. There are several things I have to know, if I'm to help you. Did the deceased leave any money or insurance?"

"No."

"Have you any money?"

"No."

"Can you borrow any?"

"I don't think so."

Mrs. Johnson sighed.

"Then the city will have to bury him."

Faye didn't comment.

"Don't you understand, child, the city will have to bury him in a pauper's grave?"

She put so much contempt into "city" and horror into "pauper" that Faye flushed and began to sob again.

Mrs. Johnson made as though to walk out, even took several steps in the direction of the door, then, changed her mind and came back.

"How much does a funeral cost?" Faye asked.

"Two hundred dollars. But you can pay on the installment plan—fifty dollars down and twenty-five a month."

Mary and Tod both spoke together.

"I'll get the money."

"I've got some."

"That's fine," Mrs. Johnson said. "You'll need at least fifty more for incidental expenses. I'll go ahead and take care of everything. Mr. Holsepp will bury your father. He'll do it right."

She shook hands with Faye, as though she were congratulating her, and hurried out of the room.

Mrs. Johnson's little business talk had apparently done Faye some good. Her lips were set and her eyes dry.

"Don't worry," Tod said. "I can raise the money."

"No, thanks," she said.

Mary opened her purse and took out a roll of bills.

"Here's some."

"No," she said, pushing it away.

She sat thinking for a while, then went to the dressing table and began to fix her tear-stained face. She wore a hard smile as she worked. Suddenly she turned, lipstick in air, and spoke to Mary.

"Can you get me into Mrs. Jenning's?"

"What for?" Tod demanded. "I'll get the money."

Both girls ignored him.

"Sure," said Mary, "you ought to done that long ago. It's a soft touch."

Faye laughed.

"I was saving it."

The change that had come over both of them startled Tod. They had suddenly become very tough.

"For a punkola like that Earle. Get smart, girlie, and lay off the cheapies. Let him ride a horse, he's a cowboy, ain't he?"

They laughed shrilly and went into the bathroom with their arms around each other.

Tod thought he understood their sudden change to slang. It made them feel worldly and realistic, and so more able to cope with serious things.

He knocked on the bathroom door.

"What do *you* want?" Faye called out.

"Listen, kid," he said, trying to imitate them. "Why go on the turf? I can get the dough."

"Oh, yeah! No thanks," Faye said.

"But listen . . ." he began again.

"Go peddle your tripe!" Mary shouted.

17

On the day of Harry's funeral Tod was drunk. He hadn't seen Faye since she went off with Mary Dove, but he knew that he was certain to find her at the undertaking parlor and he wanted to have the courage to quarrel with her. He started drinking at lunch. When he got to Holsepp's in the late afternoon, he had passed the brave state and was well into the ugly one.

He found Harry in his box, waiting to be wheeled out for exhibition in the adjoining chapel. The casket was open and the old man looked quite snug. Drawn up to a little below his shoulders and folded back to show its fancy lining was an ivory satin coverlet. Under his head was a tiny lace cushion. He was wearing a Tuxedo, or at least had on a black bow tie with his stiff shirt and wing collar. His face had been newly shaved, his eyebrows shaped and plucked and his lips and cheeks rouged. He looked like the interlocutor in a minstrel show.

Tod bowed his head as though in silent prayer when he heard someone come in. He recognized Mrs. Johnson's voice and turned carefully to face her. He caught her eye and nodded, but she ignored him. She was busy with a man in a badly fitting frock coat.

"It's the principle of the thing," she scolded. "Your estimate said bronze. Those handles ain't bronze and you know it."

"But I asked Miss Greener," whined the man. "She okayed them."

"I don't care. I'm surprised at you, trying to save a few dollars by fobbing off a set of cheap gun-metal handles on the poor child."

Tod didn't wait for the undertaker to answer. He had seen Faye pass the door on the arm of one of the Lee sisters. When he caught up with her, he didn't know what to say. She misunderstood his agitation and was touched. She sobbed a little for him.

She had never looked more beautiful. She was wearing a new, very tight black dress and her platinum hair was tucked up in a shining bun under a black straw sailor. Every so often, she carried a tiny lace handkerchief to her eyes and made it flutter there for a moment. But all he could think of was that she had earned the money for her outfit on her back.

She grew uneasy under his stare and started to edge away. He caught her arm.

"May I speak with you for a minute, alone?"

Miss Lee took the hint and left.

"What is it?" Faye asked.

"Not here," he whispered, making mystery out of his uncertainty.

He led her along the hall until he found an empty showroom. On the walls were framed photographs of important funerals and on little stands and tables were samples of coffin materials and models of tombstones and mausoleums.

Not knowing what to say, he accented his awkwardness, playing the inoffensive fool.

She smiled and became almost friendly.

"Give out, you big dope."

"A kiss . . ."

"Sure, baby," she laughed, "only don't muss me." They pecked at each other.

She tried to get away, but he held her. She became annoyed and demanded an explanation. He searched his head for one. It wasn't his head he should have searched, however.

She was leaning toward him, drooping slightly, but not from fatigue. He had seen young birches droop like that at midday when they are over-heavy with sun.

"You're drunk," she said, pushing him away.

"Please," he begged.

"Le'go, you bastard."

Raging at him, she was still beautiful. That was because her beauty was structural like a tree's, not a quality of her mind or heart. Perhaps even whoring couldn't damage it for that reason, only age or accident or disease.

In a minute she would scream for help. He had to say something. She wouldn't understand the aesthetic argument and with what values could he back up the moral one? The economic didn't make sense either. Whoring certainly paid. Half of the customer's thirty dollars. Say ten men a week.

She kicked at his shins, but he held on to her. Suddenly he began to talk. He had found an argument. Disease would destroy her beauty. He shouted at her like a Y.M.C.A. lecturer on sex hygiene.

She stopped struggling and held her head down, sobbing fitfully. When he was through, he let go of her arms and she bolted from the room. He groped his way to a carved, marble coffin.

He was still sitting there when a young man in a black jacket and gray striped trousers came in.

"Are you here for the Greener funeral?"

Tod stood up and nodded vaguely.

"The services are beginning," the man said, then opened a little casket covered with grosgrain satin and took out a dust cloth. Tod watched him go around the showroom wiping off the samples.

"Services have probably started," the man repeated with a wave at the door.

Tod understood this time and left. The only exit he could find led through the chapel. The moment he entered it, Mrs. Johnson caught him and directed him to a seat. He wanted badly to get away, but it was impossible to do so without making a scene.

Faye was sitting in the front row of benches, facing the pulpit. She had the Lee sisters on one side and Mary Dove and Abe Kusich on the other. Behind them sat the tenants of the San Berdoo, occupying about six rows. Tod was alone in the seventh. After him were several empty rows and then a scattering of men and women who looked very much out of place.

He turned in order not to see Faye's jerking shoulders and examined the people in the last rows. He knew their kind. While not torchbearers themselves, they would run behind the fire and do a great deal of the shouting. They had come to see Harry buried, hoping for a dramatic incident of some sort, hoping at least for one of the mourners to be led weeping hysterically from the chapel. It seemed to Tod that they stared back at him with an expression of vicious, acrid boredom that trembled on the edge of violence. When they began to mutter among themselves, he half turned and watched them out of the corner of his eyes.

An old woman with a face pulled out of shape by badly fitting store teeth came in and whispered to a man sucking on the handle of a home-made walking stick. He passed her message along and they all stood up and went out hurriedly. Tod guessed that some star had been seen going into a restaurant by one of their scouts. If so, they would wait outside the place for hours until the star came out again or the police drove them away.

The Gingo family arrived soon after they had left. The Gingos were Eskimos who had been brought to Hollywood to make retakes for a picture about polar exploration. Although it had been released long ago, they refused to return to Alaska. They liked Hollywood.

Harry had been a good friend of theirs and had eaten with them quite regularly, sharing the smoked salmon, white fish, marinated and maatjes herrings they bought at Jewish delicatessen stores. He also shared the great quantities of cheap brandy they mixed with hot water and salt butter and drank out of tin cups.

Mama and Papa Gingo, trailed by their son, moved down the center aisle of the chapel, bowing and waving to everyone, until they reached the front row. Here they gathered around Faye and shook hands with her, each one in turn. Mrs. Johnson tried to make them go to one of the back rows, but they ignored her orders and sat down in front.

The overhead lights of the chapel were suddenly dimmed. Simultaneously other lights went on behind imitation stained-glass windows which hung on the fake oak-paneled walls. There was a moment of hushed silence, broken only by Faye's sobs, then an electric organ started to play a recording of one of Bach's chorales, "Come Redeemer, Our Saviour."

Tod recognized the music. His mother often played a piano adaptation of it on Sundays at home. It very politely asked Christ to come, in clear and honest tones with just the proper amount of supplication. The God it invited was not the King of Kings, but a shy and gentle Christ, a maiden surrounded by maidens, and the invitation was to a lawn fete, not to the home of some weary, suffering sinner. It didn't plead; it urged with infinite grace and delicacy, almost as though it were afraid of frightening the prospective guest.

So far as Tod could tell, no one was listening to the music. Faye was sobbing and the others seemed busy inside themselves. Bach politely serenading Christ was not for them.

The music would soon change its tone and grow exciting. He wondered if that would make any difference. Already the bass was beginning to throb. He noticed that it made the Eskimos uneasy. As the bass gained in power and began to dominate the treble, he heard Papa Gingo grunt with pleasure. Mama caught Mrs. Johnson eyeing him, and put her fat hand on the back of his head to keep him quiet.

"Now come, O our Saviour," the music begged. Gone

was its diffidence and no longer was it polite. Its struggle with the bass had changed it. Even a hint of a threat crept in and a little impatience. Of doubt, however, he could not detect the slightest trace.

If there was a hint of a threat, he thought, just a hint, and a tiny bit of impatience, could Bach be blamed? After all, when he wrote this music, the world had already been waiting for its lover more than seventeen hundred years. But the music changed again and both threat and impatience disappeared. The treble soared free and triumphant and the bass no longer struggled to keep it down. It had become a rich accompaniment. "Come or don't come," the music seemed to say, "I love you and my love is enough." It was a simple statement of fact, neither cry nor serenade, made without arrogance or humility.

Perhaps Christ heard. If He did, He gave no signs. The attendants heard, for it was their cue to trundle on Harry in his box. Mrs. Johnson followed close behind and saw to it that the casket was properly placed. She raised her hand and Bach was silenced in the middle of a phrase.

"Will those of you who wish to view the deceased before the sermon please step forward?" she called out.

Only the Gingos stood up immediately. They made for the coffin in a group. Mrs. Johnson held them back and motioned for Faye to look first. Supported by Mary Dove and the Lee girls, she took a quick peek, increased the tempo of her sobs for a moment, then hurried back to the bench.

The Gingos had their chance next. They leaned over the coffin and told each other something in a series of thick, explosive gutturals. When they tried to take another look, Mrs. Johnson herded them firmly to their seats.

The dwarf sidled up to the box, made a play with his

handkerchief and retreated. When no one followed him, Mrs. Johnson lost patience, seeming to take what she understood as a lack of interest for a personal insult.

"Those who wish to view the remains of the late Mr. Greener must do so at once," she barked.

There was a little stir, but no one stood up.

"You, Mrs. Gail," she finally said, looking directly at the person named. "How about you? Don't you want a last look? Soon all that remains of your neighbor will be buried forever."

There was no getting out of it. Mrs. Gail moved down the aisle, trailed by several others.

Tod used them to cover his escape.

18

Faye moved out of the San Berdoo the day after the funeral. Tod didn't know where she had gone and was getting up the courage to call Mrs. Jenning when he saw her from the window of his office. She was dressed in the costume of a Napoleonic vivandière. By the time he got the window open, she had almost turned the corner of the building. He shouted for her to wait. She waved, but when he got downstairs she was gone.

From her dress, he was sure that she was working in the picture called "Waterloo." He asked a studio policeman where the company was shooting and was told on the back lot. He started toward it at once. A platoon of cuirassiers, big men mounted on gigantic horses, went by. He knew that they must be headed for the same set and followed them. They broke into a gallop and he was soon outdistanced.

The sun was very hot. His eyes and throat were choked with the dust thrown up by the horses' hooves and his head throbbed. The only bit of shade he could find was under an ocean liner made of painted canvas with real life boats hanging from its davits. He stood in its narrow shadow for a while, then went on toward a great forty-foot papier mâché sphinx that loomed up in the distance. He had to cross a desert to reach it, a desert that was continually being made larger by a fleet of trucks dumping white sand. He had gone only a few feet when a man with a megaphone ordered him off.

He skirted the desert, making a wide turn to the right, and came to a Western street with a plank sidewalk. On the porch of the "Last Chance Saloon" was a rocking chair. He sat down on it and lit a cigarette.

From there he could see a jungle compound with a water buffalo tethered to the side of a conical grass hut. Every few seconds the animal groaned musically. Suddenly an Arab charged by on a white stallion. He shouted at the man, but got no answer. A little while later he saw a truck with a load of snow and several malamute dogs. He shouted again. The driver shouted something back, but didn't stop.

Throwing away his cigarette, he went through the swinging doors of the saloon. There was no back to the building and he found himself in a Paris street. He followed it to its end, coming out in a Romanesque courtyard. He heard voices a short distance away and went toward them. On a lawn of fiber, a group of men and women in riding costume were picnicking. They were eating cardboard food in front of a cellophane waterfall. He started toward them to ask his way, but was stopped by a man who scowled and held up a sign—"Quiet, Please, We're Shooting." When Tod took another step forward, the man shook his fist threateningly.

Next he came to a small pond with large celluloid swans floating on it. Across one end was a bridge with a sign that read, "To Kamp Komfit." He crossed the bridge and followed a little path that ended at a Greek temple dedicated to Eros. The god himself lay face downward in a pile of old newspapers and bottles.

From the steps of the temple, he could see in the distance a road lined with Lombardy poplars. It was the one on which he had lost the cuirassiers. He pushed his way through a tangle of briars, old flats and iron junk, skirting the skeleton of a Zeppelin, a bamboo stockade, an adobe fort, the wooden horse of Troy, a flight of baroque palace stairs that started in a bed of weeds and ended against the branches of an oak, part of the Fourteenth Street elevated station, a Dutch windmill, the bones of a dinosaur, the upper half of the Merrimac, a corner of a Mayan temple, until he finally reached the road.

He was out of breath. He sat down under one of the poplars on a rock made of brown plaster and took off his jacket. There was a cool breeze blowing and he soon felt more comfortable.

He had lately begun to think not only of Goya and Daumier but also of certain Italian artists of the seventeenth and eighteenth centuries, of Salvator Rosa, Francesco Guardi and Monsu Desiderio, the painters of Decay and Mystery. Looking down hill now, he could see compositions that might have actually been arranged from the Calabrian work of Rosa. There were partially demolished buildings and broken monuments, half hidden by great, tortured trees, whose exposed roots writhed dramatically in the arid ground, and by shrubs that carried, not flowers or berries, but armories of spikes, hooks and swords.

For Guardi and Desiderio there were bridges which bridged nothing, sculpture in trees, palaces that seemed of marble until a whole stone portico began to flap in the light breeze. And there were figures as well. A hundred yards from where Tod was sitting a man in a derby hat leaned drowsily against the gilded poop of a Venetian barque and peeled an apple. Still farther on, a charwoman on a stepladder was scrubbing with soap and water the face of a Buddha thirty feet high.

He left the road and climbed across the spine of the hill to look down on the other side. From there he could see a ten-acre field of cockleburs spotted with clumps of sunflowers and wild gum. In the center of the field was a gigantic pile of sets, flats and props. While he watched, a ten-ton truck added another load to it. This was the final dumping ground. He thought of Janvier's "Sargasso Sea." Just as that imaginary body of water was a history of civilization in the form of a marine junkyard, the studio lot was one in the form of a dream dump. A Sargasso of the imagination! And the dump grew continually, for there wasn't a dream afloat somewhere which wouldn't sooner or later turn up on it, having first been made photographic by plaster, canvas, lath and paint. Many boats sink and never reach the Sargasso, but no dream ever entirely disappears. Somewhere it troubles some unfortunate person and some day, when that person has been sufficiently troubled, it will be reproduced on the lot.

When he saw a red glare in the sky and heard the rumble of cannon, he knew it must be Waterloo. From around a bend in the road trotted several cavalry regiments. They wore casques and chest armor of black cardboard and carried long horse pistols in their saddle holsters. They were

Victor Hugo's soldiers. He had worked on some of the drawings for their uniforms himself, following carefully the descriptions in "Les Miserables."

He went in the direction they took. Before long he was passed by the men of Lefebvre-Desnouttes, followed by a regiment of gendarmes d'élite, several companies of chasseurs of the guard and a flying detachment of Rimbaud's lancers.

They must be moving up for the disastrous attack on La Haite Santée. He hadn't read the scenario and wondered if it had rained yesterday. Would Grouchy or Blucher arrive? Grotenstein, the producer, might have changed it.

The sound of cannon was becoming louder all the time and the red fan in the sky more intense. He could smell the sweet, pungent odor of blank powder. It might be over before he could get there. He started to run. When he topped a rise after a sharp bend in the road, he found a great plain below him covered with early nineteenth-century troops, wearing all the gay and elaborate uniforms that used to please him so much when he was a child and spent long hours looking at the soldiers in an old dictionary. At the far end of the field, he could see an enormous hump around which the English and their allies were gathered. It was Mont St. Jean and they were getting ready to defend it gallantly. It wasn't quite finished, however, and swarmed with grips, property men, set dressers, carpenters and painters.

Tod stood near a eucalyptus tree to watch, concealing himself behind a sign that read, " 'Waterloo'—A Charles H. Grotenstein Production." Nearby a youth in a carefully torn horse guard's uniform was being rehearsed in his lines by one of the assistant directors.

"Vive l'Empereur!" the young man shouted, then

clutched his breast and fell forward dead. The assistant director was a hard man to please and made him do it over and over again.

In the center of the plain, the battle was going ahead briskly. Things looked tough for the British and their allies. The Prince of Orange commanding the center, Hill the right and Picton the left wing, were being pressed hard by the veteran French. The desperate and intrepid Prince was in an especially bad spot. Tod heard him cry hoarsely above the din of battle, shouting to the Hollande-Belgians, "Nassau! Brunswick! Never retreat!" Nevertheless, the retreat began. Hill, too, fell back. The French killed General Picton with a ball through the head and he returned to his dressing room. Alten was put to the sword and also retired. The colors of the Lunenberg battalion, borne by a prince of the family of Deux-Ponts, were captured by a famous child star in the uniform of a Parisian drummer boy. The Scotch Grays were destroyed and went to change into another uniform. Ponsonby's heavy dragoons were also cut to ribbons. Mr. Grotenstein would have a large bill to pay at the Western Costume Company.

Neither Napoleon nor Wellington was to be seen. In Wellington's absence, one of the assistant directors, a Mr. Crane, was in command of the allies. He reinforced his center with one of Chasse's brigades and one of Wincke's. He supported these with infantry from Brunswick, Welsh foot, Devon yeomanry and Hanoverian light horse with oblong leather caps and flowing plumes of horsehair.

For the French, a man in a checked cap ordered Milhaud's cuirassiers to carry Mont St. Jean. With their sabers in their teeth and their pistols in their hands, they charged. It was a fearful sight.

The man in the checked cap was making a fatal error. Mont St. Jean was unfinished. The paint was not yet dry and all the struts were not in place. Because of the thickness of the cannon smoke, he had failed to see that the hill was still being worked on by property men, grips and carpenters.

It was the classic mistake, Tod realized, the same one Napoleon had made. Then it had been wrong for a different reason. The Emperor had ordered the cuirassiers to charge Mont St. Jean not knowing that a deep ditch was hidden at its foot to trap his heavy cavalry. The result had been disaster for the French; the beginning of the end.

This time the same mistake had a different outcome. Waterloo, instead of being the end of the Grand Army, resulted in a draw. Neither side won, and it would have to be fought over again the next day. Big losses, however, were sustained by the insurance company in workmen's compensation. The man in the checked cap was sent to the dog house by Mr. Grotenstein just as Napoleon was sent to St. Helena.

When the front rank of Milhaud's heavy division started up the slope of Mont St. Jean, the hill collapsed. The noise was terrific. Nails screamed with agony as they pulled out of joists. The sound of ripping canvas was like that of little children whimpering. Lath and scantling snapped as though they were brittle bones. The whole hill folded like an enormous umbrella and covered Napoleon's army with painted cloth.

It turned into a rout. The victors of Bersina, Leipsic, Austerlitz, fled like schoolboys who had broken a pane of glass. "Sauve qui peut!" they cried, or, rather, "Scram!"

The armies of England and her allies were too deep in

scenery to flee. They had to wait for the carpenters and ambulances to come up. The men of the gallant Seventy-Fifth Highlanders were lifted out of the wreck with block and tackle. They were carted off by the stretcher-bearers, still clinging bravely to their claymores.

19

Tod got a lift back to his office in a studio car. He had to ride on the running board because the seats were occupied by two Walloon grenadiers and four Swabian foot. One of the infantrymen had a broken leg, the other extras were only scratched and bruised. They were quite happy about their wounds. They were certain to receive several extra days' pay, and the man with the broken leg thought he might get as much as five hundred dollars.

When Tod arrived at his office, he found Faye waiting to see him. She hadn't been in the battle. At the last moment, the director had decided not to use any vivandières.

To his surprise, she greeted him with warm friendliness. Nevertheless, he tried to apologize for his behavior in the funeral parlor. He had hardly started before she interrupted him. She wasn't angry, but grateful for his lecture on venereal disease. It had brought her to her senses.

She had still another surprise for him. She was living in Homer Simpson's house. The arrangement was a business one. Homer had agreed to board and dress her until she became a star. They were keeping a record of every cent he spent and as soon as she clicked in pictures, she would pay him back with six per cent interest. To make it absolutely legal, they were going to have a lawyer draw up a contract.

She pressed Tod for an opinion and he said it was a splendid idea. She thanked him and invited him to dinner for the next night.

After she had gone, he wondered what living with her would do to Homer. He thought it might straighten him out. He fooled himself into believing this with an image, as though a man were a piece of iron to be heated and then straightened with hammer blows. He should have known better, for if anyone ever lacked malleability Homer did.

He continued to make this mistake when he had dinner with them. Faye seemed very happy, talking about charge accounts and stupid sales clerks. Homer had a flower in his buttonhole, wore carpet slippers and beamed at her continually.

After they had eaten, while Homer was in the kitchen washing dishes, Tod got her to tell him what they did with themselves all day. She said that they lived quietly and that she was glad because she was tired of excitement. All she wanted was a career. Homer did the housework and she was getting a real rest. Daddy's long sickness had tired her out completely. Homer liked to do housework and anyway he wouldn't let her go into the kitchen because of her hands.

"Protecting his investment," Tod said.

"Yes," she replied seriously, "they have to be beautiful."

They had breakfast around ten, she went on. Homer brought it to her in bed. He took a housekeeping magazine and fixed the tray like the pictures in it. While she bathed and dressed, he cleaned the house. Then they went downtown to the stores and she bought all sorts of things, mostly clothes. They didn't eat lunch on account of her figure, but usually had dinner out and went to the movies.

"Then, ice cream sodas," Homer finished for her, as he came out of the kitchen.

Faye laughed and excused herself. They were going to a picture and she wanted to change her dress. When she had left, Homer suggested that they get some air in the patio. He made Tod take the deck chair while he sat on an up-turned orange crate.

If he had been careful and had acted decently, Tod couldn't help thinking, she might be living with him. He was at least better looking than Homer. But then there was her other prerequisite. Homer had an income and lived in a house, while he earned thirty dollars a week and lived in a furnished room.

The happy grin on Homer's face made him feel ashamed of himself. He was being unfair. Homer was a humble, grateful man who would never laugh at her, who was incapable of laughing at anything. Because of this great quality, she could live with him on what she considered a much higher plane.

"What's the matter?" Homer asked softly, laying one of his heavy hands on Tod's knee.

"Nothing. Why?"

Tod moved so that the hand slipped off.

"You were making faces."

"I was thinking of something."

"Oh," Homer said sympathetically.

Tod couldn't resist asking an ugly question.

"When are you two getting married?"

Homer looked hurt.

"Didn't Faye tell about us?"

"Yes, sort of."

"It's a business arrangement."

"Yes?"

To make Tod believe it, he poured out a long, disjointed argument, the one he must have used on himself. He even went further than the business part and claimed that they were doing it for poor Harry's sake. Faye had nothing left in the world except her career and she must succeed for her daddy's sake. The reason she wasn't a star was because she didn't have the right clothes. He had money and believed in her talent, so it was only natural for them to enter into a business arrangement. Did Tod know a good lawyer?

It was a rhetorical question, but would become a real one, painfully insistent, if Tod smiled. He frowned. That was wrong, too.

"We must see a lawyer this week and have papers drawn up."

His eagerness was pathetic. Tod wanted to help him, but didn't know what to say. He was still fumbling for an answer when they heard a woman shouting from the hill behind the garage.

"Adore! Adore!"

She had a high soprano voice, very clear and pure.

"What a funny name," Tod said, glad to change the subject.

"Maybe it's a foreigner," Homer said.

The woman came into the yard from around the corner of the garage. She was eager and plump and very American.

"Have you seen my little boy?" she asked, making a gesture of helplessness. "Adore's such a wanderer."

Homer surprised Tod by standing up and smiling at the woman. Faye had certainly helped his timidity.

"Is your son lost?" Homer said.

"Oh, no—just hiding to tease me."

She held out her hand.

"We're neighbors. I'm Maybelle Loomis."

"Glad to know you, ma'am. I'm Homer Simpson and this is Mr. Hackett."

Tod also shook hands with her.

"Have you been living here long?" she asked.

"No. I've just come from the East," Homer said.

"Oh, have you? I've been here ever since Mr. Loomis passed on six years ago. I'm an old settler."

"You like it then?" Tod asked.

"Like California?" she laughed at the idea that anyone might not like it. "Why, it's a paradise on earth!"

"Yes," Homer agreed gravely.

"And anyway," she went on, "I have to live here on account of Adore."

"Is he sick?"

"Oh, no. On account of his career. His agent calls him the biggest little attraction in Hollywood."

She spoke so vehemently that Homer flinched.

"He's in the movies?" Tod asked.

"I'll say," she snapped.

Homer tried to placate her.

"That's very nice."

"If it weren't for favoritism," she said bitterly, "he'd be a star. It ain't talent. It's pull. What's Shirley Temple got that he ain't got?"

"Why, I don't know," Homer mumbled.

She ignored this and let out a fearful bellow.

"Adore! Adore!"

Tod had seen her kind around the studio. She was one of that army of women who drag their children from casting office to casting office and sit for hours, weeks, months, waiting for a chance to show what Junior can do. Some of them are very poor, but no matter how poor, they always manage to scrape together enough money, often by making great sacrifices, to send their children to one of the innumerable talent schools.

"Adore!" she yelled once more, then laughed and became a friendly housewife again, a chubby little person with dimples in her fat cheeks and fat elbows.

"Have you any children, Mr. Simpson?" she asked.

"No," he replied, blushing.

"You're lucky—they're a nuisance."

She laughed to show that she didn't really mean it and called her child again.

"Adore ... Oh, Adore ..."

Her next question surprised them both.

"Who do you follow?"

"What?" said Tod.

"I mean—in the Search for Health, along the Road of Life?"

They both gaped at her.

"I'm a raw-foodist, myself," she said. "Dr. Pierce is our leader. You must have seen his ads—'Know-All Pierce-All.'"

"Oh, yes," Tod said, "you're vegetarians."

She laughed at his ignorance.

"Far from it. We're much stricter. Vegetarians eat cooked vegetables. We eat only raw ones. Death comes from eating dead things."

Neither Tod nor Homer found anything to say.

"Adore," she began again. "Adore . . ."

This time there was an answer from around the corner of the garage.

"Here I am, Mama."

A minute later, a little boy appeared dragging behind him a small sailboat on wheels. He was about eight years old, with a pale, peaked face and a large, troubled forehead. He had great staring eyes. His eyebrows had been plucked and shaped carefully. Except for his Buster Brown collar, he was dressed like a man, in long trousers, vest and jacket.

He tried to kiss his mother, but she fended him off and pulled at his clothes, straightening and arranging them with savage little tugs.

"Adore," she said sternly, "I want you to meet Mr. Simpson, our neighbor."

Turning like a soldier at the command of a drill sergeant, he walked up to Homer and grasped his hand.

"A pleasure, sir," he said, bowing stiffly with his heels together.

"That's the way they do it in Europe," Mrs. Loomis beamed, "Isn't he cute?"

"What a pretty sailboat!" Homer said, trying to be friendly.

Both mother and son ignored his comment. She pointed to Tod, and the child repeated his bow and heel-click.

"Well, we've got to go," she said.

Tod watched the child, who was standing a little to one side of his mother and making faces at Homer. He rolled his eyes back in his head so that only the whites showed and twisted his lips in a snarl.

Mrs. Loomis noticed Tod's glance and turned sharply. When she saw what Adore was doing, she yanked him by the arm, jerking him clear off the ground.

"Adore!" she yelled.

To Tod she said apologetically, "He thinks he's the Frankenstein monster."

She picked the boy up, hugging and kissing him ardently. Then she set him down again and fixed his rumpled clothing.

"Won't Adore sing something for us?" Tod asked.

"No," the little boy said sharply.

"Adore," his mother scolded, "sing at once."

"That's all right, if he doesn't feel like it," Homer said.

But Mrs. Loomis was determined to have him sing. She could never permit him to refuse an audience.

"Sing, Adore," she repeated with quiet menace. "Sing 'Mama Doan Wan' No Peas.' "

His shoulders twitched as though they already felt the strap. He tilted his straw sailor over one eye, buttoned up his jacket and did a little strut, then began:

> *"Mama doan wan' no peas,*
> *An' rice, an' cocoanut oil,*
> *Just a bottle of brandy handy all the day.*
> *Mama doan wan' no peas,*
> *Mama doan wan' no cocoanut oil."*

His singing voice was deep and rough and he used the broken groan of the blues singer quite expertly. He moved his body only a little, against rather than in time with the music. The gestures he made with his hands were extremely suggestive.

"Mama doan wan't no gin,
Because gin do make her sin,
Mama doan wan' no glass of gin,
Because it boun' to make her sin,
An' keep her hot and bothered all the day."

He seemed to know what the words meant, or at least his body and his voice seemed to know. When he came to the final chorus, his buttocks writhed and his voice carried a top-heavy load of sexual pain.

Tod and Homer applauded. Adore grabbed the string of his sailboat and circled the yard. He was imitating a tugboat. He tooted several times, then ran off.

"He's just a baby," Mrs. Loomis said proudly, "but he's got loads of talent."

Tod and Homer agreed.

She saw that he was gone again and left hurriedly. They could hear her calling in the brush back of the garage.

"Adore! Adore . . ."

"That's a funny woman," Tod said.

Homer sighed.

"I guess it's hard to get a start in pictures. But Faye is awfully pretty."

Tod agreed. She appeared a moment later in a new flower print dress and picture hat and it was his turn to sigh. She was much more than pretty. She posed, quivering and balanced, on the doorstep and looked down at the two men in the patio. She was smiling, a subtle half-smile uncontaminated by thought. She looked just born, everything moist and fresh, volatile and perfumed. Tod suddenly became very conscious of his dull, insensitive feet bound in dead skin and of his hands, sticky and thick, holding a heavy, rough felt hat.

He tried to get out of going to the pictures with them, but couldn't. Sitting next to her in the dark proved the ordeal he expected it to be. Her self-sufficiency made him squirm and the desire to break its smooth surface with a blow, or at least a sudden gesture, became irresistible.

He began to wonder if he himself didn't suffer from the ingrained, morbid apathy he liked to draw in others. Maybe he could only be galvanized into sensibility and that was why he was chasing Faye.

He left hurriedly, without saying good-by. He had decided to stop running after her. It was an easy decision to make, but a hard one to carry out. In order to manage it, he fell back on one of the oldest tricks in the very full bag of the intellectual. After all, he told himself, he had drawn her enough times. He shut the portfolio that held the drawings he had made of her, tied it with a string, and put it away in his trunk.

It was a childish trick, hardly worthy of a primitive witch doctor, yet it worked. He was able to avoid her for several months. During this time, he took his pad and pencils on a continuous hunt for other models. He spent his nights at the different Hollywood churches, drawing the worshipers. He visited the "Church of Christ, Physical" where holiness was attained through the constant use of chestweights and spring grips; the "Church Invisible" where fortunes were told and the dead made to find lost objects; the "Tabernacle of the Third Coming" where a woman in male clothing preached the "Crusade Against Salt"; and the "Temple Moderne" under whose glass and

chromium roof "Brain-Breathing, the Secret of the Az-
tecs" was taught.

As he watched these people writhe on the hard seats of
their churches, he thought of how well Alessandro Magnasco would dramatize the contrast between their drained-
out, feeble bodies and their wild, disordered minds. He
would not satirize them as Hogarth or Daumier might, nor
would he pity them. He would paint their fury with respect, appreciating its awful, anarchic power and aware
that they had it in them to destroy civilization.

One Friday night in the "Tabernacle of the Third Coming," a man near Tod stood up to speak. Although his name
most likely was Thompson or Johnson and his home town
Sioux City, he had the same countersunk eyes, like the
heads of burnished spikes, that a monk by Magnasco might
have. He was probably just in from one of the colonies in
the desert near Soboba Hot Springs where he had been
conning over his soul on a diet of raw fruit and nuts. He
was very angry. The message he had brought to the city was
one that an illiterate anchorite might have given decadent
Rome. It was a crazy jumble of dietary rules, economics
and Biblical threats. He claimed to have seen the Tiger of
Wrath stalking the walls of the citadel and the Jackal of
Lust skulking in the shrubbery, and he connected these
omens with "thirty dollars every Thursday" and meat eating.

Tod didn't laugh at the man's rhetoric. He knew it was
unimportant. What mattered were his messianic rage and
the emotional response of his hearers. They sprang to their
feet, shaking their fists and shouting. On the altar someone
began to beat a bass drum and soon the entire congregation
was singing "Onward Christian Soldiers."

20

As time went on, the relationship between Faye and Homer began to change. She became bored with the life they were leading together and as her boredom deepened, she began to persecute him. At first she did it unconsciously, later maliciously.

Homer realized that the end was in sight even before she did. All he could do to prevent its coming was to increase his servility and his generosity. He waited on her hand and foot. He bought her a coat of summer ermine and a light blue Buick runabout.

His servility was like that of a cringing, clumsy dog, who is always anticipating a blow, welcoming it even, and in a way that makes overwhelming the desire to strike him. His generosity was still more irritating. It was so helpless and unselfish that it made her feel mean and cruel, no matter how hard she tried to be kind. And it was so bulky that she was unable to ignore it. She had to resent it. He was destroying himself, and although he didn't mean it that way, forcing her to accept the blame.

They had almost reached a final crisis when Tod saw them again. Late one night, just as he was preparing for bed, Homer knocked on his door and said that Faye was downstairs in the car and that they wanted him to go to a night club with them.

The outfit Homer wore was very funny. He had on loose blue linen slacks and a chocolate flannel jacket over a yellow polo shirt. Only a Negro could have worn it without looking ridiculous, and no one was ever less a Negro than Homer.

Tod drove with them to the "Cinderella Bar," a little stucco building in the shape of a lady's slipper, on Western Avenue. Its floor show consisted of female impersonators.

Faye was in a nasty mood. When the waiter took their order, she insisted on a champagne cocktail for Homer. He wanted coffee. The waiter brought both, but she made him take the coffee back.

Homer explained painstakingly, as he must have done many times, that he could not drink alcohol because it made him sick. Faye listened with mock patience. When he finished, she laughed and lifted the cocktail to his mouth.

"Drink it, damn you," she said.

She tilted the glass, but he didn't open his mouth and the liquor ran down his chin. He wiped himself, using the napkin without unfolding it.

Faye called the waiter again.

"He doesn't like champagne cocktails," she said. "Bring him brandy."

Homer shook his head.

"Please, Faye," he whimpered.

She held the brandy to his lips, moving the glass when he turned away.

"Come on, sport—bottoms up."

"Let him alone," Tod finally said.

She ignored him as though she hadn't even heard his protest. She was both furious and ashamed of herself. Her shame strengthened her fury and gave it a target.

"Come on, sport," she said savagely, "or Mama'll spank."

She turned to Tod.

"I don't like people who won't drink. It isn't sociable. They feel superior and I don't like people who feel superior."

"I don't feel superior," Homer said.

"Oh, yes, you do. I'm drunk and you're sober and so you feel superior. God-damned, stinking superior."

He opened his mouth to reply and she poured the brandy into it, then clapped her hand over his lips so that he couldn't spit it back. Some of it came out of his nose.

Still without unfolding the napkin, he wiped himself. Faye ordered another brandy. When it came, she held it to his lips again, but this time he took it and drank it himself, fighting the stuff down.

"That's the boy," Faye laughed. "Well done, sloppy-boppy."

Tod asked her to dance in order to give Homer a moment alone. When they reached the floor, she made an attempt to defend herself.

"That guy's superiority is driving me crazy."

"He loves you," Tod said.

"Yeah, I know, but he's such a slob."

She started to cry on his shoulder and he held her very tight. He took a long chance.

"Sleep with me."

"No, baby," she said sympathetically.

"Please, please . . . just once."

"I can't, honey. I don't love you."

"You worked for Mrs. Jenning. Make believe you're still working for her."

She didn't get angry.

"That was a mistake. And anyway, that was different. I only went on call enough times to pay for the funeral and besides those men were complete strangers. You know what I mean?"

"Yes. But please, darling. I'll never bother you again. I'll go East right after. Be kind."

"I can't."

"Why . . . ?"

"I just can't. I'm sorry, darling. I'm not a tease, but I can't like that."

"I love you."

"No, sweetheart, I can't."

They danced until the number finished without saying anything else. He was grateful to her for having behaved so well, for not having made him feel too ridiculous.

When they returned to the table, Homer was sitting exactly as they had left him. He held the folded napkin in one hand and the empty brandy glass in the other. His helplessness was extremely irritating.

"You're right about the brandy, Faye," Homer said. "It's swell! Whoopee!"

He made a little circular gesture with the hand that held the glass.

"I'd like a Scotch," Tod said.

"Me, too," Faye said.

Homer made another gallant attempt to get into the spirit of the evening.

"Garsoon," he called to the waiter, "more drinks."

He grinned at them anxiously. Faye burst out laughing and Homer did his best to laugh with her. When she stopped suddenly, he found himself laughing alone and turned his laugh into a cough, then hid the cough in his napkin.

She turned to Tod.

"What the devil can you do with a slob like that?"

The orchestra started and Tod was able to ignore her question. All three of them turned to watch a young man in a tight gown of red silk sing a lullaby.

> *"Little man, you're crying,*
> *I know why you're blue,*
> *Someone took your kiddycar away;*
> *Better go to sleep now,*
> *Little man, you've had a busy day . . ."*

He had a soft, throbbing voice and his gestures were matronly, tender and aborted, a series of unconscious caresses. What he was doing was in no sense parody; it was too simple and too restrained. It wasn't even theatrical. This dark young man with his thin, hairless arms and soft, rounded shoulders, who rocked an imaginary cradle as he crooned, was really a woman.

When he had finished, there was a great deal of applause. The young man shook himself and became an actor again. He tripped on his train, as though he weren't used to it, lifted his skirts to show he was wearing Paris garters, then strode off swinging his shoulders. His imitation of a man was awkward and obscene.

Homer and Tod applauded him.

"I hate fairies," Faye said.

"All women do."

Tod meant it as a joke, but Faye was angry.

"They're dirty," she said.

He started to say something else, but Faye had turned to Homer again. She seemed unable to resist nagging him. This time she pinched his arm until he gave a little squeak.

"Do you know what a fairy is?" she demanded.

"Yes," he said hesitatingly.

"All right, then," she barked. "Give out! What's a fairy?"

Homer twisted uneasily, as though he already felt the ruler on his behind, and looked imploring at Tod, who tried to help him by forming the word "homo" with his lips.

"Momo," Homer said.

Faye burst out laughing. But his hurt look made it impossible not to relent, so she patted his shoulder.

"What a hick," she said.

He grinned gratefully and signaled the waiter to bring another round of drinks.

The orchestra began to play and a man came over to ask Faye to dance. Without saying a word to Homer, she followed him to the floor.

"Who's that?" Homer asked, chasing them with his eyes.

Tod made believe he knew and said that he had often seen him around the San Berdoo. His explanation satisfied Homer, but at the same time set him to thinking of something else. Tod could almost see him shaping a question in his head.

"Do you know Earle Shoop?" Homer finally asked.

"Yes."

Homer then poured out a long, confused story about a dirty black hen. He kept referring to the hen again and again, as though it were the one thing he couldn't stand about Earle and the Mexican. For a man who was incapable of hatred, he managed to draw a pretty horrible picture of the bird.

"You never saw such a disgusting thing, the way it squats and turns its head. The roosters have torn all the feathers off its neck and made its comb all bloody and it has scabby feet covered with warts and it cackles so nasty when they drop it into the pen."

"Who drops it into what pen?"

"The Mexican."

"Miguel?"

"Yes. He's almost as bad as his hen."

"You've been to their camp?"

"Camp?"

"In the mountains?"

"No. They're living in the garage. Faye asked me if I minded if a friend of hers lived in the garage for a while because he was broke. But I didn't know about the chickens or the Mexican. . . . Lots of people are out of work nowadays."

"Why don't you throw them out?"

"They're broke and they have no place to go. It isn't very comfortable living in a garage."

"But if they don't behave?"

"It's just that hen. I don't mind the roosters, they're pretty, but that dirty hen. She shakes her dirty feathers each time and clucks so nasty."

"You don't have to look at it."

"They do it every afternoon at the same time when I'm usually sitting in the chair in the sun after I get back from shopping with Faye and just before dinner. The Mexican knows I don't like to see it so he tries to make me look just for spite. I go into the house, but he taps on the windows and calls me to come out and watch. I don't call that fun. Some people have funny ideas of what's fun."

"What's Faye say?"

"She doesn't mind the hen. She says it's only natural."

Then, in case Tod should mistake this for criticism, he told him what a fine, wholesome child she was. Tod agreed, but brought him back to the subject.

"If I were you," he said, "I'd report the chickens to the police. You have to have a permit to keep chickens in the city. I'd do something and damned quick."

Homer avoided a direct answer.

"I wouldn't touch that thing for all the money in the world. She's all over scabs and almost naked. She looks like a buzzard. She eats meat. I saw her one time eating some meat that the Mexican got out of the garbage can. He feeds the roosters grain but the hen eats garbage and he keeps her in a dirty box."

"If I were you, I'd throw those bastards out and their birds with them."

"No, they're nice enough young fellows, just down on their luck, like a lot of people these days, you know. It's just that hen . . ."

He shook his head wearily, as though he could smell and taste her.

Faye was coming back. Homer saw that Tod was going to speak to her about Earle and the Mexican and signaled desperately for him not to do it. She, however, caught at it and was curious.

"What have you guys been chinning about?"

"You, darling," Tod said. "Homer has a t.l. for you."

"Tell me, Homer."

"No, first you tell me one."

"Well, the man I just danced with asked me if you were a movie big shot."

Tod saw that Homer was unable to think of a return compliment so he spoke for him.

"I said you were the most beautiful girl in the place."

"Yes," Homer agreed. "That's what Tod said."

"I don't believe it. Tod hates me. And anyway, I caught you telling him to keep quiet. You were shushing him."

She laughed.

"I bet I know what you were talking about." She mimicked Homer's excited disgust. "That dirty black hen, she's all over scabs and almost naked."

Homer laughed apologetically, but Tod was angry.

"What's the idea of keeping those guys in the garage?" he demanded.

"What the hell is it your business?" she replied, but not with real anger. She was amused.

"Homer enjoys their company. Don't you, sloppy-boppy?"

"I told Tod they were nice fellows just down on their luck like a lot of people these days. There's an awful lot of unemployment going around."

"That's right," she said. "If they go, I go."

Tod had guessed as much. He realized there was no use in saying anything. Homer was again signaling for him to keep quiet.

For some reason or other, Faye suddenly became ashamed of herself. She apologized to Tod by offering to dance with him again, flirting as she suggested it. Tod refused.

She broke the silence that followed by a eulogy of

Miguel's chickens, which was really meant to be an excuse for herself. She described what marvelous fighters the birds were, how much Miguel loved them and what good care he took of them.

Homer agreed enthusiastically. Tod remained silent. She asked him if he had ever seen a cock fight and invited him to the garage for the next night. A man from San Diego was coming North with his birds to pit them against Miguel's.

When she turned to Homer again, he leaned away as though she were going to hit him. She flushed with shame at this and looked at Tod to see if he had noticed. The rest of the evening, she tried to be nice to Homer. She even touched him a little, straightening his collar and patting his hair smooth. He beamed happily.

21

When Tod told Claude Estee about the cock fight, he wanted to go with him. They drove to Homer's place together.

It was one of those blue and lavender nights when the luminous color seems to have been blown over the scene with an air brush. Even the darkest shadows held some purple.

A car stood in the driveway of the garage with its headlights on. They could see several men in the corner of the building and could hear their voices. Someone laughed, using only two notes, ha-ha and ha-ha, over and over again.

Tod stepped ahead to make himself known, in case they were taking precautions against the police. When he entered the light, Abe Kusich and Miguel greeted him but Earle didn't.

"The fights are off," Abe said. "That stinkola from Diego didn't get here."

Claude came up and Tod introduced him to the three

men. The dwarf was arrogant, Miguel gracious and Earle his usual wooden, surly self.

Most of the garage floor had been converted into a pit, an oval space about nine feet long and seven or eight wide. It was floored with an old carpet and walled by a low, ragged fence made of odd pieces of lath and wire. Faye's coupe stood in the driveway, placed so that its headlights flooded the arena.

Claude and Tod followed Abe out of the glare and sat down with him on an old trunk in the back of the garage. Earle and Miguel came in and squatted on their heels facing them. They were both wearing blue denims, polka-dot shirts, big hats and high-heeled boots. They looked very handsome and picturesque.

They sat smoking silently, all of them calm except the dwarf, who was fidgety. Although he had plenty of room, he suddenly gave Tod a shove.

"Get over, lard-ass," he snarled.

Tod moved, crowded against Claude, without saying anything. Earle laughed at Tod rather than the dwarf, but the dwarf turned on him anyway.

"Why, you punkola! Who you laughing at?"

"You," Earle said.

"That so, hah? Well, listen to me, you pee-hole bandit, for two cents I'd knock you out of them prop boots."

Earle reached into his shirt pocket and threw a coin on the ground.

"There's a nickel," he said.

The dwarf started to get off the trunk, but Tod caught him by the collar. He didn't try to get loose, but leaned forward against his coat, like a terrier in a harness, and wagged his great head from side to side.

"Go on," he sputtered, "you fugitive from the Western Costume Company, you . . . you louse in a fright-wig, you."

Earle would have been much less angry if he could have thought of a snappy comeback. He mumbled something about a half-pint bastard, then spat. He hit the instep of the dwarf's shoe with a big gob of spittle.

"Nice shot," Miguel said.

This was apparently enough for Earle to consider himself the winner, for he smiled and became quiet. The dwarf slapped Tod's hand away from his collar with a curse and settled down on the trunk again.

"He ought to wear gaffs," Miguel said.

"I don't need them for a punk like that."

They all laughed and everything was fine again.

Abe leaned across Tod to speak to Claude.

"It would have been a swell main," he said. "There was more than a dozen guys here before you come and some of them with real dough. I was going to make book."

He took out his wallet and gave him one of his business cards.

"It was in the bag," Miguel said. "I got five birds that would of won easy and two sure losers. We would of made a killing."

"I've never seen a chicken fight," Claude said. "In fact, I've never even seen a game chicken."

Miguel offered to show him one of his birds and left to get it. Tod went down to the car for the bottle of whiskey they had left in a side pocket. When he got back, Miguel was holding Jujutla in the light. They all examined the bird.

Miguel held the cock firmly with both hands, somewhat in the manner that a basketball is held for an underhand toss. The bird had short, oval wings and a heart-shaped tail that stood at right angles to its body. It had a triangular head, like a snake's, terminating in a slightly curved beak, thick at the base and fine at the point. All its feathers were so tight and hard that they looked as though they had been varnished. They had been thinned out for fighting and the lines of its body, which was like a truncated wedge, stood out plainly. From between Miguel's fingers dangled its long, bright orange legs and its slightly darker feet with their horn nails.

"Juju was bred by John R. Bowes of Lindale, Texas," Miguel said proudly. "He's a six times winner. I give fifty dollars and a shotgun for him."

"He's a nice bird," the dwarf said grudgingly, "but looks ain't everything."

Claude took out his wallet.

"I'd like to see him fight," he said. "Suppose you sell me one of your other birds and I put it against him."

Miguel thought a while and looked at Earle, who told him to go ahead.

"I've got a bird I'll sell you for fifteen bucks," he said.

The dwarf interfered.

"Let me pick the bird."

"Oh, I don't care," Claude said, "I just want to see a fight. Here's your fifteen."

Earle took the money and Miguel told him to get Hermano, the big red.

"That red'll go over eight pounds," he said, "while Juju won't go more than six."

Earle came back carrying a large rooster that had a silver shawl. He looked like an ordinary barnyard fowl.

When the dwarf saw him, he became indignant.

"What do you call that, a goose?"

"That's one of Street's Butcher Boys," Miguel said.

"I wouldn't bait a hook with him," the dwarf said.

"You don't have to bet," Earle mumbled.

The dwarf eyed the bird and the bird eyed him. He turned to Claude.

"Let me handle him for you, mister," he said.

Miguel spoke quickly.

"Earle'll do it. He knows the cock."

The dwarf exploded at this.

"It's a frame-up!" he yelled.

He tried to take the red, but Earle held the bird high in the air out of the little man's reach.

Miguel opened the trunk and took out a small wooden box, the kind chessmen are kept in. It was full of curved gaffs, small squares of chamois with holes in their centers and bits of waxed string like that used by a shoemaker.

They crowded around to watch him arm Juju. First he wiped the short stubs on the cock's legs to make sure they were clean and then placed a leather square over one of them so that the stub came through the hole. He then fitted a gaff over it and fastened it with a bit of the soft string, wrapping very carefully. He did the same to the other leg.

When he had finished, Earle started on the big red.

"That's a bird with lots of cojones," Miguel said. "He's won plenty fights. He don't look fast maybe, but he's fast all right and he packs an awful wallop."

"Strictly for the cook stove, if you ask me," the dwarf said.

Earle took out a pair of shears and started to lighten the red's plumage. The dwarf watched him cut away most of the bird's tail, but when he began to work on the breast, he caught his hand.

"Leave him be!" he barked. "You'll kill him fast that way. He needs that stuff for protection."

He turned to Claude again.

"Please, mister, let me handle him."

"Make him buy a share in the bird," Miguel said.

Claude laughed and motioned for Earle to give Abe the bird. Earl didn't want to and looked meaningly at Miguel.

The dwarf began to dance with rage.

"You're trying to cold-deck us!" he screamed.

"Aw, give it to him," Miguel said.

The little man tucked the bird under his left arm so that his hands were free and began to look over the gaffs in the box. They were all the same length, three inches, but some had more pronounced curves than the others. He selected a pair and explained his strategy to Claude.

"He's going to do most of his fighting on his back. This pair'll hit right that way. If he could get over the other bird, I wouldn't use them."

He got down on his knees and honed the gaffs on the cement floor until they were like needles.

"Have we a chance?" Tod asked.

"You can't ever tell," he said, shaking his extra large head. "He feels almost like a dead bird."

After adjusting the gaffs with great care, he looked the bird over, stretching its wings and blowing its feathers in order to see its skin.

"The comb ain't bright enough for fighting condition," he said, pinching it, "but he looks strong. He may have been a good one once."

He held the bird in the light and looked at its head. When Miguel saw him examining its beak, he told him anxiously to quit stalling. But the dwarf paid no attention and went on muttering to himself. He motioned for Tod and Claude to look.

"What'd I tell you!" he said, puffing with indignation. "We've been cold-decked."

He pointed to a hair line running across the top of the bird's beak.

"That's not a crack," Miguel protested, "it's just a mark."

He reached for the bird as though to rub its beak and the bird pecked savagely at him. This pleased the dwarf.

"We'll fight," he said, "but we won't bet."

Earle was to referee. He took a piece of chalk and drew three lines in the center of the pit, a long one in the middle and two shorter ones parallel to it and about three feet away.

"Pit your cocks," he called.

"No, bill them first," the dwarf protested.

He and Miguel stood at arm's length and thrust their birds together to anger them. Juju caught the big red by the comb and held on viciously until Miguel jerked him away. The red, who had been rather apathetic, came to life and the dwarf had trouble holding him. The two men thrust their birds together again, and again Juju caught the red's comb. The big cock became frantic with rage and struggled to get at the smaller bird.

"We're ready," the dwarf said.

He and Miguel climbed into the pit and set their birds down on the short lines so that they faced each other. They held them by the tails and waited for Earle to give the signal to let go.

"Pit them," he ordered.

The dwarf had been watching Earle's lips and he had his bird off first, but Juju rose straight in the air and sank one spur in the red's breast. It went through the feathers into the flesh. The red turned with the gaff still stuck in him and pecked twice at his opponent's head.

They separated the birds and held them to the lines again.

"Pit 'em!" Earle shouted.

Again Juju got above the other bird, but this time he missed with his spurs. The red tried to get above him, but couldn't. He was too clumsy and heavy to fight in the air. Juju climbed again, cutting and hitting so rapidly that his legs were a golden blur. The red met him by going back on his tail and hooking upward like a cat. Juju landed again and again. He broke one of the red's wings, then practically severed a leg.

"Handle them," Earle called.

When the dwarf gathered the red up, its neck had begun to droop and it was a mass of blood and matted feathers. The little man moaned over the bird, then set to work. He spit into its gaping beak and took the comb between his lips and sucked the blood back into it. The red began to regain its fury, but not its strength. Its beak closed and its neck straightened. The dwarf smoothed and shaped its plumage. He could do nothing to help the broken wing or the dangling leg.

"Pit 'em," Earle said.

The dwarf insisted that the birds be put down beak to beak on the center line, so that the red would not have to move to get at his opponent. Miguel agreed.

The red was very gallant. When Abe let go of its tail, it made a great effort to get off the ground and meet Juju in the air, but it could only thrust with one leg and fell over on its side. Juju sailed above it, half turned and came down on its back, driving in both spurs. The red twisted free, throwing Juju, and made a terrific effort to hook with its good leg, but fell sideways again.

Before Juju could get into the air, the red managed to drive a hard blow with its beak to Juju's head. This slowed the smaller bird down and he fought on the ground. In the pecking match, the red's greater weight and strength evened up for his lack of a leg and a wing. He managed to give as good as he got. But suddenly his cracked beak broke off, leaving only the lower half. A large bubble of blood rose where the beak had been. The red didn't retreat an inch, but made a great effort to get into the air once more. Using its one leg skillfully, it managed to rise six or seven inches from the ground, not enough, however, to get its spurs into play. Juju went up with him and got well above, then drove both gaffs into the red's breast. Again one of the steel needles stuck.

"Handle them," Earle shouted.

Miguel freed his bird and gave the other back to the dwarf. Abe, moaning softly, smoothed its feathers and licked its eyes clean, then took its whole head in his mouth. The red was finished, however. It couldn't even hold its neck straight. The dwarf blew away the feathers from under its tail and pressed the lips of its vent together hard. When that didn't seem to help, he inserted his little finger and scratched the bird's testicles. It fluttered and made a gallant effort to straighten its neck.

"Pit birds."

Once more the red tried to rise with Juju, pushing hard with its remaining leg, but it only spun crazily. Juju rose, but missed. The red thrust weakly with its broken bill. Juju went into the air again and this time drove a gaff through one of the red's eyes into its brain. The red fell over stone dead.

The dwarf groaned with anguish, but no one else said anything. Juju pecked at the dead bird's remaining eye.

"Take off that stinking cannibal!" the dwarf screamed.

Miguel laughed, then caught Juju and removed its gaffs. Earle did the same for the red. He handled the dead cock gently and with respect.

Tod passed the whiskey.

22

They were well on their way to getting drunk when Homer came out to the garage. He gave a little start when he saw the dead chicken sprawled on the carpet. He shook hands with Claude after Tod introduced him, and with Abe Kusich, then made a little set speech about everybody coming in for a drink. They trooped after him.

Faye greeted them at the door. She was wearing a pair of green silk lounging pajamas and green mules with large pompons and very high heels. The top three buttons of her jacket were open and a good deal of her chest was exposed but nothing of her breasts; not because they were small, but because they were placed wide apart and their thrust was upward and outward.

She gave Tod her hand and patted the dwarf on the top of the head. They were old friends. In acknowledging Homer's awkward introduction of Claude, she was very much the lady. It was her favorite role and she assumed it whenever she met a new man, especially if he were someone whose affluence was obvious.

"Charmed to have you," she trilled.

The dwarf laughed at her.

In a voice stiff with hauteur, she then ordered Homer into the kitchen for soda, ice and glasses.

"A swell layout," announced the dwarf, putting on the hat he had taken off in the doorway.

He climbed into one of the big Spanish chairs, using his knees and hands to do it, and sat on the edge with his feet dangling. He looked like a ventriloquist's dummy.

Earle and Miguel had remained behind to wash up. When they came in, Faye welcomed them with stilted condescension.

"How do you do, boys? The refreshments will be along in a jiffy. But perhaps you prefer a liqueur, Miguel?"

"No, mum," he said, a little startled. "I'll have what the others have."

He followed Earle across the room to the couch. Both of them took long, wooden steps, as though they weren't used to being in a house. They sat down gingerly with their backs straight, their big hats on their knees and their hands under their hats. They had combed their hair before leaving the garage and their small round heads glistened prettily.

Homer took the drinks around on a small tray.

They all made a show of manners, all but the dwarf, that is, who remained as arrogant as ever. He even commented on the quality of the whiskey. As soon as everyone had been served, Homer sat down.

Faye alone remaining standing. She was completely self-possessed despite their stares. She stood with one hip thrown out and her hand on it. From where Claude was sitting he could follow the charming line of her spine as it swooped into her buttocks, which were like a heart upside down.

He gave a low whistle of admiration and everyone agreed by moving uneasily or laughing.

"My dear," she said to Homer, "perhaps some of the men would like cigars?"

He was surprised and mumbled something about there being no cigars in the house but that he would go to the store for them if . . . Having to say all this made him unhappy and he took the whiskey around again. He poured very generous shots.

"That's a becoming shade of green," Tod said.

Faye peacocked for them all.

"I thought maybe it was a little gaudy . . . vulgar you know."

"No," Claude said enthusiastically, "it's stunning."

She repaid him for his compliment by smiling in a peculiar, secret way and running her tongue over her lips. It was one of her most characteristic gestures and very effective. It seemed to promise all sorts of undefined intimacies, yet it was really as simple and automatic as the word thanks. She used it to reward anyone for anything, no matter how unimportant.

Claude made the same mistake Tod had often made and jumped to his feet.

"Won't you sit here?" he said, waving gallantly at his chair. She accepted by repeating the secret smile and the tongue caress. Claude bowed, but then, realizing that everyone was watching him, added a little mock flourish to make himself less ridiculous. Tod joined them, then Earle and

Miguel came over. Claude did the courting while the others stood by and stared at her.

"Do you work in pictures, Mr. Estee?" she asked.

"Yes. You're in pictures, of course?"

Everyone was aware of the begging note in his voice, but no one smiled. They didn't blame him. It was almost impossible to keep that note out when talking to her. Men used it just to say good morning.

"Not exactly, but I hope to be," she said. "I've worked as an extra, but I haven't had a real chance yet. I expect to get one soon. All I ask is a chance. Acting is in my blood. We Greeners, you know, were all theatre people from away back."

She didn't let Claude finish, but he didn't care.

"Not musicals, but real dramas. Of course, maybe light comedies at first. All I ask is a chance. I've been buying a lot of clothes lately to make myself one. I don't believe in luck. Luck is just hard work, they say, and I'm willing to work as hard as anybody."

"You have a delightful voice and you handle it well," he said.

He couldn't help it. Having once seen her secret smile and the things that accompanied it, he wanted to make her repeat it again and again.

"I'd like to do a show on Broadway," she continued. "That's the way to get a start nowadays. They won't talk to you unless you've had stage experience."

She went on and on, telling him how careers are made in the movies and how she intended to make hers. It was all nonsense. She mixed bits of badly understood advice from the trade papers with other bits out of the fan magazines and compared these with the legends that surrounded the

activities of screen stars and executives. Without any no-
ticeable transition, possibilities became probabilities and
wound up as inevitabilities. At first she occasionally stopped
and waited for Claude to chorus a hearty agreement, but
when she had a good start, all her questions were rhetorical
and the stream of words rippled on without a break.

None of them really heard her. They were all too busy
watching her smile, laugh, shiver, whisper, grow indignant,
cross and uncross her legs, stick out her tongue, widen and
narrow her eyes, toss her head so that her platinum hair
splashed against the red plush of the chair back. The
strange thing about her gestures and expressions was that
they didn't really illustrate what she was saying. They were
almost pure. It was as though her body recognized how
foolish her words were and tried to excite her hearers into
being uncritical. It worked that night; no one even thought
of laughing at her. The only move they made was to narrow their circle about her.

Tod stood on the outer edge, watching her through the
opening between Earle and the Mexican. When he felt a
light tap on his shoulder, he knew it was Homer, but didn't
turn. When the tap was repeated, he shrugged the hand
away. A few minutes later, he heard a shoe squeak behind
him and turned to see Homer tiptoeing off. He reached a
chair safely and sank into it with a sigh. He put his heavy
hands on the knees, one on each, and stared for a while at
their backs. He felt Tod's eyes on him and looked up and
smiled.

His smile annoyed Tod. It was one of those irritating
smiles that seem to say: "My friend, what can you know of
suffering?" There was something very patronizing and superior about it, and intolerably snobbish.

He felt hot and a little sick. He turned his back on Homer and went out the front door. His indignant exit wasn't very successful. He wobbled quite badly and when he reached the sidewalk, he had to sit down on the curb with his back against a date palm.

From where he was sitting, he couldn't see the city in the valley below the canyon, but he could see the reflection of its lights, which hung in the sky above it like a batik parasol. The unlighted part of the sky at the edge of the parasol was a deep black with hardly a trace of blue.

Homer followed him out of the house and stood standing behind him, afraid to approach. He might have sneaked away without Tod's knowing it, if he had not suddenly looked down and seen his shadow.

"Hello," he said.

He motioned for Homer to join on the curb.

"You'll catch cold," Homer said.

Tod understood his protest. He made it because he wanted to be certain that his company was really welcome. Nevertheless, Tod refused to repeat the invitation. He didn't even turn to look at him again. He was sure he was wearing his long-suffering smile and didn't want to see it.

He wondered why all his sympathy had turned to malice. Because of Faye? It was impossible for him to admit it. Because he was unable to do anything to help him? This reason was a more comfortable one, but he dismissed it with even less consideration. He had never set himself up as a healer.

Homer was looking the other way, at the house, watching the parlor window. He cocked his head to one side when someone laughed. The four short sounds, ha-ha and again ha-ha, distinct musical notes, were made by the dwarf.

"You could learn from him," Tod said.

"What?" Homer asked, turning to look at him.

"Let it go."

His impatience both hurt and puzzled Homer. He saw that and motioned for him to sit down, this time emphatically.

Homer obeyed. He did a poor job of squatting and hurt himself. He sat nursing his knee.

"What is it?" Tod finally said, making an attempt to be kind.

"Nothing, Tod, nothing."

He was grateful and increased his smile. Tod couldn't help seeing all its annoying attributes, resignation, kindliness, and humility.

They sat quietly, Homer with his heavy shoulders hunched and the sweet grin on his face, Tod frowning, his back pressed hard against the palm tree. In the house the radio was playing and its blare filled the street.

They sat for a long time without speaking. Several times Homer started to tell Tod something but he didn't seem able to get the words out. Tod refused to help him with a question.

His big hands left his lap, where they had been playing "here's the church and here the steeple," and hid in his armpits. They remained there for a moment, then slid under his thighs. A moment later they were back in his lap. The right hand cracked the joints of the left, one by one, then the left did the same service for the right. They seemed easier for a moment, but not for long. They started "here's the church" again, going through the entire performance and ending with the joint manipulation as before. He started a third time, but catching Tod's eyes, he stopped and trapped his hands between his knees.

It was the most complicated tic Tod had ever seen. What made it particularly horrible was its precision. It wasn't pantomime, as he had first thought, but manual ballet.

When Tod saw the hands start to crawl out again, he exploded.

"For Christ's sake!"

The hands struggled to get free, but Homer clamped his knees shut and held them.

"I'm sorry," he said.

"Oh, all right."

"But I can't help it, Tod. I have to do it three times."

"Okay with me."

He turned his back on him.

Faye started to sing and her voice poured into the street.

> *"Dreamed about a reefer five feet long*
> *Not too mild and not too strong,*
> *You'll be high, but not for long,*
> *If you're a viper—a vi-paah."*

Instead of her usual swing delivery, she was using a lugubrious one, wailing the tune as though it were a dirge. At the end of every stanza, she shifted to an added minor.

> *"I'm the queen of everything,*
> *Gotta be high before I can swing,*
> *Light a tea and let it be,*
> *If you're a viper—a vi-paah."*

"She sings very pretty," Homer said.

"She's drunk."

"I don't know what to do, Tod," Homer complained. "She's drinking an awful lot lately. It's that Earle. We used to have a lot of fun before he came, but now we don't have any fun any more since he started to hang around."

"Why don't you get rid of him?"

"I was thinking about what you said about the license to keep chickens."

Tod understood what he wanted.

"I'll report them to the Board of Health tomorrow."

Homer thanked him, then insisted on explaining in detail why he couldn't do it himself.

"But that'll only get rid of the Mexican," Tod said. "You have to throw Earle out yourself."

"Maybe he'll go with his friend?"

Tod knew that Homer was begging him to agree so that he could go on hoping, but he refused.

"Not a chance. You'll have to throw him out."

Homer accepted this with his brave, sweet smile.

"Maybe . . ."

"Tell Faye to do it," Tod said.

"Oh, I can't."

"Why the hell not? It's your house."

"Don't be mad at me, Toddie."

"All right, Homie, I'm not mad at you."

Faye's voice came through the open window.

> *"And when our throat gets dry,*
> *You know you're high,*
> *If you're a viper."*

The others harmonized on the last word, repeating it.

"Vi-paah . . ."

"Toddie," Homer began, "if . . ."

"Stop calling me Toddie, for Christ's sake!"

Homer didn't understand. He took Tod's hand.

"I didn't mean nothing. Back home we call . . ."

Tod couldn't stand his trembling signals of affection. He tore free with a jerk.

"Oh, but, Toddie, I . . ."

"She's a whore!"

He heard Homer grunt, then heard his knees creak as he struggled to his feet.

Faye's voice came pouring through the window, a reedy wail that broke in the middle with a husky catch.

> *"High, high, high, high, when you're high,*
> *Everything is dandy,*
> *Truck on down to the candy store,*
> *Bust your conk on peppermint candy!*
> *Then you know your body's sent,*
> *Don't care if you don't pay rent,*
> *Sky is high and so am I,*
> *If you're a viper—a vi-paah."*

23

When Tod went back into the house, he found Earle, Abe Kusich and Claude standing together in a tight group, watching Faye dance with Miguel. She and the Mexican were doing a slow tango to music from the phonograph. He held her very tight, one of his legs thrust between hers, and they swayed together in long spirals that broke rhythmically at the top of each curve into a dip. All the buttons on her lounging pajamas were open and the arm he had around her waist was inside her clothes.

Tod stood watching the dancers from the doorway for a moment, then went to a little table on which the whiskey bottle was. He poured himself a quarter of a tumblerful, tossed it off, then poured another drink. Carrying the glass, he went over to Claude and the others. They paid no attention to him; their heads moved only to follow the dancers, like the gallery at a tennis match.

"Did you see Homer?" Tod asked, touching Claude's arm.

Claude didn't turn, but the dwarf did. He spoke as though hypnotized.

"What a quiff! What a quiff!"

Tod left them and went to look for Homer. He wasn't in the kitchen, so he tried the bedrooms. One of them was locked. He knocked lightly, waited, then repeated the knock. There was no answer, but he thought he heard someone move. He looked through the keyhole. The room was pitch dark.

"Homer," he called softly.

He heard the bed creak, then Homer replied.

"Who is it?"

"It's me—Toddie."

He used the diminutive with perfect seriousness.

"Go away, please," Homer said.

"Let me in for a minute. I want to explain something."

"No," Homer said, "go away, please."

Tod went back to the living room. The phonograph record had been changed to a fox-trot and Earle was now dancing with Faye. He had both his arms around her in a bear hug and they were stumbling all over the room, bumping into the walls and furniture. Faye, her head thrown back, was laughing wildly. Earle had both eyes shut tight.

Miguel and Claude were also laughing, but not the dwarf. He stood with his fist clenched and his chin stuck out. When he couldn't stand any more of it, he ran after the dancers to cut in. He caught Earle by the seat of his trousers.

"Le'me dance," he barked.

Earle turned his head, looking down at the dwarf from over his shoulder.

"Git! G'wan, git!"

Faye and Earle had come to a halt with their arms around each other. When the dwarf lowered his head like a goat and tried to push between them, she reached down and tweaked his nose.

"Le'me dance," he bellowed.

They tried to start again, but Abe wouldn't let them. He had his hands between them and was trying frantically to pull them apart. When that wouldn't work, he kicked Earle sharply in the shins. Earle kicked back and his boot landed in the little man's stomach, knocking him flat on his back. Everyone laughed.

The dwarf struggled to his feet and stood with his head lowered like a tiny ram. Just as Faye and Earle started to dance again, he charged between Earle's legs and dug upward with both hands. Earle screamed with pain, and tried to get at him. He screamed again, then groaned and started to sink to the floor, tearing Faye's silk pajamas on his way down.

Miguel grabbed Abe by the throat. The dwarf let go his hold and Earle sank to the floor. Lifting the little man free, Miguel shifted his grip to his ankles and dashed him against the wall, like a man killing a rabbit against a tree. He swung the dwarf back to slam him again, but Tod caught his arm. Then Claude grabbed the dwarf and together they pulled him away from the Mexican.

He was unconscious. They carried him into the kitchen and held him under the cold water. He came to quickly, and began to curse. When they saw he was all right, they went back to the living room.

Miguel was helping Earle over to the couch. All the tan

had drained from his face and it was covered with sweat. Miguel loosened his trousers while Claude took off his necktie and opened his collar.

Faye and Tod watched from the side.

"Look," she said, "my new pajamas are ruined."

One of the sleeves had been pulled almost off and her shoulder stuck through it. The trousers were also torn. While he stared at her, she undid the top of the trousers and stepped out of them. She was wearing tight black lace drawers. Tod took a step toward her and hesitated. She threw the pajama bottoms over her arm, turned slowly and walked toward the door.

"Faye," Tod gasped.

She stopped and smiled at him.

"I'm going to bed," she said. "Get that little guy out of here."

Claude came over and took Tod by the arm.

"Let's blow," he said.

Tod nodded.

"We'd better take the homunculus with us or he's liable to murder the whole household."

Tod nodded again and followed him into the kitchen. They found the dwarf holding a big piece of ice to the side of his head.

"There's some lump where that greaser slammed me."

He made them finger and admire it.

"Let's go home," Claude said.

"No," said the dwarf, "let's go see some girls. I'm just getting started."

"To hell with that," snapped Tod. "Come on."

He pushed the dwarf toward the door.

"Take your hands off, punk!" roared the little man.

Claude stepped between them.

"Easy there, citizen," he said.

"All right, but no shoving."

He strutted out and they followed.

Earle still lay stretched on the couch. He had his eyes closed and was holding himself below the stomach with both hands. Miguel wasn't there.

Abe chuckled, wagging his big head gleefully.

"I fixed that buckeroo."

Out on the sidewalk he tried again to get them to go with him.

"Come on, you guys—we'll have some fun."

"I'm going home," Claude said.

They went with the dwarf to his car and watched him climb in behind the wheel. He had special extensions on the clutch and brake so that he could reach them with his tiny feet.

"Come to town?"

"No, thanks," Claude said politely.

"Then to hell with you!"

That was his farewell. He let out the brake and the car rolled away.

24

Tod woke up the next morning with a splitting headache. He called the studio to say he wouldn't be in and remained in bed until noon, then went downtown for breakfast. After several cups of hot tea, he felt a little better and decided to visit Homer. He still wanted to apologize.

Climbing the hill to Pinyon Canyon made his head throb and he was relieved when no one answered his repeated knocks. As he started away, he saw one of the curtains move and went back to knock once more. There was still no answer.

He went around to the garage. Faye's car was gone and so were the game chickens. He went to the back of the house and knocked on the kitchen door. Somehow the silence seemed too complete. He tried the handle and found that the door wasn't locked. He shouted hello a few times, as a warning, then went through the kitchen into the living room.

The red velvet curtains were all drawn tight, but he could see Homer sitting on the couch and staring at the backs of his hands which were cupped over his knees. He wore an old-fashioned cotton nightgown and his feet were bare.

"Just get up?"

Homer neither moved nor replied.

Tod tried again.

"Some party!"

He knew it was stupid to be hearty, but he didn't know what else to be.

"Boy, have I got a hang-over," he went on, even going so far as to attempt a chuckle.

Homer paid absolutely no attention to him.

The room was just as they had left it the night before. Tables and chairs were overturned and the smashed picture lay where it had fallen. To give himself a reason for staying, he began to tidy up. He righted the chairs, straightened the carpet and picked up the cigarette butts that littered the floor. He also threw aside the curtains and opened a window.

"There, that's better, isn't it?" he asked cheerfully.

Homer looked up for a second, then down at his hands again. Tod saw that he was coming out of his stupor.

"Want some coffee?" he asked.

He lifted his hands from his knees and hid them in his armpits, clamping them tight, but didn't answer.

"Some hot coffee—what do you say?"

He took his hands from under his arms and sat on them. After waiting a little while he shook his head no, slowly, heavily, like a dog with a foxtail in its ear.

"I'll make some."

Tod went to the kitchen and put the pot on the stove. While it was boiling, he took a peek into Faye's room. It had been stripped. All the dresser drawers were pulled out and there were empty boxes all over the floor. A broken flask of perfume lay in the middle of the carpet and the place reeked of gardenia.

When the coffee was ready, he poured two cups and carried them into the living room on a tray. He found Homer just as he had left him, sitting on his hands. He moved a small table close to him and put the tray on it.

"I brought a cup for myself, too," he said. "Come on—drink it while it's hot."

Tod lifted a cup and held it out, but when he saw that he was going to speak, he put it down and waited.

"I'm going back to Wayneville," Homer said.

"A swell idea—great!"

He pushed the coffee at him again. Homer ignored it. He gulped several times, trying to swallow something that was stuck in his throat, then began to sob. He cried without covering his face or bending his head. The sound was like an ax chopping pine, a heavy, hollow, chunking noise. It was repeated rhythmically but without accent. There was no progress in it. Each chunk was exactly like the one that preceded. It would never reach a climax.

Tod realized that there was no use trying to stop him. Only a very stupid man would have the courage to try to do it. He went to the farthest corner of the room and waited.

Just as he was about to light a second cigarette, Homer called him.

"Tod!"

"I'm here, Homer."

He hurried over to the couch again.

Homer was still crying, but he suddenly stopped even more abruptly than he had started.

"Yes, Homer?" Tod asked encouragingly.

"She's left."

"Yes, I know. Drink some coffee."

"She's left."

Tod knew that he put a great deal of faith in sayings, so he tried one.

"Good riddance to bad rubbish."

"She left before I got up," he said.

"What the hell do you care? You're going back to Wayneville."

"You shouldn't curse," Homer said with the same lunatic calm.

"I'm sorry," Tod mumbled.

The word "sorry" was like dynamite set off under a dam. Language leaped out of Homer in a muddy, twisting torrent. At first, Tod thought it would do him a lot of good to pour out in this way. But he was wrong. The lake behind the dam replenished itself too fast. The more he talked the greater the pressure grew because the flood was circular and ran back behind the dam again.

After going on continuously for about twenty minutes, he stopped in the middle of a sentence. He leaned back, closed his eyes and seemed to fall asleep. Tod put a cushion under his head. After watching him for a while, he went back to the kitchen.

He sat down and tried to make sense out of what Homer had told him. A great deal of it was gibberish. Some of it, however, wasn't. He hit on a key that helped when he realized that a lot of it wasn't jumbled so much as timeless. The words went behind each other instead of after. What he had taken for long strings were really one thick word and not a sentence. In the same way several sentences were simultaneous and not a paragraph. Using this key, he was able to arrange a part of what he had heard so that it made the usual kind of sense.

After Tod had hurt him by saying that nasty thing about Faye, Homer ran around to the back of the house and let himself in through the kitchen, then went to peek into the parlor. He wasn't angry with Tod, just surprised and upset because Tod was a nice boy. From the hall that led into the parlor he could see everybody having a good time and he was glad because it was kind of dull for Faye living with an old man like him. It made her restless. No one noticed him peeking there and he was glad because he didn't feel much like joining the fun, although he liked to watch people enjoy themselves. Faye was dancing with Mr. Estee and they made a nice pair. She seemed happy. Her face shone like always when she was happy. Next she danced with Earle. He didn't like that because of the way he held her. He couldn't see what she saw in that fellow. He just wasn't nice, that's all. He had mean eyes. In the hotel business they used to watch out for fellows like that and never gave them credit because they would jump their bills. Maybe he couldn't get a job because nobody would trust him, although it was true as Faye said that a lot of people were out of work nowadays. Standing there peeking at the party, enjoying the laughing and singing, he saw Earle catch Faye and bend her back and kiss her and everybody laughed although you could see Faye didn't like it because she slapped his face. Earle didn't care, he just kissed her again, a long nasty one. She got away from him and ran toward the door where he was standing. He tried to hide, but she caught him. Although he didn't say anything, she said he was nasty spying on her and wouldn't listen when he tried to explain. She went into her room and he followed to tell about the peeking, but she carried on awful and cursed him some more as she put red on her lips. Then she knocked over the perfume. That made her twice as mad. He tried to explain but she wouldn't listen and just went on calling him all sorts of dirty things. So he went to his room and got undressed and tried to go to sleep. Then Tod woke him up and wanted to come and talk. He wasn't angry, but didn't feel like talking just then, all he wanted to do was go to sleep. Tod went away and no sooner had he climbed back into bed when there was some awful screaming and banging. He was afraid to go out and see and he thought of calling the police, but he was scared to go in the hall where the phone was so he started to get dressed to climb out of the window and go for help because it sounded like murder but before he finished putting his shoes on, he heard Tod talking to Faye and he figured that it must be all right or she wouldn't be laughing so he got undressed and went back to bed again. He couldn't fall asleep wondering what had happened, so when the house was quiet, he took a chance and knocked on Faye's door to find out. Faye let him in. She was curled up in bed like a little girl. She called him Daddy and kissed him and said that she wasn't angry at him at all. She said there had been a fight but nobody got hurt much and for him to go back to bed and that they would talk more in the morning. He went back like she said and fell asleep, but he woke up again as it was just breaking daylight. At first he wondered why he was up because when he once fell asleep, usually he didn't get up before the alarm clock rang. He knew that something had happened, but he didn't know what until he heard a noise in Faye's room. It was a moan and he thought he was dreaming, but he heard it again. Sure enough, Faye was moaning all right. He thought she must be sick. She moaned again like in pain. He got out of bed and went to her door and knocked and asked if she was sick. She didn't answer and the moaning stopped so he went back to bed. A little later she moaned again so he got out of bed, thinking she might want the hot water bottle or some aspirin and a drink of water or something and knocked on her door again, only meaning to help her. She heard him and said something. He didn't understand what but he thought she meant for him to go in. Lots of times when she had a headache he brought her an aspirin and a glass of water in the middle of the night. The door wasn't locked. You'd have thought she would have locked the door because the Mexican was in bed with her, both of them naked and she had her arms around him. Faye saw him and pulled the sheets over her head without saying anything. He didn't know what to do, so he backed out of the room and closed the door. He was standing in the hall, trying to figure out what to do, feeling so ashamed, when Earle appeared with his boots in his hand. He must have been sleeping in the parlor. He wanted to know what the trouble was. "Faye's sick," he said, "and I'm getting her a glass of water." But then Faye moaned again and Earle heard it. He pushed open the door. Faye screamed. He could hear Earle and Miguel cursing each other and fighting. He was afraid to call the police on account of Faye and didn't know what to do. Faye kept on screaming. When he opened the door again, Miguel fell out with Earle on top of him and both of them tearing at each other. He ran inside the room and locked the door. She had the sheets over her head, screaming. He could hear Earle and Miguel fighting in the hall and then he couldn't hear them any more. She kept the sheets over her head. He tried to talk to her but she wouldn't answer. He sat down on a chair to guard her in case Earle and Miguel came back, but they didn't and after a while she pulled the sheets away from her face and told him to get out. She pulled the sheets over her face again when he answered, so then he waited a little longer and again she told him to get out without letting him see her face. He couldn't hear either Miguel or Earle. He opened the door and looked out. They were gone. He locked the doors and windows and went to his room and lay down on his bed. Before he knew it he fell asleep and when he woke up she was gone. All he could find was Earle's boots in the hall. He threw them out the back and this morning they were gone.

25

Tod went into the living room to see how Homer was getting on. He was still on the couch, but had changed his position. He had curled his big body into a ball. His knees were drawn up almost to his chin, his elbows were tucked in close and his hands were against his chest. But he wasn't relaxed. Some inner force of nerve and muscle was straining to make the ball tighter and still tighter. He was like a steel spring which has been freed of its function in a machine and allowed to use all its strength centripetally. While part of a machine the pull of the spring had been used against other and stronger forces, but now, free at last, it was striving to attain the shape of its original coil.

Original coil . . . In a book of abnormal psychology borrowed from the college library, he had once seen a picture of a woman sleeping in a net hammock whose posture was much like Homer's. "Uterine Flight," or something like that, had been the caption under the photograph. The woman had been sleeping in the hammock without changing her position, that of the foetus in the womb, for a great many years. The doctors of the insane asylum had been able to awaken her for only short periods of time and those months apart.

He sat down to smoke a cigarette and wondered what he ought to do. Call a doctor? But after all Homer had been awake most of the night and was exhausted. The doctor would shake him a few times and he would yawn and ask what the matter was. He could try to wake him up himself. But hadn't he been enough of a pest already? He was so much better off asleep, even if it was a case of "Uterine Flight."

What a perfect escape the return of the womb was. Better by far than Religion or Art or the South Sea Islands. It was so snug and warm there, and the feeding was automatic. Everything perfect in that hotel. No wonder the memory of those accommodations lingered in the blood and nerves of everyone. It was dark, yes, but what a warm, rich darkness. The grave wasn't in it. No wonder one fought so desperately against being evicted when the nine months' lease was up.

Tod crushed his cigarette. He was hungry and wanted his dinner, also a double Scotch and soda. After he had eaten, he would come back and see how Homer was. If he was still asleep, he would try to wake him. If he couldn't, he might call a doctor.

He took another look at him, then tiptoed out of the cottage, shutting the door carefully.

26

Tod didn't go directly to dinner. He went first to Hodge's saddlery store thinking he might be able to find out something about Earle and through him about Faye. Calvin was standing there with a wrinkled Indian who had long hair held by a bead strap around his forehead. Hanging over the Indian's chest was a sandwich board that read—

TUTTLE'S TRADING POST
for
GENUINE RELICS OF THE OLD WEST

*Beads, Silver, Jewelry, Moccasins,
Dolls, Toys, Rare Books, Postcards.*

TAKE BACK A SOUVENIR
from
TUTTLE'S TRADING POST

Calvin was always friendly.
"Lo, thar," he called out, when Tod came up.

"Meet the chief," he added, grinning. "Chief Kiss-My-Towkus."

The Indian laughed heartily at the joke.

"You gotta live," he said.

"Earle been around today?" Tod asked.

"Yop. Went by an hour ago."

"We were at a party last night and I . . ."

Calvin broke in by hitting his thigh a wallop with the flat of his palm.

"That must've been some shindig to hear Earle tell it. Eh, Skookum?"

"Vas you dere, Sharley?" the Indian agreed, showing the black inside of his mouth, purple tongue and broken orange teeth.

"I heard there was a fight after I left."

Calvin smacked his thigh again.

"Sure musta been. Earle got himself two black eyes, lulus."

"That's what comes of palling up with a dirty greaser," said the Indian excitedly.

He and Calvin got into a long argument about Mexicans. The Indian said that they were all bad. Calvin claimed he had known quite a few good ones in his time. When the Indian cited the case of the Hermanos brothers who had killed a lonely prospector for half a dollar, Calvin countered with a long tale about a man called Tomas Lopez who shared his last pint of water with a stranger when they both were lost in the desert.

Tod tried to get the conversation back to what interested him.

"Mexicans are very good with women," he said.

"Better with horses," said the Indian. "I remember one time along the Brazos, I . . ."

Tod tried again.

"They fought over Earle's girl, didn't they?"

"Not to hear him tell it," Calvin said. "He claims it was dough—claims the Mex robbed him while he was sleeping."

"The dirty, thievin' rat," said the Indian, spitting.

"He claims he's all washed up with that bitch," Calvin went on. "Yes, siree, that's his story, to hear him tell it."

Tod had enough.

"So long," he said.

"Glad to meet you," said the Indian.

"Don't take any wooden nickels," Calvin shouted after him.

Tod wondered if she had gone with Miguel. He thought it more likely that she would go back to work for Mrs. Jenning. But either way she would come out all right. Nothing could hurt her. She was like a cork. No matter how rough the sea got, she would go dancing over the same waves that sank iron ships and tore away piers of reinforced concrete. He pictured her riding a tremendous sea. Wave after wave reared its ton on ton of solid water and crashed down only to have her spin gaily away.

When he arrived at Musso Frank's restaurant, he ordered a steak and a double Scotch. The drink came first and he sipped it with his inner eye still on the spinning cork.

It was a very pretty cork, gilt with a glittering fragment of mirror set in its top. The sea in which it danced was beautiful, green in the trough of the waves and silver at their tips. But for all their moondriven power, they could do no more than net the bright cork for a moment in a spume of intricate lace. Finally it was set down on a strange shore where a savage with pork-sausage fingers and a pimpled butt picked it up and hugged it to his sagging belly. Tod recognized the fortunate man; he was one of Mrs. Jenning's customers.

The waiter brought his order and paused with bent back for him to comment. In vain. Tod was far too busy to inspect the steak.

"Satisfactory, sir?" asked the waiter.

Tod waved him away with a gesture more often used on flies. The waiter disappeared. Tod tried the same gesture on what he felt, but the driving itch refused to go. If only he had the courage to wait for her some night and hit her with a bottle and rape her.

He knew what it would be like lurking in the dark in a vacant lot, waiting for her. Whatever that bird was that sang at night in California would be bursting its heart in theatrical runs and quavers and the chill night air would smell of spice pink. She would drive up, turn the motor off, look up at the stars, so that her breasts reared, then toss her head and sigh. She would throw the ignition keys into her purse and snap it shut, then get out of the car. The long step she took would make her tight dress pull up so that an inch of glowing flesh would show above her black stocking. As he approached carefully, she would be pulling her dress down, smoothing it nicely over her hips.

"Faye, Faye, just a minute," he would call.

"Why, Tod, hello."

She would hold her hand out to him at the end of her long arm that swooped so gracefully to join her curving shoulder.

"You scared me!"

She would look like a deer on the edge of the road when a truck comes unexpectedly around a bend.

He could feel the cold bottle he held behind his back and the forward step he would take to bring . . .

"Is there anything wrong with it, sir?"

The fly-like waiter had come back. Tod waved at him, but this time the man continued to hover.

"Perhaps you would like me to take it back, sir?"

"No, no."

"Thank you, sir."

But he didn't leave. He waited to make sure that the customer was really going to eat. Tod picked up his knife and cut a piece. Not until he had also put some boiled potato in his mouth did the man leave.

Tod tried to start the rape going again, but he couldn't feel the bottle as he raised it to strike. He had to give it up.

The waiter came back. Tod looked at the steak. It was a very good one, but he wasn't hungry any more.

"A check, please."

"No dessert, sir?"

"No, thank you, just a check."

"Check it is, sir," the man said brightly as he fumbled for his pad and pencil.

27

When Tod reached the street, he saw a dozen great violet shafts of light moving across the evening sky in wide crazy sweeps. Whenever one of the fiery columns reached the lowest point of its arc, it lit for a moment the rose-colored domes and delicate minarets of Kahn's Persian Palace Theatre. The purpose of this display was to signal the world premiere of a new picture.

Turning his back on the searchlights, he started in the opposite direction, toward Homer's place. Before he had gone very far, he saw a clock that read a quarter past six and changed his mind about going back just yet. He might as well let the poor fellow sleep for another hour and kill some time by looking at the crowds.

When still a block from the theatre, he saw an enormous electric sign that hung over the middle of the street. In letters ten feet high he read that—

"MR. KAHN A PLEASURE DOME DECREED"

Although it was still several hours before the celebrities would arrive, thousands of people had already gathered. They stood facing the theatre with their backs toward the gutter in a thick line hundreds of feet long. A big squad of policemen was trying to keep a lane open between the front rank of the crowd and the façade of the theatre.

Tod entered the lane while the policeman guarding it was busy with a woman whose parcel had torn open, dropping oranges all over the place. Another policeman shouted for him to get the hell across the street, but he took a chance and kept going. They had enough to do without chasing him. He noticed how worried they looked and how careful they tried to be. If they had to arrest someone, they joked good-naturedly with the culprit, making light of it until they got him around the corner, then they whaled him with their clubs. Only so long as the man was actually part of the crowd did they have to be gentle.

Tod had walked only a short distance along the narrow lane when he began to get frightened. People shouted, commenting on his hat, his carriage, and his clothing. There was a continuous roar of catcalls, laughter and yells, pierced occasionally by a scream. The scream was usually followed by a sudden movement in the dense mass and part of it would surge forward wherever the police line was weakest. As soon as that part was rammed back, the bulge would pop out somewhere else.

The police force would have to be doubled when the stars started to arrive. At the sight of their heroes and heroines, the crowd would turn demoniac. Some little gesture, either too pleasing or too offensive, would start it moving and then nothing but machine guns would stop it. Individually the purpose of its members might simply be to get a souvenir, but collectively it would grab and rend.

A young man with a portable microphone was describing the scene. His rapid, hysterical voice was like that of a revivalist preacher whipping his congregation toward the ecstasy of fits.

"What a crowd, folks! What a crowd! There must be ten thousand excited, screaming fans outside Kahn's Persian tonight. The police can't hold them. Here, listen to them roar."

He held the microphone out and those near it obligingly roared for him.

"Did you hear it? It's a bedlam, folks. A veritable bedlam! What excitement! Of all the premières I've attended, this is the most . . . the most . . . stupendous, folks. Can the police hold them? Can they? It doesn't look so, folks . . ."

Another squad of police came charging up. The sergeant pleaded with the announcer to stand further back so the people couldn't hear him. His men threw themselves at the crowd. It allowed itself to be hustled and shoved out of habit and because it lacked an objective. It tolerated the police, just as a bull elephant does when he allows a small boy to drive him with a light stick.

Tod could see very few people who looked tough, nor could he see any working men. The crowd was made up of the lower middle classes, every other person one of his torchbearers.

Just as he came near the end of the lane, it closed in front of him with a heave, and he had to fight his way through. Someone knocked his hat off and when he stooped to pick it up, someone kicked him. He whirled around angrily and found himself surrounded by people who were laughing at him. He knew enough to laugh with them. The crowd became sympathetic. A stout woman slapped him on the back, while a man handed him his hat, first brushing it carefully with his sleeve. Still another man shouted for a way to be cleared.

By a great deal of pushing and squirming, always trying to look as though he were enjoying himself, Tod finally managed to break into the open. After rearranging his clothes, he went over to a parking lot and sat down on the low retaining wall that ran along the front of it.

New groups, whole families, kept arriving. He could see a change come over them as soon as they had become part of the crowd. Until they reached the line, they looked diffident, almost furtive, but the moment they had become part of it, they turned arrogant and pugnacious. It was a mistake to think them harmless curiosity seekers. They were savage and bitter, especially the middle-aged and the old, and had been made so by boredom and disappointment.

All their lives they had slaved at some kind of dull, heavy labor, behind desks and counters, in the fields and at tedious machines of all sorts, saving their pennies and dreaming of the leisure that would be theirs when they had enough. Finally that day came. They could draw a weekly income of ten or fifteen dollars. Where else should they go but California, the land of sunshine and oranges?

Once there, they discover that sunshine isn't enough. They get tired of oranges, even of avocado pears and passion fruit. Nothing happens. They don't know what to do with their time. They haven't the mental equipment for leisure, the money nor the physical equipment for pleasure. Did they slave so long just to go to an occasional Iowa picnic? What else is there? They watch the waves come in at Venice. There wasn't any ocean where most of them came from, but after you've seen one wave, you've seen them all. The same is true of the airplanes at Glendale. If only a plane would crash once in a while so that they could watch the passengers being consumed in a "holocaust of flame," as the newspapers put it. But the planes never crash.

Their boredom becomes more and more terrible. They realize that they've been tricked and burn with resentment. Every day of their lives they read the newspapers and went to the movies. Both fed them on lynchings, murder, sex crimes, explosions, wrecks, love nests, fires, miracles, revolutions, wars. This daily diet made sophisticates of them. The sun is a joke. Oranges can't titillate their jaded palates. Nothing can ever be violent enough to make taut their slack minds and bodies. They have been cheated and betrayed. They have slaved and saved for nothing.

Tod stood up. During the ten minutes he had been sitting on the wall, the crowd had grown thirty feet and he was afraid that his escape might be cut off if he loitered much longer. He crossed to the other side of the street and started back.

He was trying to figure what to do if he were unable to wake Homer when, suddenly he saw his head bobbing above the crowd. He hurried toward him. From his appearance, it was evident that there was something definitely wrong.

Homer walked more than ever like a badly made automaton and his features were set in a rigid, mechanical grin. He had his trousers on over his nightgown and part of it hung out of his open fly. In both of his hands were suitcases. With each step, he lurched to one side then the other, using the suitcases for balance weights.

Tod stopped directly in front of him, blocking his way.

"Where're you going?"

"Wayneville," he replied, using an extraordinary amount of jaw movement to get out this single word.

"That's fine. But you can't walk to the station from here. It's in Los Angeles."

Homer tried to get around him, but he caught his arm.

"We'll get a taxi. I'll go with you."

The cabs were all being routed around the block because of the preview. He explained this to Homer and tried to get him to walk to the corner.

"Come on, we're sure to get one on the next street."

Once Tod got him into a cab, he intended to tell the driver to go to the nearest hospital. But Homer wouldn't budge, no matter how hard he yanked and pleaded. People stopped to watch them, others turned their heads curiously. He decided to leave him and get a cab.

"I'll come right back," he said.

He couldn't tell from either Homer's eyes or expression whether he heard, for they both were empty of everything, even annoyance. At the corner he looked around and saw that Homer had started to cross the street, moving blindly. Brakes screeched and twice he was almost run over, but he didn't swerve or hurry. He moved in a straight diagonal. When he reached the other curb, he tried to get on the sidewalk at a point where the crowd was very thick and was shoved violently back. He made another attempt and this time a policeman grabbed him by the back of the neck and hustled him to the end of the line. When the policeman let go of him, he kept on walking as though nothing had happened.

Tod tried to get over to him, but was unable to cross until the traffic lights changed. When he reached the other side, he found Homer sitting on a bench, fifty or sixty feet from the outskirts of the crowd.

He put his arm around Homer's shoulder and suggested that they walk a few blocks further. When Homer didn't answer, he reached over to pick up one of the valises. Homer held on to it.

"I'll carry it for you," he said, tugging gently.

"Thief!"

Before Homer could repeat the shout, he jumped away. It would be extremely embarrassing if Homer shouted thief in front of a cop. He thought of phoning for an ambulance. But then, after all, how could he be sure that Homer was crazy? He was sitting quietly on the bench, minding his own business.

Tod decided to wait, then try again to get him into a cab. The crowd was growing in size all the time, but it would be at least half an hour before it over-ran the bench. Before that happened, he would think of some plan. He moved a short distance away and stood with his back to a store window so that he could watch Homer without attracting attention.

About ten feet from where Homer was sitting grew a large eucalyptus tree and behind the trunk of the tree was a little boy. Tod saw him peer around it with great caution, then suddenly jerk his head back. A minute later he repeated the maneuver. At first Tod thought he was playing hide and seek, then noticed that he had a string in his hand which was attached to an old purse that lay in front of Homer's bench. Every once in a while the child would jerk the string, making the purse hop like a sluggish toad. Its torn lining hung from its iron mouth like a furry tongue and a few uncertain flies hovered over it.

Tod knew the game the child was playing. He used to play it himself when he was small. If Homer reached to pick up the purse, thinking there was money in it, he would yank it away and scream with laughter.

When Tod went over to the tree, he was surprised to discover that it was Adore Loomis, the kid who lived across the street from Homer. Tod tried to chase him, but he dodged around the tree, thumbing his nose. He gave up and went back to his original position. The moment he left, Adore got busy with his purse again. Homer wasn't paying any attention to the child, so Tod decided to let him alone.

Mrs. Loomis must be somewhere in the crowd, he thought. Tonight when she found Adore, she would give him a hiding. He had torn the pocket of his jacket and his Buster Brown collar was smeared with grease.

Adore had a nasty temper. The completeness with which Homer ignored both him and his pocketbook made him frantic. He gave up dancing it at the end of the string and approached the bench on tiptoes, making ferocious faces, yet ready to run at Homer's first move. He stopped when about four feet away and stuck his tongue out. Homer ignored him. He took another step forward and ran through a series of insulting gestures.

If Tod had known that the boy held a stone in his hand, he would have interfered. But he felt sure that Homer wouldn't hurt the child and was waiting to see if he wouldn't move because of his pestering. When Adore raised his arm, it was too late. The stone hit Homer in the face. The boy turned to flee, but tripped and fell. Before he could scramble away, Homer landed on his back with both feet, then jumped again.

Tod yelled for him to stop and tried to yank him away. He shoved Tod and went on using his heels. Tod hit him as hard as he could, first in the belly, then in the face. He ignored the blows and continued to stamp on the boy. Tod hit him again and again, then threw both arms around him and tried to pull him off. He couldn't budge him. He was like a stone column.

The next thing Tod knew, he was torn loose from Homer and sent to his knees by a blow in the back of the head that spun him sideways. The crowd in front of the theatre had charged. He was surrounded by churning legs and feet. He pulled himself erect by grabbing a man's coat, then let himself be carried along backwards in a long, curving swoop. He saw Homer rise above the mass for a moment, shoved against the sky, his jaw hanging as though he wanted to scream but couldn't. A hand reached up and caught him by his open mouth and pulled him forward and down.

There was another dizzy rush. Tod closed his eyes and fought to keep upright. He was jostled about in a hacking cross surf of shoulders and backs, carried rapidly in one direction and then in the opposite. He kept pushing and hitting out at the people around him, trying to face in the direction he was going. Being carried backwards terrified him.

Using the eucalyptus tree as a landmark, he tried to work toward it by slipping sideways against the tide, pushing hard when carried away from it and riding the current when it moved toward his objective. He was within only a few feet of the tree when a sudden, driving rush carried him far past it. He struggled desperately for a moment, then gave up and let himself be swept along. He was the spearhead of a flying wedge when it collided with a mass going in the opposite direction. The impact turned him around. As the two forces ground against each other, he was turned again and again, like a grain between millstones. This didn't stop until he became part of the opposing force. The pressure continued to increase until he thought he must collapse. He was slowly pushed into the air. Although relief for his cracking ribs could be gotten by continuing to rise, he fought to keep his feet on the ground. Not being able to touch was an even more dreadful sensation than being carried backwards.

There was another rush, shorter this time, and he found himself in a dead spot where the pressure was less and equal. He became conscious of a terrible pain in his left leg, just above the ankle, and tried to work it into a more comfortable position. He couldn't turn his body, but managed to get his head around. A very skinny boy, wearing a Western Union cap, had his back wedged against his shoulder. The pain continued to grow and his whole leg as high as the groin throbbed. He finally got his left arm free and took the back of the boy's neck in his fingers. He twisted as hard as he could. The boy began to jump up and down in his clothes. He managed to straighten his elbow, by pushing at the back of the boy's head, and so turn half way around and free his leg. The pain didn't grow less.

There was another wild surge forward that ended in another dead spot. He now faced a young girl who was sobbing steadily. Her silk print dress had been torn down the front and her tiny brassiere hung from one strap. He tried by pressing back to give her room, but she moved with him every time he moved. Now and then, she would jerk violently and he wondered if she was going to have a fit. One of her thighs was between his legs. He struggled to get free of her, but she clung to him, moving with him and pressing against him.

She turned her head and said, "Stop, stop," to someone behind her.

He saw what the trouble was. An old man, wearing a Panama hat and horn-rimmed glasses, was hugging her. He had one of his hands inside her dress and was biting her neck.

Tod freed his right arm with a heave, reached over the girl and brought his fist down on the man's head. He couldn't hit very hard but managed to knock the man's hat off, also his glasses. The man tried to bury his face in the girl's shoulder, but Tod grabbed one of his ears and yanked. They started to move again. Tod held on to the ear as long as he could, hoping that it would come away in his hand. The girl managed to twist under his arm. A piece of her dress tore, but she was free of her attacker.

Another spasm passed through the mob and he was carried toward the curb. He fought toward a lamp-post, but he was swept by before he could grasp it. He saw another man catch the girl with the torn dress. She screamed for help. He tried to get to her, but was carried in the opposite direction. This rush also ended in a dead spot. Here his neighbors were all shorter than he was. He turned his head upward toward the sky and tried to pull some fresh air into his aching lungs, but it was all heavily tainted with sweat.

In this part of the mob no one was hysterical. In fact,

most of the people seemed to be enjoying themselves. Near him was a stout woman with a man pressing hard against her from in front. His chin was on her shoulder, and his arms were around her. She paid no attention to him and went on talking to the woman at her side.

"The first thing I knew," Tod heard her say, "there was a rush and I was in the middle."

"Yeah. Somebody hollered, 'Here comes Gary Cooper,' and then wham!"

"That ain't it," said a little man wearing a cloth cap and pullover sweater. "This is a riot you're in."

"Yeah," said a third woman, whose snaky gray hair was hanging over her face and shoulders. "A pervert attacked a child."

"He ought to be lynched."

Everybody agreed vehemently.

"I come from St. Louis," announced the stout woman, "and we had one of them pervert fellers in our neighborhood once. He ripped up a girl with a pair of scissors."

"He must have been crazy," said the man in the cap. "What kind of fun is that?"

Everybody laughed. The stout woman spoke to the man who was hugging her.

"Hey, you," she said. "I ain't no pillow."

The man smiled beatifically but didn't move. She laughed, making no effort to get out of his embrace.

"A fresh guy," she said.

The other woman laughed.

"Yeah," she said, "this is a regular free-for-all."

The man in the cap and sweater thought there was another laugh in his comment about the pervert.

"Ripping up a girl with scissors. That's the wrong tool."

He was right. They laughed even louder than the first time.

"You'd a done it different, eh, kid?" said a young man with a kidney-shaped head and waxed mustaches.

The two women laughed. This encouraged the man in the cap and he reached over and pinched the stout woman's friend. She squealed.

"Lay off that," she said good-naturedly.

"I was shoved," he said.

An ambulance siren screamed in the street. Its wailing moan started the crowd moving again and Tod was carried along in a slow, steady push. He closed his eyes and tried to protect his throbbing leg. This time, when the movement ended, he found himself with his back to the theatre wall. He kept his eyes closed and stood on his good leg. After what seemed like hours, the pack began to loosen and move again with a churning motion. It gathered momentum and rushed. He rode it until he was slammed against the base of an iron rail which fenced the driveway of the theatre from the street. He had the wind knocked out of him by the impact, but managed to cling to the rail. He held on desperately, fighting to keep from being sucked back. A woman caught him around the waist and tried to hang on. She was sobbing rhythmically. Tod felt his fingers slipping from the rail and kicked backwards as hard as he could. The woman let go.

Despite the agony in his leg, he was able to think clearly about his picture, "The Burning of Los Angeles." After his quarrel with Faye, he had worked on it continually to escape tormenting himself, and the way to it in his mind had become almost automatic.

As he stood on his good leg, clinging desperately to the

iron rail, he could see all the rough charcoal strokes with which he had blocked it out on the big canvas. Across the top, parallel with the frame, he had drawn the burning city, a great bonfire of architectural styles, ranging from Egyptian to Cape Cod colonial. Through the center, winding from left to right, was a long hill street and down it, spilling into the middle foreground, came the mob carrying baseball bats and torches. For the faces of its members, he was using the innumerable sketches he had made of the people who come to California to die; the cultists of all sorts, economic as well as religious, the wave, airplane, funeral and preview watchers—all those poor devils who can only be stirred by the promise of miracles and then only to violence. A super "Dr. Know-All Pierce-All" had made the necessary promise and they were marching behind his banner in a great united front of screwballs and screwboxes to purify the land. No longer bored, they sang and danced joyously in the red light of the flames.

In the lower foreground, men and women fled wildly before the vanguard of the crusading mob. Among them were Faye, Harry, Homer, Claude and himself. Faye ran proudly, throwing her knees high. Harry stumbled along behind her, holding on to his beloved derby hat with both hands. Homer seemed to be falling out of the canvas, his face half-asleep, his big hands clawing the air in anguished pantomime. Claude turned his head as he ran to thumb his nose at his pursuers. Tod himself picked up a small stone to throw before continuing his flight.

He had almost forgotten both his leg and his predicament, and to make his escape still more complete he stood on a chair and worked at the flames in an upper corner of the canvas, modeling the tongues of fire so that they licked even more avidly at a corinthian column that held up the palmleaf roof of a nutburger stand.

He had finished one flame and was starting on another when he was brought back by someone shouting in his ear. He opened his eyes and saw a policeman trying to reach him from behind the rail to which he was clinging. He let go with his left hand and raised his arm. The policeman caught him by the wrist, but couldn't lift him. Tod was afraid to let go until another man came to aid the policeman and caught him by the back of his jacket. He let go of the rail and they hauled him up and over it.

When they saw that he couldn't stand, they let him down easily to the ground. He was in the theatre driveway. On the curb next to him sat a woman crying into her skirt. Along the wall were groups of other disheveled people. At the end of the driveway was an ambulance. A policeman asked him if he wanted to go to the hospital. He shook his head no. He then offered him a lift home. Tod had the presence of mind to give Claude's address.

He was carried through the exit to the back street and lifted into a police car. The siren began to scream and at first he thought he was making the noise himself. He felt his lips with his hands. They were clamped tight. He knew then it was the siren. For some reason this made him laugh and he began to imitate the siren as loud as he could.

A Note on the Type

The principal text of this Modern Library edition
was set in a digitized version of Janson,
a typeface that dates from about 1690 and was cut by Nicholas Kis,
a Hungarian working in Amsterdam. The original matrices have
survived and are held by the Stempel foundry in Germany.
Hermann Zapf redesigned some of the weights and sizes for Stempel,
basing his revisions on the original design.